Cathe

Afloat

Afloat

JENNIFER McCARTNEY

HAMISH HAMILTON
an imprint of
PENGUIN BOOKS

HAMISH HAMILTON

Published by the Penguin Group
Penguin Books Ltd, 80 Strand, London WC2R ORL, England
Penguin Group (USA) Inc., 375 Hudson Street, New York, New York 10014, USA
Penguin Group (Canada), 90 Eglinton Avenue East, Suite 700, Toronto, Ontario, Canada M4P 2Y3
(a division of Pearson Penguin Canada Inc.)
Penguin Ireland, 25 St Stephen's Green, Dublin 2, Ireland
(a division of Penguin Books Ltd)
Penguin Group (Australia), 250 Camberwell Road, Camberwell, Victoria 3124, Australia
(a division of Pearson Australia Group Pty Ltd)
Penguin Books India Pvt Ltd, 11 Community Centre, Panchsheel Park, New Delhi – 110 017, India
Penguin Group (NZ), 67 Apollo Drive, Mairangi Bay, Auckland 1310, New Zealand
(a division of Pearson New Zealand Ltd)
Penguin Books (South Africa) (Pty) Ltd, 24 Sturdee Avenue, Rosebank, Johannesburg 2196, South Africa

Penguin Books Ltd, Registered Offices: 80 Strand, London WC2R ORL, England

www.penguin.com

First published 2007
I

Set in 12/14.75 pt Monotype Dante
Typeset by Rowland Phototypesetting Ltd, Bury St Edmunds, Suffolk
Printed in Great Britain by Clays Ltd, St Ives plc

A CIP catalogue record for this book is available from the British Library

ISBN 978-0-241-14344-5

For Mrs Holder

'O – at Mackinaw! That fairy island, which I shall never see again! and which I should have dearly liked to filch from the Americans, and carry home to you in my dressing box.'

Anna Brownell Jameson, *Winter Studies and Summer Rambles in Canada, 1838*

LEHI m
Usage: Biblical, Mormon
From an Old Testament place name meaning 'jawbone' in Hebrew. It is also used in the Books of Mormon as the name of a prophet.

The Utah Baby Namer

Your right hand, palm inward, thumb out, is the state of Michigan.

Mackinac Island is off the tip of your middle finger. Green and heavy, this limestone outcrop of land lies in the straits of Mackinac between the lakes of Huron and Michigan. The island is nine miles around with forest in the middle and it takes one hour to circle it by bicycle. You cannot travel by car, because there are none. The narrow road surrounding the island, the M-185, is the only highway in North America on which there has never been a motor-vehicle accident, although the cemetery is full. The weather intrudes like a clenched fist. During the winters the five hundred horses are taken away to a southern state.

It was May. The island lay underneath a sky shaded like the underbelly of a fish.

As the ferryboat angled towards the pier I watched my summer becoming larger, the houses clearer, the postcard image of horse-and-carriage suddenly alive on modern, gray-paved streets. The air was cold on the top deck, and everything was sharp, clear, and bright. The island's green crown, thick with forests, was welcoming. White seagulls turned pin-wheels in the sky and the lake was calm as we docked – the horn loud. Descending to the wooden jetty to collect my suitcase, then tugging it behind me onto the cement sidewalk, I approached the building I had, until now, seen only in photographs.

★

I will tell you everything that comes next, the exact events of that summer, so you can understand what I am waiting for now. It is 12:05 p.m. I have six hours until my visitor arrives. Enough time for everything to happen again.

Mackinac

Gracing the top of the document stapled to the front gate is the delicate, embossed image of a golden canoe.

WE APOLOGIZE FOR THE INCONVENIENCE BUT THE TIPPECANOE (EXCLUDING THE FRONT GATE) HAS BEEN FRESHLY WHITENED FOR YOUR ENJOYMENT THIS SEASON. PLEASE DO NOT TOUCH ANYTHING.

The wet paint sign is not hand-lettered – it looks professionally commissioned.

I set my luggage next to the wooden bike rack which says, TIPPECANOE GUESTS ONLY, PLEASE, and turn to the building, which months earlier had occupied an entire page of St. Paul's *Pioneer Press*. Its two stories are incongruous next to the slightly dingy Pancake House and the half-full marina. The metal plaque affixed to the entrance dates the building back to 1926, and though the restaurant is closed until tomorrow the front door is open. The fumes are overwhelming.

The owner's hair is dyed black in a long sharp ponytail which does not swing as she advances towards me. She extends a perfect hand, and when she smiles her teeth are white. It's impossible to determine her age as she is rich enough to have had any number of surgeries. She could be thirty-five or fifty-five.

My teeth are not as white as hers.

'Good morning,' she says. 'Welcome to the Tippecanoe.'

'Thank you,' I say.

She continues smiling as she sweeps me into the restaurant,

pointing towards a low, leather armchair that cannot be easy to extricate oneself from after a night of cocktails. Other new arrivals are already sitting properly in the half-circle arrangement, and among these even the men are beautiful. I wonder how she accomplished this as we were all hired over the phone.

The interior has hardwood pine floors, clean lines, and soaring ceilings – the perfect design and symmetry the handsome result of renovation, investment, and impossibly high standards. Glass, leather, and wood all seem to glow with natural light. The only questionable item of taste is the cocktail bar's appearance – the façade a glossy wooden half of a canoe.

'Authentic,' she assures me.

Seated, I scratch the leather armrest with a fingernail and then rub the mark with my thumb. The lake looks black beneath textured gray clouds and in the marina beside the restaurant is a fantastic yacht flying a French flag. A girl with long blonde hair and eyes drawn black with eyeliner leans over to me and whispers while nodding towards the boat, 'Who do you have to fuck to get a ride on that thing?'

As an introduction the owner tells us she used to be a ballet instructor on Cape Cod and gives a slight curtsy in her pointed high heels. She is dressed in perfect black like a monochrome painting, and there is no sign of lint anywhere. Her name is Velvet.

The Tippecanoe is not a roast-beef restaurant. The menu we are given to study displays venison, smoked salmon, elk pepper steaks, and different sauces, most of which I've never heard of. Dishes are finished with pear walnut crème, fig confit or garlic sabayon. There is the full array of cutlery, including the shrimp fork: no corners are cut. The tablecloths are crisp and white, napkins the same. Crystal goblets are polished by hand. Velvet tells us apologetically that some tourists will

4

have to leave after being seated, realizing they cannot afford the restaurant. The clientele *do* fit the image for the most part however, Velvet assures us. I imagine men with business credit cards drinking Manhattans, and women with earrings and outfits purchased all at once, so that nothing is left to chance.

After a long speech and lots of handouts, we begin our hands-on training. My table of pretend guests is having tonic water, a glass of champagne, and a Brie and biscuit platter. In hushed whispers everyone is searching the kitchen, trying to complete their assigned tasks.

Where's the whipped cream?

What the hell is Abalone? Is that the hot line or the cold line?

How do I make this napkin look like a swan?

Velvet corners me by the espresso machine. Someone has left the grinder running and the air is hot and caffeinated. Smiling, she switches the machine off, then turns to me. She is much taller than I am.

'You brought out tonic water without a lime,' she says. 'All soft drinks must be served with one black straw, and one slice of lime.'

I nod. These are the details that must be remembered.

Velvet informs a young man wearing a baseball hat that for seventy-six years the sugar cubes at this restaurant have been presented to the guests in a china bowl, on a china plate, with an accompanying silver doily. The ketchup also goes on a doily plate – as does mayonnaise, syrup, hot sauce, salad dressing, soup, tea bags, and teapots. *When in doubt, doily.* She emphasizes her D's.

When Velvet leaves the dining area to retrieve our written tests, the hat-wearing waiter says, 'Fuck the doilies,' and puts one in his mouth.

He is still chewing when Velvet returns with the stack of papers.

As she distributes the tests, she reminds us that the Tippecanoe is the *first* restaurant on the island to open for the summer season, and the last to close for the winter. It is one of the top six restaurants in Michigan. I receive a perfect score on the Chamber of Commerce's standardized exam for new island employees.

The island has four hundred and three year-round residents. The visitors in the summer number over one million.

There are seventeen pubs, most of them on Main Street, which runs the length of the town and is parallel to the water.

There are three ferry lines running boats into the harbor every fifteen minutes.

There are bike rental shops that charge by the half hour.

There is an old British fort on a cliff that is open to visitors.

There is a taxi service of horse-drawn carriages.

There is one red-brick school.

There is a medical center.

One of the girls gets four out of twenty and has to write the test again.

What www.mackinac.com never told me, and what the written test excludes, is the incredible atmosphere. The streets in town are chaos, with ringing bike bells, and music pouring out of each pub and ferry horns blaring and school groups screaming and taxi drivers in their horse-drawn carriages shouting at tourists taking pictures in the middle of the road.

Conversely, everything is calm, green, the water is everywhere. There are no traffic lights and no exhaust fumes and no daily headlines save the weekly *Town Crier* and nothing is fast enough to be a problem.

At the end of this first day the espresso machine bears a sign, DON'T FORGET TO TURN ME OFF.

★

My first night on the island I am alone. The other girls are in their apartments, already friends. I met them all during training, our nametags a strange exercise in alliteration: Brenna, Blue, Bailey. Bell. Blue said her parents let her two-year-old sister choose her name. Brenna, the girl who commented about the yacht, told me that as soon as she gets her first pay check she's getting her roots done.

The bedroom, bathroom, and kitchen don't feel like my own yet. I leave my suitcase closed on the bed, unzipping only the flat compartment at the front to retrieve the last items I packed: the calendar and a box of thumbtacks. I press the month of May firmly to an empty white wall. The carpet's a hotel-shade of pink and each room is adorned with laminated instructions about the fridge, microwave, and kettle, reminders about remembering to lock the front door and close all the windows, a warning about ants. It smells as if other people lived here once but have been away a long time.

Through the open doorway of my suite the grounds are illuminated by old-fashioned lampposts, two of which are working. The long gravel road is lined with weeds and pine trees, the sign at the entrance reads, MACKINAC PINE SUITES. The bike racks are full, my father's mountain bike indistinguishable from the rest. There are beer cans in the garden, and it has the atmosphere of a place that is cared for but not invested in, tucked conveniently amongst the trees and away from the eyes of tourists. I wander out a bit further, guessing the long building must hold about thirty apartments and I wonder who else is alone tonight. Directly above me is an apartment on the second floor with a balcony. It's filled with light and people, but the stairs are steep and I wasn't invited. A bare ass appears at one of the windows, followed by shrieks. A silhouette calls out, 'You're new?'

'I'm new,' I say.

'Come on up, grab a beer.'

I climb the cement stairs at a pace that doesn't appear too eager, but when I get to the top he isn't looking at me. On his white T-shirt is a large blue ribbon that says, 1st Place County Fair. There's no hemp necklace or gold chain or earring in one ear, and though his top front teeth are crooked he is passably handsome. He turns, tells me his name, wiping his palm on his jeans before shaking my hand. The accent is from Michigan, and I wonder which part.

'Want a drink?'

I shrug, smiling, and I still haven't brushed my teeth. I stop smiling. The beer cooler outside the door is full of melting ice, and he gives me a wet can. 'Thanks.'

I pull the tab, trying to remember when I last drank beer from a can. I think it was in high school, and I hope he doesn't crush the can on his forehead when he's finished. I don't ask about the ribbon.

Leaning our elbows on the metal railing, we stare out over the tops of the trees. He tells me Velvet bought the Pine Suites after someone killed his family in one of the guest rooms, and no one wanted to stay here anymore.

'Killed them all with an axe,' he says.

We consider this.

'Imagine bringing an axe with you on vacation,' I say.

He laughs, nodding. 'Sunglasses, bug spray, unwieldy murder weapon . . .' He counts the items on his fingers.

The island seems full of things I'd like to discover and it's only been eight hours.

'Which suite was it?' I ask.

Bryce winks at me. 'You're in suite eight, right? Just don't be in your bedroom after midnight.'

I punch him in the arm. 'Fuck off.'

He rubs his arm. 'He'll be waiting for you.'

Someone inside is yelling for him, and Bryce excuses himself. I stay at the top of the stairs feeling alone, and I should have followed him in, but it's too late now. After a while he returns in a light-blue shirt that buttons down the front, but he hasn't unbuttoned it too far. The county fair ribbon is gone.

'You want to come down to the bars with us?' he asks.

'I don't drink,' I say, handing him my empty can.

He puts it in the plastic bag he's allotted for recyclables.

A group gathers and we wander down into town, everyone electing to walk the mile or so instead of riding bikes as there are so many of us. It becomes second nature to sidestep the wet piles of horseshit. They rarely get a chance to harden as there are men employed with brushes and wheelbarrows and shovels to scoop the piles out of sight. Tourists taking pictures of the carriages don't like to smell horseshit, I imagine, not at the prices they've paid to come here. These men are everywhere, wearing gray coveralls and standing beside their rapidly filling wheelbarrows. Bryce tells us that last summer immigration officials took most of these men away. They were chained by their ankles in the middle of the road, and led onto a waiting coast-guard boat. People took pictures. More men arrived to take their place.

One of the girls at the front of the group thinks this is totally sad.

At the bar the couches are leather and I sit by myself, wondering whose bare ass I was witness to earlier. Someone with a pink martini is talking to Bryce, and in the dim light I notice her long luminous nails, legs crossed towards him. He nods encouragingly for a few minutes while I wish for anyone to join me, to save me and talk about their city or cat or the poetry they write in spiral notebooks labelled POETRY. Anything so there isn't empty space around me. When the girl with long nails retreats to the bathroom on wobbly stilettos, Bryce sits beside me.

'Looks like she forgot to finish getting dressed,' he says, nodding towards her backless top tied with string.

The couch seats two comfortably.

'Not your favorite person?' I ask.

'I try and stay away.'

I cross my legs towards him. 'Why the name Bryce?'

'It's a canyon in Utah. My family's Mormon.'

'Just your family?'

'You can't be Mormon and drink beer at the same time. Cheers.'

I imagine running my hands through his beautiful hay-colored hair as our beers click together. They are huge, bigger than a pint, and I have trouble lifting the glass with one hand. He is drinking Miller Light. I am drinking Labatt Blue.

Seated, Bryce and I are the same height.

The opening night of Velvet's restaurant is a carefully orchestrated event. Soft jazz plays through small expensive speakers mounted near the ceiling. The new menus stand sleek and upright in their leather jackets next to the cream-colored candles, the napkins are folded to look like swans. The air smells of orchid, fresh pesto, and starched linen, and the front door has been propped open with a tiny brass doorstop in the shape of a galloping horse. The sounds of cutlery and tinkling glassware and laughter echo with perfect pitch as the room fills. Nothing is too loud.

In a smooth black skirt and turtleneck, Velvet spends the evening air-kissing her friends and hissing instructions at the staff.

'Nicole and Alan, *welcome*! Nicole, you look wonderful in that shade of beige, or is it more of an ecru?'

Then turning smoothly, with a sixth sense for incompetence as I pass with my tray, 'Soup spoon, soup spoon, soup spoon!'

Rummy from Canada is nervous. He lives in apartment seven at the Pine Suites, and when you ask Rummy what time it is, he says things like, 'time for a beer,' or, 'time for you to get a watch.'

This makes me think of my father.

He has a round easy face and thick earlobes, not pierced or decorated, and his build reminds me of a baseball player, his thighs solid under his uniform. He confides this is his first job in the hospitality industry – the exchange rate on the American dollar allowing him to maximize his savings for school. With the guests he is enthusiastic because he means it, not because he has to be. The more experienced servers, the ones whose names I cannot yet keep straight, will smack open the swinging door to the kitchen and announce, 'Water and a main course to *share*.'

They're looking for sympathy, and it's too early to know yet which servers I will wish this fate on, *the cheap table*, so I nod.

Rummy arrives as I'm retrieving my second forgotten soup spoon of the night.

'Is there a drink called a gin at seven?' he asks.

'Gin *and* seven. With Seven Up. Why?'

'Shit. I thought he said, gin *at seven*. And I asked if he wanted his gin at seven o'clock.'

'You're joking.'

He shakes his head.

Chef Walter, a large African–American man from Kansas, turns to me as I'm laughing. He points a quiet finger at me, thick and careful, as if not only his kitchen but his body too is disciplined.

'Which one are you?' he asks.

Before I can tell him my name, he turns back to the hot line, waving me away. 'I don't even care, just shut the fuck up.'

Mortified, I follow Rummy out into the dining room where my table of two is still finishing their Chilled Cranberry and Raspberry Soup with Grated Nutmeg. They've been enjoying their tiny bowls for thirty-five minutes, but at least the soup is intended to be cold. Next to them, Rummy approaches table five with a gin and seven on his tray. The two men ask Rummy where he's from.

'Canada, eh?' The first man raises his gin towards Rummy as if making a toast. 'Our fifty-first state!'

The other man sips his vodka tonic and chuckles, and I think I hear the word *Igloo*. Rummy then points out that their assumptions regarding his enjoyment of the warm Michigan weather are misplaced, as the island is actually five hours north of where he grew up. The men are from Connecticut, and as my table finally finishes their soup I see Rummy using his right hand to show them where exactly his home is in Ontario in relation to Michigan.

He finds me later by the canoe bar as I wait for a Manhattan on the rocks and tells me how, over their dessert of Figs Poached in Cabernet Sauvignon and Served with Almond Ice Cream, one of the men had conceded: 'You guys got a great prime minister up there though, that Trudeau guy is really something.'

Rummy informed the man that Trudeau died earlier this month.

'Oh right,' he said. 'Well, who you got running the place now then?'

We snicker at this, which makes me feel like I can't ask Rummy who Trudeau was. Wanting to know, and annoyed that I don't, I will look it up on the Internet later.

The restaurant fills quickly. Women with bodies that look too sleek to have borne children arrive on the arms of men wearing linen clothing and smelling of pre-dinner cocktails. Each elegant couple raise toasts across their immaculate tables, ordering hors d'oeuvres as well as desserts, and each check is well over one hundred dollars. When I finish at eleven, I feel there will never be enough time in my lifetime to learn everything I need to know about food, wine, and luxury.

The changing room is hot, loud, and crowded with female bodies in bras, wearing socks, putting on lipstick and body spray. The room begins to smell of deodorant, hair gel, and scents like 'passion' and 'ocean.' I kick off my black work shoes and strip off my apron, already stained with salad dressing, sauce, and wine. The closet behind me says 'Tuxedo Shirts' and I take a hanger, buttoning the shirt to the neck and placing it back in the closet for it to be cleaned by a professional laundry service in St. Ignace. This convenience comes out of my pay check.

Tonight Brenna isn't wearing underwear, just a thin black strip of pubic hair visible before she pulls up her pants.

'I can't stand wearing them,' she claims.

Blue, a tiny girl with dark hair and a delicate silver cross which she wears on the outside of her uniform, disagrees, maintaining that vaginas are like feet.

'It's like wearing no socks with running shoes,' she says, scrunching her nose. 'And then your feet start sweating.'

I have never considered *not* wearing panties and, despite this warning, I make up my mind not to wear any tomorrow.

★

The pub I'd been to on my first night turns out to be the employee bar of choice. Its proper title is the Cockpit Club, but it has obtained an affectionate nickname over the years.

Rummy and I agree to meet at the Cock after work, as it also happens to be the closest bar to the restaurant. The two buildings face one another on Main Street, and the time elapsed from clocking out to having your first sip of beer is about five minutes. It is maybe twenty feet from the door of the Tippecanoe to the front door of the Cock, but I ride my bike anyway, pedaling quickly for ten feet and then coasting the last ten. I park a suitable distance away from the bike I know belongs to Bryce. I do not lock it.

It's a cold northern Michigan night, and I'm wearing a bright sweater the color of a new leaf. He sees me through the glass doors before I open them, and inside the bar is thick with warmth, almost hot. John the bartender doesn't recognize me yet but gives me a nod, and Bryce is standing by the jukebox.

'Hey, come help me pick songs,' he says. He feeds a bill into the machine. 'You first,' he tells me.

I flip the selections back and forth taking my time, and I finally choose 'Hollywood Nights' by Bob Seger, a song I always pick first. He presses F8, a song by James Brown. We both agree on Michael Jackson for the last one. My song begins suddenly, the line about the girl standing bright as the sun. Bryce motions to a couch full of people I haven't met yet.

The girls in his group are singing along, 'he was a Midwestern boy', and waving their martini glasses in time to the music.

I glance at them, then back at Bryce. 'Thanks,' I say. 'But I'm meeting Rummy.'

He smiles at me. 'Well, you're welcome to join me. I promise not to sing.'

★

I am half pleased at appearing so indifferent and half mortified to have refused his offer. Sitting up at the bar alone as the sing-along turns into shrieking giggles, I decide if Rummy doesn't arrive soon I'll have to pretend to talk on my phone. Taking it from my bag, there is no signal.

The Cock is small, and caters to the island workers, not the tourists. It is brightly lit by fluorescent bulbs, and the chairs and tables are white plastic. Against the left wall and out of place are two leather couches – probably cast-offs from a family living room – and against the right wall the bar extends the length of the room.

Rummy arrives when I am halfway through my first pint.

'He'll have a gin and seven up,' I tell the bartender.

Rummy sits down heavily on his stool, sweat on his face even though it's cool outside. He shakes his head.

'I've never had such a stressful job before,' he says.

John sets the gin and seven in front of him and Rummy eyes it warily before pulling out the straw and draining the glass.

'I'd rather have my rye and ginger,' he says.

He motions to John and asks for a shot of rye whisky in his ginger ale. John shrugs. Rummy turns back to me.

'So have you ever heard of Hamilton, Ontario?'

I think for a moment. 'I've heard of Newfoundland. My parents saw a moose there, a huge one by the side of the road.'

He decides to ignore this. 'That's a different province. Do you like Lifesavers?'

'The candy?'

'They were made in Hamilton. For seventy years, every Lifesaver sold in North America was made in a factory down the street from my house.'

'No shit,' I say.

I lean back on my stool and turn my head slightly to see what Bryce is doing, while Rummy continues.

'You could tell what flavor they were making because of the smell. On the days when they made butterscotch, the whole street would be lined with people. Neighbors. Kids. Standing around. Sniffing.'

Bryce is sitting back on the couch, looking relaxed and, I think, a bit bored amid the shouts of the girls around him. He looks over and nods. I lean forward again and look at Rummy.

'I like the green Lifesavers,' I say.

He rolls his eyes at me. 'Green is not a flavor.'

Drunk already from the vodka he sips during work, Trainer joins us, slamming his empty water bottle proudly on the surface of the bar. He slides into the high-backed barstool next to Rummy, slinging his backpack off his shoulder. Trainer is tall, large, and bearded, his Cleveland Indians hat frayed at the edges and lined with sweat stains. He looks at me, then at Rummy.

'You're the Canadian,' he says, as a statement.

Rummy says *yes* as if he's resigned himself to this new identity.

'Where are you from again?' Rummy asks.

'Sandusky. You know Cedar Point?'

'No.'

'The amusement park.'

'Sorry.'

'Well, it's in Sandusky.'

Trainer turns and looks straight ahead, sipping his Belvedere and soda until Rummy asks if he's ever heard of Hamilton. Trainer hasn't, but has been to Toronto. They begin discussing the city while I concentrate on appearing interested, wondering if I should go to the bathroom so I can pass by the leather couch. Soon, however, Trainer's favorite haunts in Ontario's capital command my attention. He orders another drink, and attempts to enlighten Rummy and myself.

'Well, my first time I was eighteen. I'd been chatting with this guy from TO online, and we'd agreed to meet. He was thirty-six. I told my mom I was going to see the Hockey Hall of Fame.'

'That's in Canada?' I ask.

Trainer ignores me and continues. 'Got there after nine hours on the Greyhound, and he takes me to this pretty seedy place.' He pauses. 'Well, pretty much any bathhouse I've been in is seedy. We bypassed the slurp ramp for the hot tubs. You guys know what a slurp ramp is?'

Rummy and I shake our heads.

'It's like this platform with curtains all around you, and in the curtains are slits about waist high to stick your dick through.'

I imagine Trainer naked, fitting his penis through a hole in a stiff curtain. Immediately his life seems much more interesting than mine.

'So, whatever, that's not my bag, we went to the hot tub. It's like, really crowded. I had to walk down the steps with my wang flopping from side to side until I reached the surface. So the hot tub's just full of these floating dicks, literally.'

'So what do you do when you're in there?' I want to know.

'Whatever you want.'

His second drink finished already, he orders a Bud this time, and winks as he lifts the bottle to his lips. 'Predictable is boring,' he says.

Although I roll my eyes when he says this, I'm often susceptible to the type of people who make these sweeping pronouncements.

John's Yellow Submarine is the drink special, written on a chalkboard next to the Pac Man video game. The ingredients are listed as blended vanilla ice cream, Baileys, and banana liqueur. I order one of these next, and it comes with half a banana stuck upright onto the side of the glass.

Trainer confides that he trusts Rummy because he's from Canada. There is no particular logic to this, only Trainer's perception of Canadians as being the coolest people in the world.

'Canadians are funnier than us,' he states. 'And I don't feel like a homo in Toronto.'

'And we make great Lifesavers,' Rummy adds.

Trainer wants to know what the hell he's talking about.

'I like the green ones,' I say again.

Bryce arrives beside me at the bar to pay his tab, and tells me he's meeting someone down the street.

'A buddy of mine,' he says. 'You'll probably meet him.'

I want to go with him, to pretend I was just leaving myself, but he's bought me a beer and I can't leave it.

He sets it in front of me saying, 'Labbatt's, right?'

I nod and thank him, and, without breaking eye contact, he says, 'No problem. The first of many.'

I don't turn to watch him go, but I know when he's gone.

'He seems nice,' Rummy says.

When I leave the bar at two thirty alone, Trainer is walking with difficulty up Main Street, held up by someone half his size.

He gives me a wave and yells, 'Juan here is helping me home tonight because Juan is so fucking hot. Isn't that right, Juan?'

Juan nods and looks pleased.

As I walk towards my bike, I have a sense of how important

this all is. Of how each star is warm and the night is good and the sound of bikes and horses should be recorded so that everyone can hear, everyone can know how important this all is. These thoughts are interrupted by me falling over.

St. Paul, 12:57 p.m.

That's what it was like in the beginning; the magic of new people and the openness of sky. The flicker burning of discovery and the sensation of everything way ahead and waiting. It's funny how quickly I adapted that summer. How easily I slid into the flow of things, like stepping into a river and letting myself be carried away. I learned the customs instantly, the job in a single day. I envied the other girls for their quick opinions, long nails, and loud laughter that turned heads. I suppose I always stood out though – my straight hair that wasn't blonde, eyebrows that weren't plucked too thin and with a way of listening hard that made people tell me things, even when I had nothing to say in return. But now I am glad for that.

I do a lot of thinking these days, when I'm not busy with everything else. It is the island I think of most; sometimes my hands feel tired and bloody from battering on the door of the past, begging to be let back in.

After all these years I still have my tea in the same mug, washing it after every use by hand. With a small black picture of a birch bark canoe, the elaborate cursive script of *The Tippecanoe* is still visible, perhaps only because I know where it is. I pour half a cup of boiling water over the teabag and poke it about with a spoon, the scent of bergamot rising as the water turns black, bitter. Steam from the kettle clouds the kitchen window white and wet.

Outside the oak leaves have turned brown but have not fallen. The yellowing grass is not quite dead. St. Paul in the fall. Hunting season is just beginning: bear, snipe, trout, deer. Crossbow hunting only, for the adult bucks. Not that I've ever gone near a rifle, but I know enough to make small talk with the neighbors when I'm forced to. Althea next door is ninety-six and owns a lever-action Marlin 336 SS. 'The components are stainless steel so it'll survive anything,' she explained of her fifty-year-old deer rifle. 'Now pretend that pumpkin is someone's head,' she told me, pointing into her backyard and hoisting the gun up to her shoulder. Two days later I was still scraping pumpkin guts from the siding of my house. Althea keeps the rifle loaded under her bed in case a foul-weather hunter decides to become an opportunist. I go over sometimes to help her read her mail.

These last fifteen years hunters have become a common sight in our neighborhood backyards, out for deer or raccoons when the city is shut down. I keep my pantry stocked and my head down. I'm too old to play with guns.

Having nothing else to do, I begin worrying briefly about the weather predicted for this evening, the hurricane of snow bright red on the digital radar, descending south from Alberta in the mad mix of hail, rain, high winds, and huge drifts of snow we have come to expect.

Worry gives a small thing a big shadow, my mother would say in her odd, cheerful wisdom. In her day she would have been right. But the storm is two hundred miles across, fully equipped with its own shadow. A 6.5 capable of darkening two states at a time.

Taking a bottle from under the sink I fill the Tippecanoe cup to the top. Even if the storm descends, the new armored city snowplows will be out along with the high-capacity salt trucks and national guard weather vehicles; I decide it will probably miss St. Paul altogether. It must. When it does, I will indulge myself – wondering thoughtfully if my own determination to *believe* can alter an omnipotent predetermined outcome. This morning it's still about ten degrees, and almost sunny.

Anna appears in the kitchen with a denim jacket over her sweatshirt, dark hair in a bun, huge purse bulging with items gleaned from our morning's work. It seems like we have been clearing for weeks – sorting, throwing everything away.

'I'm off. Be safe tonight, Mom.'

'Is that a new purse?' I ask.

She checks the thermostat, then lines up my afternoon pills on the kitchen counter.

'It *is* new,' I say. 'It's a *leather* purse.' I make a mooing sound and she rolls her eyes.

'I don't *eat* cows, Mother, but I've decided I don't mind wearing them.'

'You're getting old,' I tell her, pleased.

She pats me on the shoulder. 'No more ice cream before bed, remember.'

This morning I answered the door to Anna in my nightgown, ice cream stained all down the front from last night when I fell asleep watching television. The last of the carton melted all over me, but I'd been too tired to get up and change. It was a cold, sticky sleep. Anna had looked at the material, and up at me. 'Mom, why do you look like you took a chocolate bath?'

'It leaked.'

She helped me with my bath then, though I could have washed myself.

'Keep an eye on the weather,' she tells me now. 'It's a 6.5.'

We both look out the window.

'It will be fine,' I say, confidently. 'Look, a blue jay.'

She doesn't see it, but she didn't look either.

The front door shuts behind her and she walks into the wind chimes that are hanging too low from the roof's overhang.

'Goddamn you,' she says matter-of-factly.

The hollow pitch of the chimes echoes in my head long after I hear her car start and drive away.

In the quiet minutes that pass in her absence, the blue jay in the oak tree is still, and I wonder if it isn't a branch after all. If I could lift my arms properly and be sure I had a proper grip on the rock, I would go outside to see if I had imagined him, or if the bird would fly away.

I want Anna to come back, to make her watercress and banana sandwiches on multi-grain bread and talk about the advanced downward dog *asana* she is practicing for yoga and the different essential oils she uses on her mat. *Lavender and geranium. For balance.* I want another voice besides my own internal narrator – someone aloud and real to keep me from pulling up anchor and sailing into the past. *Wallowing*, Anna calls it. *Remembering* is different from wallowing, I told her once.

'Not when you do it for weeks at a time,' she said.

But who's to judge? I map my veins as they come and go, down through my arms, into my wrists, thick and blue over the tops of my knuckles. My hands look swollen, and remembering my water pills, I take two and retreat to the bathroom to wait. I bought the ones with calcium included to help strengthen my bones. Two years ago I fell, breaking my collarbone in two places, but I haven't broken anything since. Sitting straight with my hands on my naked thighs I inspect each swollen finger, waiting for them to deflate as my body drains. Absently I wish we'd been bold enough to paint the house a dramatic color instead of opting for off-white. When we moved in we did all the decorating and painting ourselves – wallpaper, paint, everything. Everything white. Clean. Empty. Our first place together – we thought we might upgrade in a few years and the real estate agent advised white houses sell better. That's what we did. Moved in thinking about moving out. We bought it the year Anna was born.

'It's like living in an egg,' Alan had said approvingly, tapping the walls with a knuckle.

'What happens when we hatch?' I'd asked.

He had raised an eyebrow at me then, a talent for facial contortion that I lack.

Anna's just done her house in terracotta and yellows, each room like a vacation. 'I couldn't resist,' she said. 'Now I'm on my own I can do the walls whatever color I want.' 'Join the club,' I said.

My system flushed, I return to the kitchen, taking a sip from my mug and breathing the fumes back quickly. The tea is too hot, and, still, I am not quite ready for what lies before me on the table.

I put the mug back on its coaster, part of a set we received for Christmas years ago from Anna and her then-husband. They bought them during an eco-vacation in Venezuela and, according to Anna, the coasters are made of fair trade wood and painted with organic paints. The one under my mug has the stylized image of a naked woman on it, holding what looks like a bucket and spade and standing underneath a palm tree. Her nipples are round blobs of brown paint, and they are both the same size.

I think I will get rid of these too, never having liked them much in the first place. Moving my mug off the coaster I test its weight, smooth and light in my hand, before awkwardly flinging it into the hallway like a Frisbee, listening with satisfaction as it smacks against the wall.

Funny what we hang onto because it never occurs to us to let it go.

Mackinac

The first evening Bryce and I spend alone together, we walk. My bike has been stolen. I was told to buy a lock but I didn't, feeling that rich tourists must be above thieving. It is now probably in the harbor, the victim of a drunken employee joy ride. This doesn't stop me examining every bicycle that goes by – a few BMX bikes like Bryce's from the eighties; some old-school Raleigh Choppers mostly owned by island kids; tourists on tandems; one Schwinn Sting Ray which Bryce points out to me, impressed; a few mountain bikes; one or two sixties-era Free Spirits from Sears. But none of them are mine, and it's exhausting. We are walking to a place called Sunset Rock, but we've missed the sunset.

Above us the clouds are gray illuminated trails, still and waiting. In the sharp promise of evening we leave behind the tourists, carriages, drunks, and the wide street curves up and away, becoming a narrow path with just enough space for one carriage to pass. He is taking me into the heart of the island, secret and isolated from the town that stands busy and erect by the water. Beyond Main Street, Bryce tells me, the land is inhabited by year-round and summer residents, and that's where the real island begins. He points out the grand façade of a million-dollar summer home, planted secretly among a stand of trees, and it is perfect with a front porch, stone chimney, lavender plants, and lemon-colored paint. There is a gate, but no garage, which makes sense but still strikes me as odd. We pass five more like it. Soon there's only forest on either side, the trees labeled every so often with black placards – sugar maple, silver maple, balsam fir, yellow birch. The paved road turns to gravel, the sound of our passage marked by the crunching under our feet. Birds sing in the trees, hidden.

We follow the signs for the National Park, the Post Cemetery, and the rock formations. We follow the network of paths named and laid out and marched upon by British and American soldiers.

Above us to the north is Canada, and below us our entire country.

It is dusk, and it doesn't seem possible the island can stretch so far. We veer off into deep grass that is slightly trampled, then into the forest. The canopy of trees absorbs the evening light. He loses his way and flicks his cigarette lighter. The ground cover is leafy and black, and we can't find the trail. The metal keeps burning his hand; each time it lights we search the undergrowth.

'There are only a few bears on the island, so we should be okay,' he says.

Then he points. 'There.'

As if we are walking through a crowd and I need to be led, he reaches his hand back to grab mine, and I follow him onto the path.

Sunset Rock is a man-made balcony built into a steep hill overlooking the lake. It is made of both cement and rock and the words 'Sunset Rock' are spelled out in pebbles embedded along the ledge. It faces southwest, and the sky is gray now. I can see Mackinac Bridge in the distance, crossing the straits and connecting the hand of Michigan to its upper peninsula. It is the third longest suspension bridge in the world although I'd never heard of it until now. Bryce tells me that in 1977, twenty years after it opened, a gust of high wind swept a woman and her Toyota right off the bridge into the water. Her car was found although her body never was.

Lights from the mainland are starting to become visible. Headlights move far away along the bridge. There are no sounds except for the wind and the lake. Of all the Blues and Brennas, it is me who is here.

From the bushes Bryce retrieves a bottle of red wine and two glasses.

'I didn't know whether to buy red or white.'

'Holy shit. Come here often?'

He pretends to be hurt.

'I don't even like wine,' he says. 'But it seemed better than bringing cans of beer.'

I have to agree with him.

Despite his planning he has forgotten a corkscrew, so we improvise with his penknife, gouging out small pieces of cork until it finally drops down into the neck of the bottle. We strain the bits of cork through our teeth.

After half the bottle, I set my empty wine glass on the pebbled balcony, enjoying the pleasant sound as it scrapes the stone. Bryce does the same and we lean on our elbows, staring out together into the horizon.

As we talk he doesn't ask what my favorite color is, whether I have a birthmark somewhere on my body, and he doesn't want to know my middle name. He does not ask and then say, *I could tell you were an Aquarius.*

Instead he points to something on the rocky beach below us.

'Look.'

I can't see anything. Bryce moves closer to me, our cheeks touch as I look down the length of his arm to where he is pointing. Then, slowly, it moves. Backside waddling carefully, tail flat and serene, the black shape reaches the water, wades in, and disappears. We stay silent, watching, but nothing else moves except the waves.

'Nice beaver,' Bryce says, and I punch him in the arm.

We talk more about the island and he mentions all the things he'd like me to see.

'We have lots of time,' he says.

And we do. By the time we finish the wine it is black out. It is too cool for mosquitoes but we think we hear a raccoon.

'Let's toss our glasses.'

This is my suggestion; I want to hear them break. He agrees without hesitating.

'On three, ready?'

He starts to count. I hold the fat part of my glass upside down in the palm of my hand like a baseball, the stem extending between my knuckles. We reach back and throw together. There is nothing to reflect the light as they spin out into the night. His lands in the water with a far-away swallowing sound. My throw is shorter and the glass smashes on the narrow lane of the M-185 below.

'Do you think that'll shred some kid's bike tires?' I wonder.

He thinks it probably will.

Then he tells me he borrowed the wine glasses with Velvet's permission, promising their return. He shrugs.

On the walk back, I break my shoe. It's only a black flip-flop made of plastic and can be easily replaced. I leave them both behind, feeling carefree. We are ten minutes into the twenty-minute walk when the path turns to gravel. The wine doesn't keep this from hurting.

An unforgiving sunrise illuminates his narrow bed the next morning and I leave it reluctantly, moving slowly. The feel of the thick white scar running down his left bicep stays on the end of my tongue – the place where his sister's ice skate opened his skin when he was ten. The ridge of flesh where it healed is uneven, soft, and oily to taste. I myself have a scar from my uncle's threshing machine, but we didn't discuss this.

I have just enough time to throw up, find my clothes and run to my apartment to find my work clothes before leaving for my eight a.m. shift.

From the Pine Suites I turn right on the road into town. Except for a few early morning workers coasting past, tires whizzing, feet motionless on the pedals and disappearing in seconds, the wide street is empty. The small blue house on my left is used as staff quarters for one of the souvenir shops downtown, a dozen bicycles lie on the lawn and by the front door. Five minutes further on, the road is lined with red and yellow tulips, the golf course wet with morning dew on the left. The air smells of clean laundry and sweet fudge and the lake. Wet and alive and calm. I am relieved of the guilt accumulated from childhood science projects on pollution; this air is separate from industry.

By the time I reach town the morning mist is lifting, taking with it my hangover. Almost.

Turning left, Main Street is straight and long, with porches, balconies, and wide sidewalks. There is no place for modernity here it seems; everything built recently matches the architecture from the past. The older buildings have been carefully preserved and are all made of wood, whitewashed, and joined together in rows. Though most of the doorways enter into pubs there are also stores selling candy, ice cream, and fudge. Interspersed between these are the Tippecanoe's competitors – the Lakeview, the Carriage House, the Island House. There are flags everywhere. Stylish old-fashioned banners, half circles of red, white, and blue hang from atop buildings. These banners have a historical feel to them, and I imagine in sepia tones a presidential parade with everyone on fine horses, the president munching on a half pound slice of peanut butter fudge.

I give a nod to one of the trash collectors. I don't know his name, but he has an eight ball tattooed onto his forehead, and a long black pool cue complementing this on his cheekbone. The trash collectors come around once a week, sitting atop massive dumpsters pulled by a team of horses. Free from the stigma this occupation carries at home, this man has risen to the top of the island's job chain. Or so Bryce has told me. The guy with the spider-web head stops at every establishment on the island, picking up the trash from restaurants and pubs, and making drop-offs to his clientele. This is how the drugs circulate the island. A weekly pick-up and delivery service.

By the store that sells plastic shot glasses I walk past a woman in a sweatshirt holding a camera and wearing American flag shoes. They are flat slip-on shoes made of canvas. The day's first ferryboat must have arrived.

The school groups, the bus tours, and the families who can't really afford the island arrive very early in the morning and leave on the last ferryboat home. They come for the fudge, the beer, the guided tours, and the main street. The visitors with money are the businessmen, the retired couples, the yachters, and the politicians. Sleeping off hangovers in their expensive island hotels and floating mansions during the day, they emerge at night for the food, the wine, and the fairytale.

I walk into work, through the back into the changing room. Velvet gives me a brief nod as I meet her in the hallway.

'Five minutes late,' she says, as she passes.

Trainer emerges from the bathroom in the hall and cheerfully gives both middle fingers to Velvet's retreating form. Then he takes a closer look at me.

31

'You look freshly fucked,' he says.

The weather will be warm today, I can feel it.

Five hours later my hands still smell like orchids. Velvet has her favorite purple orchids flown in every morning from a flower shop in Chicago. A man who I hear was late for delivery only once, and never again, delivers them to the restaurant from the airport. My job is to fill the square glass vases on each table with one cup of water, and one flowering purple orchid. These are knocked over every other night by drunk customers as the vases are really too tall for the tables, but the tradition continues proudly in the face of common sense. Bryce tells me this practice costs her over a thousand dollars a day. When the weather prevents the plane from making its daily delivery, we learn to stay out of her way.

The further inland I walk from the Tippecanoe the more the tourist/nature divide becomes evident. The forest is thick and silent with no bicyclists or carriages, and the hot sweat of work becomes easy to forget. The only reminder is the thick perfume on my hands, and I decide never to buy orchids for any reason in my lifetime or stoop to smell them wherever they may be. The afternoon is now mine, and I have a lead on a bicycle. Tom, one of the cooks from the restaurant, said he stashed his old bike at the airport last year, and this year returned with a new one. Over six feet tall, Tom had winked at me from behind the hot line this morning.

'It's yours if you want it,' he said.

Then, seemingly to himself: 'What I wouldn't give to be a bike seat some days.'

I walk through the forest following the arrow-shaped 'airport' signs, until the paved path turns to grass. There is a long field and one building. The two runways are inexplicably numbered 'eight' and 'twenty-six.' In front of the building is

Tom's bike, unlocked, as he'd described it. I suppose the airport is too far to travel for common thievery.

Because of my perfect score on the Chamber of Commerce Test for New Island Employees, I know the airport averages about sixty-five flights a day in high season, all of the planes small twin engines and expensive. About three quarters of these flights are private, usually men flying in from Chicago or Cleveland. They radio their approximate arrival time to the one airport employee, requesting a taxi when they touch down. When I serve these men at the restaurant they look at their wristwatches. *Just flew in for the day*, they say over their shrimp cocktails and tumblers of Oban.

I wonder sometimes at the luxury I am allowed to mingle with here, and if it will ever be mine.

The rest of the flights are air taxis from the mainland. Rummy took one over the other night after he missed the last ferry, and he said the floor of the plane had rusted away in spots and was covered by wooden planks. A metal folding chair was set up in the back for him to sit on. He suspected the pilot might be drunk.

'The pretentious part of me wanted to make fun of it,' he said. 'But I was shitting my pants the whole time.'

Twenty minutes later after a wind-buffeted landing, he resolved never to miss the last ferry ever again.

I sit on my new mode of transport with pride, marveling that while I lost an expensive mountain bike, this vintage model is like something from an old French movie where girls in long black skirts and red lipstick ride about through cobble-stoned streets, and there's even a basket. The wide seat is made of cracked white canvas, the silver fenders brown with rust. It also has a kickstand. Navy blue with solid metal bars, this bike looks like it will last forever.

I get lost trying to ride back, but taking the trails that run downhill I eventually reach the lake. Emerging from the trees about five minutes from town, I ride casually over to the Tippecanoe to look at Bryce through the window. It's not too busy and he notices my bike, giving the thumbs up. After looking over his shoulder for Velvet, he points to his crotch, then taps his watch.

We will meet at the Cock when he's done work. Nodding to show him I understand, he smiles then continues the complicated napkin fold for the swan at table eleven. I begin the ride back uphill to Tippecanoe housing, wishing my new bike had more than one gear.

I shower, shave, and lotion, debating my choice of underwear, finally deciding on a pink lacy thong. I've just discovered that bike seats and no underwear are not a pleasant combination.

I also think it is better to be naked in stages.

Brushing my teeth twice, I make sure to get the back of my tongue and the spaces between my gums and wisdom teeth. A drop of concealer covers the mole by my eyebrow that is slightly too dark.

At ten I leave my apartment door unlocked and ride into town, my hair straight and long in the wind, and the feeling of the island in my veins. I careen downhill around nervous tourists with baby carriers attached to bikes, and though my hands are on the brakes I never use them.

Main Street is busy with the sounds of Friday, and the dark road is illuminated on either side with lights from the bars. Bicycles line the curbs in a chaos of silver and color and wheels and Bryce is waiting for me inside the Cock with two brandy glasses in front of him.

The Flambouie is a ritual that newcomers to the island are initiated with, he explains. It is a shot of Drambuie liqueur heated in a glass with a lighter, and then a second glass is placed atop the first to capture the alcohol fumes before they escape. Typically a crowd of well-wishers will gather to shout encouragement. I have two, whipping the top glass off of each shot, breathing the fumes quickly as if it's a drug, and then downing the hot liqueur in a swallow. My stomach burns and it feels like living.

John pours me another, for free.

We sit on the leather couches and this time I belong. The large television near the bar shows a gold-colored football team playing a blue one with the sound turned down. Someone that Bryce knows falls off her barstool, but she's okay and orders another beer. An elderly couple walk in and then out again, looking for a different, perhaps more sophisticated Mackinac experience, and I imagine the woman is looking for 'a glass of your house chardonnay', and the man will try a local beer because he's on holiday and feeling adventurous. Beside the couch Rummy is talking to Blue who is drinking orange juice, her dark hair layered attractively around her face, the silver of her cross resting between the delicate points of her collarbone.

'I hear people from Canada say "hoser" a lot?' she asks him.

Rummy smiles, and I can tell he's making allowances for her.

'Lots of rumors about us Canadians,' he says. 'Whatever you've heard it's all true.'

He leers at her, and she laughs nervously, poking her orange-juice straw around her glass. When she is done he gets her another one.

The jukebox is loud and continuous, the sound of the Pac-Man video game bleeps in the background and Bryce wants to know where my adorable mole went, the one by my eyebrow. I laugh and rub away the concealer. Sober I might have been mortified, but instead feel only mild embarrassment. Bryce leans over and licks it.

When I stumble up to the bar for another drink I notice Trainer, sitting by himself.

'You lucky bitch,' he says, and I smile.

At the end of the night Bryce pays our tab and helps me out the door, telling me to follow him. There is a trail he says, a not so short cut that he wants to show me. He makes sure I am steady on my bike before retrieving his.

'It's too hard to stay straight,' I say, feeling that I could probably stay straight just fine.

'Once you start pedaling,' he says, 'you'll be perfect. You see this?'

He points to a thin sliver of line on the left side of his chin.

'The tequila did me in last summer, went right off the street and into a lamppost.'

'That's not comforting me.'

'But it's because I forgot to pedal. So just remember to keep pedaling and you'll be fine. I promise.'

'I really like my new bike,' I say.

We leave the town behind. Instead of continuing up the paved road to the Pine Suites, he veers to the right across some gravel and behind the massive barn owned by the carriage company. The noise of the horses echoes off the high wooden rafters, the sound mournful and loud. Then we are past the barn and the silence encompasses us again as we pedal up an incline towards the trees. I cannot see the path anymore as we enter the forest. If I look up I can see where the trees meet the sky, though just barely, and in the darkness the oak and pine are all one massive wall. There are no streetlights, no sounds, and my entire world is this. We are hurtling too fast through the darkness together and I am afraid of not being fast enough to keep up. I pedal furiously to stay right behind his back tire. As our bikes glide around the curves of the trail he looks back to see if I am keeping up. He keeps looking back and I want to yell:

I can do it!

I'm here!

I won't be left behind!

I want to laugh and say, 'I'm not a girl that you need to take care of, Bryce.'

But I don't say it because I wouldn't mean it. I don't say it because he is looking after me and I never asked him to. He gives a shit whether or not I am behind him and he is checking to make sure. I trust him because I have to and he is not fucking off and riding too fast and I am almost crying because it is such a relief to have this.

Pedaling into infinity, this island feels more real than any other place I have lived. I work every day and drink every night and excess is expected and encouraged and *there is not enough time*, but that's exactly the point. My friendships here are lively and spontaneous compared to the girls at St. Kat's now far away and boring with too much education, and there is a man in front of me, a quick ghostly form turned solid and safe in the darkness, and I am beginning to think of him as mine.

St. Paul, 1:35 p.m.

With my chocolate-covered nightgown in the garbage, Anna helped choose my outfit this morning. The decision of what to wear was difficult. If the storm arrived as predicted I would need to be warm, which meant unflattering woolen socks, full cotton underwear and a long-sleeved shirt, which in turn meant unearthing the large Tupperware container marked WINTER CLOTHING from the basement. If the storm veered or dissipated, as they often did, the temperature would stay relatively the same. Rapid Weather Patterns, the government calls them. Appearing fully formed on radar and disappearing as quickly, they are exact, perfect storms with a disciplined set of precipitation rings that destroy everything underneath. I've experienced only one, though there have been many warnings.

The first three appeared in rapid succession over a period of two days in California, and the images were fantastic. Buildings covered in ice, flooded with three feet of water, everything glistening in the quiet aftermath, holes punched through cars and roofs by hailstones. The property values for the homes left standing dropped so quickly, those who weren't displaced simply left. Santa Fe and Salt Lake took most of the influx – the first city by choice, the second by charity.

I was in Monterey for the opening of the Sun Palms, the first of the big resorts the government built to bring in revenue for the rebuilding effort. Meredith and I went in expensive bikinis, drank too much, and met a military man. He'd been from the bay area, which was still underwater, and when the cannonballs of hail hit he'd been walking his dog Mobius – a real pretty beagle, the man told us. When the hail stopped there was nothing left on the end of his leash but pulp, and he was barely conscious anyway, floating down his own neighborhood street in thirteen hours' worth of rain, hail, and snow. I wanted to know what happened next, and he said a family in Bountiful had taken him in, their ward helping him through *his journey*. A Mormon family, and I nodded. We all looked out over the water together. What I wouldn't give for a boiled egg, he told us. But all the chickens had died years ago from the flu.

When I left California, its border rendered as arbitrary as I guess it ever was, I brought a T-shirt for Alan that said, *I survived California's RWPs and all I got was this lousy T-shirt.* But he wouldn't wear it, and I suppose he was right. He usually kept my poor taste in check.

My optimism about the likelihood of the storm veering off course, and also because I was too tired to retrieve my winter clothes from the basement, led me to choose a short-sleeve knitted pullover in a solid wine color, dark and flattering against my pale skin.

'This color really takes the years off,' said Anna, plucking approvingly at the material.

I decided to wear jeans because they made me feel younger.

What's missing is a flat abdomen and suntanned arms, though I never tanned very well, and now there's no sweat on the backs of my legs or low-slung pants to barely conceal my pubic hair. What's gone is the feeling of everything years and years ahead, and here I am counting down the hours to an evening.

I'll take what I can get.

My tea's gone cold.

I have all of my old journals, two from that Mackinac

summer, although I don't know how I ever found the time to write. The seventy-five books are on a shelf in the hall closet, and will remain there until I die. I wonder what will happen to them when I am gone. If Anna will find them and throw them away, or if she will sit and read, taking an afternoon, then an evening, a weekend, to know me better.

One Saturday, years ago, while Anna and her father were at the Tomahawk Ropes Course in Mankato, I did a meticulous search of her bedroom and found her journal, feeling embarrassed I was so curious and disappointed there seemed to be nothing else to find. My daughter was a mysterious woman, and what I did not know about her seemed suddenly astounding that afternoon; it was irresponsible to be so ignorant. In the drawer of her bedside table, where I found one green apple-flavored condom, was a clean white book with a quotation on the cover – *The Past and Future are Illusions. They Exist in the Present. Which is What there is and All there is.* The beginning of her interest in Zen; she was just fourteen. Sitting on her bed and locking the door, I decided to start at the end. I still remember the words exactly, written in anger and outlining her opinion of me. I snapped the book shut, humiliated. In the bathroom I ran a hot shower and cried, while afterwards, standing naked in front of the steamed-up mirror I turned and strained to see the soft blue mark of the tattoo from so long ago. I rubbed moisturizer into my face with an upward motion, careful not to tug the skin. I was snippy with Alan for a week.

Would I have been upset if it weren't true?

I imagine with a delicious horror the skeletons that might jump out from the pages of my own past, an army waving words like knives and stabbing everyone that's left – although recently too many of these skeletons have been aired, their bones brittle but hard in the sunlight.

40

Journal number 18, the year after the island:

Test negative. This entry was followed by a drawing of a bare-breasted woman with angry pubic hair.

Journal number 36, right after we slept together:

Alan's penis is marginally better than Dan's. A bit longer. Great Lakes birthmark, nice hands.

Journal number 46, right after I started at the office:

Russ took me to 22 Musgrave. Drink Drink. Roast Chicken. Government Amex.* Remember to ask Patty about his lazy eye*

An unnumbered journal, from my thirties:

The hailstones are here, big as babies. In the basement. Anna won't stop crying.

I sorted through the books earlier today after boxing up the old bed linens. My purple sheets from college had been in that closet for almost fifty years along with my mother's handmade quilts, some old board games, and an instruction booklet for playing gin rummy. The entire top shelf had been stuffed with sad and oily plush toys Anna had insisted I keep, claiming there was no room in her own house for such things. I called her over and she emerged from my bedroom stopping to perform what she called 'the forward bend' *asana.*

'You're just touching your toes,' I pointed out.

She ignored me for a moment, exhaling loudly with her face between her knees before straightening.

'Yoga would really help your quality of life, Mother. We could do it together.'

At times, watching Anna makes me wish for my reclining chair, a place to sit, surrounded by my empty house with nothing around me to confuse or contradict my own understanding of the world.

I shook my head and pointed to the top shelf of the closet.

'Your animals,' I said.

'Oh my God!' Reaching up, she brought down a green rabbit. 'Holy shit, it's Bugsby!'

I told her that if she didn't pick one they were all going in the garbage. She rummaged through them, smelling their fur, finally putting them all in a garbage bag to take back to her house. She knew each one by name. Anna had created nametags for all her toys, printing the letters with black marker and affixing the *hello my name is* sticker to the plush and plastic breasts.

When the shelf was empty, Anna wrote her name in capital letters on a strip of masking tape and stuck it to the plastic bag, so that it wasn't confused with the others. She looked at me defiantly and said, 'Well, I won't keep *all* of them. I'll sort them out later.'

To which I replied, 'Yeah, right.'

She eyed my journals as she bagged up the animals, but did not say anything.

They sit alone in the closet now, except for a change of pillowcases and some extra blankets for the guest bedroom. An entire closet filled with my own words. I suppose the cupboard is haunted, in a way.

But I'm ready for them now.

The first is as blue as water, the other red and bound in cloth, both absent of any clever quotations. So much of my past in these pages, ready to be discovered, and I will read each page to remember the summer as it was, to help my guest and I to reminisce when he arrives after his long drive.

It is not yet two, the weather is steady in my backyard.

Reading back in time is tedious, tiring, deciphering the horrible handwriting, drunken handwriting, drunken thoughts. Nothing is dated, all the days run together. Beneath the words, *eight shots don't know how I got home fucking bike*, I have written, more coherently:

I am in love not because it is Saturday
or spring
not because I am drunk
or alone
not because he is what I was waiting for
but because I am here.

These words have not lost their importance to me, even written so long ago. And what better reason to love?

I run my fingers over the page, but I can't feel the depression of the letters anymore.

Mackinac

The sun reflects off the water and the roads, and brightens the white buildings. It bakes the island dry and dusty, so by the end of the day the streets are covered in a thin layer of dried horseshit that the men with their wheelbarrows are unable to collect. The dust creeps up pant legs and covers toes and sandals and I *know* that it's shit, but it looks like dust so it's okay.

When I sit to examine my dirty feet closely, I see the brown bits of undigested hay, like tiny slivers of sawdust. Unlike Main Street, scooped, shoveled, and washed clean at night with the town fire hose to emerge pristine and slightly damp the next morning, the shit builds up around our apartments, the flies loud and buzzing. Our road only qualifies for a once a week cleaning.

Inside, away from the breeze off the lake, the Pine Suites heat up with stagnant air, laundry begins to smell, leftover food brings ants (as Velvet's laminated warning signs had predicted) and the walls seem to be sweating. Our room smells of bodies.

Bryce makes us a pitcher of purple juice and we finish it quickly. When he swallows I can hear the liquid in his throat, and he makes an *ahhh* sound after every sip. I wonder if after a while this would get annoying, but he's too new, too good for me to wonder for very long. We lie on his bed, the one sheet shoved to the floor. He licks me with his tongue to see if it will leave a purple mark.

I reach under the bed for my journal. The cover is clean

and blue, the new paper white and stiff; I am trying not to fill its pages with things like, *laundry detergent*, or *remember my red shirt*. The sweat from my palm sticks to the fresh pages. Bryce wants to know what I'm writing.

'Secrets.'

'Tell me.'

I turn the pages as if looking for a specific passage.

June fourth, I read, *I think Bryce is just dreamy.*

'Fuck off. What are you writing, really?'

June fifth, I continue, *sometimes Bryce swears at me and it makes me sad.*

I am worried he might snatch the book from me. Instead he reaches absently across the bed to poke me in the back.

'You're very soft,' he says.

'Tell me about being Mormon,' I ask.

He stops poking. 'I don't think so.'

'I want to know. Do you have churches?'

'We have churches.'

'So what's the deal? Why Utah?'

'Wouldn't you rather have sex?' he asks.

I roll my eyes at him, and he sighs and then recites as if from a brochure:

Joseph Smith is the founder of the Church of the Latter Day Saints. The angel Moroni visited him in upstate New York, and the angel showed him a set of tablets, which laid the foundation for the Mormon religion.

'Where are they?'

'Where are what?'

'The tablets?'

'In heaven.'

'And this happened in upstate New *York*?'

'That's the story.'

'And Salt Lake City?'

'Good skiing,' he says.

'What was on the tablets?'

'Shit, it's one o'clock. The game's on.'

Bryce rolls off the bed, his chest tanned and wet with sweat, and punches the television on. His loose jeans reveal the tops of his boxers: a red and white heart pattern. He notices me noticing.

'They're functional, not sentimental,' he says, anticipating my question.

I decide to see his point. In the kitchen, he pulls a beer from the fridge and then returns, tossing something towards me.

'What's this?'

The magnet is plastic, and shows a man in eighteenth-century dress leading a wagon train and pointing. The magnet says, 'This is the place.'

'It's Brigham Young leading the Mormons to Salt Lake. I got it when I was there. You can have it, if you want.'

'It's fucking hideous. I don't want it.'

When I look up he winks at me, and I throw it at him.

'Who's Brigham Young?' I ask.

'I'm watching the game,' he says, climbing back into bed. He takes my hand absently, and kisses my knuckles as the red team beats the blue team in a game that goes into overtime.

Tonight the chef special is *duck confit*. Chef Walter refuses to tell me what *confit* means and I have to look it up in his special dictionary, its pages smeared with food and oil. *Confit* means, 'roasted in its own juices.'

'Isn't that what *picatta* means too?'

Chef Walter stares at me, then says, 'Look it up.'

I do, and *piccatta* means '*seared* in its own juices.' I tell Rummy and Trainer as they arrive what *confit* means.

The Tippecanoe is almost empty and it's raining gray drizzle outside. The heat from the early afternoon has evaporated taking the tourists with it, and I remember we left the bedroom windows open. Everyone stands around polishing silverware, drinking coffee, and helping each other with the *USA Today* crossword. We are stuck on twenty-three across, for which the clue reads: the abbreviation for a western state. We can't decide which states constitute western states, or if the clue includes places which are southwest, like New Mexico. We agree on UT, WA, MT, and NV, but we won't know which is right until the puzzle is almost done.

'The woman at table twelve has fake tits,' Brenna announces, as she enters the kitchen.

Rummy immediately goes out to check and reports back with the authority of an expert that they are most likely fake. A few of the girls go out to look as well, while Trainer says, 'It's got to be Utah, because thirteen down is Ukulele.'

He uses his black pen to fill in the spaces.

'Did I tell you I got a new bike?'

'Spare me,' Trainer says.

When I go out to check on my two tables, the couple that was sitting at table number five is now outside on the patio, the gray slate black and slick from the earlier afternoon rain. In fact the entire restaurant is outside, looking up. The air is wet with mist and there is a rainbow. A full arc seems to be projecting from the top of the lighthouse and curving over the entire expanse of the sky to fall somewhere by the last ferry dock at the other end of the island. Everyone is speaking softly, standing in groups. Table number five gives me their disposable camera, posing by the railing overlooking the water with the end of the rainbow falling behind them. As the mechanism makes a tiny clicking noise, I have a strange feeling in my throat.

Trainer appears beside me, licking black crossword ink from his fingers.

'God. A rainbow,' he says. 'What a fucking cliché.'

Velvet comes to get me, making careful high-heeled steps across the slate. Her black blouse is unbuttoned in such a way the pale beginnings of her breasts are visible, and she tells me the water glasses on table nineteen are empty. Table nineteen has already paid and refused my last offer to refill their glasses. There is no point in telling Velvet this. I take one more look at the sky before I follow her in.

As I approach the table, Velvet watching to ensure I do as she instructed, the couple are discussing the lighthouse. They turn to look at me.

'Which one is the famous one?' the woman wants to know.

'Sorry?'

'Well, there's the big white one, right there in the lake, and the little red one out there on the island across from us.'

I squint out the window, disbelieving. 'There's two?'

The couple look at me, and then out the window. The woman points: 'That one, and then that one.'

She points out the bright-red building and the lighthouse tower beside it. From a distance it looks like a house.

'Oh,' I say. 'I only ever noticed the big white one.'

I could never figure out why the white one was called Round Island Lighthouse when it wasn't on an island.

Realizing I have pointed out the Round Island Lighthouse incorrectly now to over a dozen guests, I instinctively look over my shoulder to make sure Velvet can't hear our conversation from where she is standing. Still holding the water pitcher, I awkwardly fill up their glasses without asking them, and retreat to the back of the restaurant where I decide I like the modern white lighthouse better than the famous one. Alone in the lake, the massive structure reflects the weather perfectly, glowing gold and pink with the sun, and turning gray with the storms. To me this is more valuable.

Trainer stands next to me for a while, his only table having a relaxed dinner with Mango Carpaccio appetizers and Glazed Walnut and Arugula salads before the main course. There are three couples, all the men gray-haired, the women lipsticked. The sort of table where it's awkward to drop the check, three hands reaching at once, everyone winking at you.

'Guess how much their bill is?' he asks.

'I don't know. Did you know there were two lighthouses?'

He looks at me. 'What the fuck are you talking about?'

I shake my head. 'Four hundred?' I guess.

'Six fifty,' he says.

As he starts to calculate his tip I look out the window, but the rainbow is gone.

Bryce tells me later on when I get out of work that he had seen the rainbow too, and had thought of me.

Then he says:

'I fucking nailed Brenna with a water balloon today.'

'That's the third rainbow I've ever seen in my life,' I say.

He puts an arm around me. 'You'll see tons more this summer, I promise.'

I like that he feels he can promise me this.

Then he adds grinning, 'She was soaked.'

Brenna is reading a book in which the narrator talks about waiters being a 'bad emotional risk.' These male waiters travel from restaurant to resort to hotel, learning, loving, hating, then moving on. This transient lifestyle has trained them to be incapable of longevity. They'll be pleasant to your face and then spit on your relationship behind your back. And they like to sample lots of different dishes.

'It's so true,' says Brenna. 'It's *so* my ex-boyfriend, Matt. He's such a cheating piece of shit.'

The other girls nod sympathetically and she turns to me.

'You're really lucky,' she says. 'Bryce is, like, husband material.'

Blue says she can't wait until she gets married. Her boyfriend's name is Jeremy.

Does the job make the man, or does the man take the job? I am optimistic. Bryce is a waiter, but he is very picky about what he eats. And I have it on good authority that he never spits in anyone's food.

St. Paul, 1:45 p.m.

June something: days steady, heat really hot. Bryce wants to buy a log cabin outside of Grayling and raise emus for a living. Rummy says Canada is our largest trading partner. Ingrown hair.

I never mothered my dolls when I was younger; I never changed their diapers or fed them plastic bottles. My toys were always teenagers, the stuffed bears on their way to the mall while the fat monkey got ready for dates with Applejack, the only male pony in the My Little Pony collection.

Then when I was older I kept abortion in my back pocket like a condom, just in case. Bryce and I even talked about it, both of us feeling we were being responsible by discussing the possibilities. A mini baby. A cell blob. A clot of blood. That was all. We laughed about it back then.

But when I was thirty I had no excuse for not wanting a baby anymore. Four years I had protested, while Alan would smile at babies and then look at me. There were times, I admit, when they made eye contact, warm and innocent in their new envelope of skin, that I wondered. But I was content to wonder.

Pregnancy crushed me – by the eighth month my belly was so distended I looked like a starving child. In complete denial of the upcoming event – my body expelling a human being from between my legs – I spared my *bump* all volumes and editions of the Womb Symphonies, the Pea-in-a-Pod aroma-therapy creams, the books designed to speed learning when read aloud to the fetus, and I continued working and drinking as if there was nothing else inside me but the things that belonged. Kidneys, liver, lungs.

I did let Alan read the newspaper in a loud voice though, towards the end.

I became too big to hide from the hands that would descend upon me in supermarkets. My black T-shirts and sweaters were long enough to cover all the skin of my stomach but not the shape of it, and still, bizarrely, the material would be lifted and strange female hands placed on either side of my bellybutton as if gaining access to some universal truth. As if this ability to grow other people under our skin connected us somehow. These joyful women were nothing like me, betraying me with wonderful, hopeful stories of childbirths that made them look off into the bags of frozen corn and smile.

Listen, baby, I would say alone, to my stomach. *Don't fuck with me.*

The depression afterwards nearly killed me. For the first few months, in the least violent of my dreams, I abandoned Alan and the baby in the middle of the night while leaking blood from between my legs. Before I could get out the door the leaking turned to gushing and I started to run, not even looking back at the crib as it began to float away on the rising tide of my own insides.

We only had one child. I told Alan if I got pregnant again I would stab myself through the stomach. He patted my knee and said he thought the doctors had less intrusive methods these days.

The *New York Times* had an article once long ago, about an elephant at the Calgary zoo that abandoned her calf, not knowing what to do with it. The staff made her watch as they cared for it, hoping to 'kick-start her maternal instincts.' Animal scientists came to study the mother, speculating as to what went wrong with nature. I wonder, really, just how unusual that is after all.

Now Anna sits before me day after day, organizing me. Saving me. Fit and full-figured, her long hair dyed chestnut, she arrives each morning to rid me of my past. Her determination to purge these memories makes me wonder if she's afraid I'm in danger of drowning – too many love letters, campaign buttons, and pressed maple leaves to sink my good judgment and understanding of time.

From eight until noon, we put shoes in garbage bags, place cufflinks aside for charity, and discuss healthcare and the weather and current events. Some days I will nap in my leather recliner and when I awake in the afternoon she is gone. After wandering around the house calling her name, I will return to my chair to await her evening phone call.

It is all the same to me, these constant and recycled day-light hours. Today is the exception. Anna understood I was nervous, though not the reason for it, and indulged me. She spoke clearly, gently, guiding me by the elbow from bedroom to bathroom to kitchen. She worries needlessly I believe, for whatever my physical ailments my mind is here, solid and thinking and faithful to the realities of which I need to be aware.

Sometimes, I admit, she will see things I do not.

'You have to get rid of these curtains from your bedroom,' she said. 'There was a spider's nest in them. I tried Raid, but now they're smelly and full of dead spiders.'

I looked, and she was right. Anna's Buddhist nature does not extend its generosity to the world of spiders. I tried to imagine they looked peaceful, thin sharp legs clustered together in the folds of my once expensive purchase. But they were dead and did not belong there, settling in the safety of my curtains and living with me, uninvited.

'Shit,' I said. 'How did they get in there?'

She shrugged. 'Who knows anymore.'

As a young woman Anna took my youth and made so much more of it – for that I am proud, but also envious. In Oregon she was a volunteer firefighter, the next summer she taught rock climbing in Jackson Hole and the next it was Death Valley to participate in the movement to declare California a sovereign nation after the government's attempt to redraw its borders and continued mismanagement of the RWP aftermath. The last winter, before she met Michael, she spent in the Florida Everglades giving riverboat tours among the alligators. We'd put up her letters on the fridge, searching each area online so we'd know where she was and what everything looked like. We suggested things she could go see, but of course she had already seen them. Just over a year ago she and Michael had returned from the opening celebrations at Crazy Horse Memorial in South Dakota, the mountain finally whittled away, much grander than Mount Rushmore and postcard worthy, the man's long arm stretched out in answer to the white man's question: Where are your lands now?

My lands are where my dead lie buried.

His index finger broke off during a miscalculated blast of explosives, Anna explained in the postcard, his reach not quite complete.

In my journal I wrote: *One hundred years to carve a man into a mountain. Michael did not sign the postcard.*

This year is the first time since I was twelve that I have not kept a journal. My days are empty pages, which is not the same as having nothing to do. It's the quality of life that's changed.

I flip the pages of my Mackinac life, switching over to the red journal, the brief scribbled memories containing whole worlds within them, but *still* the time goes slowly. St. Paul's massive air-raid siren sounds suddenly, then again in thirty-second intervals, wailing into the quiet of my kitchen oasis. Without checking the city-issued pamphlet on the fridge, the sound registers as a warning, to turn the television to one of Minnesota's weather channels; to call 1–800-RWP-INFO; to drive carefully as the National Guard weather vehicles are out; to keep children inside under a government-regulated roof. Alan and I had ours redone after the first storm with a cellulose-and-concrete-based shingle that's still under warranty – *With KEVLAR Roofing your home is your port in the storm.* But this afternoon there is still no rain and no change in the lighting. A warning. It will pass. And soon the doorbell will ring, because it must. I look from the clock back to my past and, even as I calculate the hours I have left, it comes back, everything comes back, and the feeling so strange that *I'm there* and I can physically feel the aching. The air is what I remember most, the scent of summer, sugar, horseshit, and lake water – and the pages *do* smell of something, they must, and it's not just the hallway closet.

After a shopping list for Mackinac Mart that reads:
beer
that round cheese
tampons
I find a page filled with just one word written over and over and over again. In sprawling, capital letters, the word is: MORE.

Mackinac

The island gets busier as the summer progresses. There are more people, more boats heavy with families, more dinner reservations, more bicycles on the street, more tourists crossing in front of carriages without looking both ways, more money to be made, and more reasons to get drunk in the evenings.

I have a table of children out on the patio. It is much too bright for a morning, almost hot and not yet eight thirty, which makes me annoyed that I spent from seven to eight wiping all the dew and mist from the patio furniture. The children are relatives of Velvet's, and I realize I always pictured her springing forth full-grown from the pinnacle of a New York skyscraper, free from the messiness of youth and family. But here they are, staying as guests at one of the hotels down the road. Their parents have given the oldest daughter money to go out for breakfast, but Aunt Velvet tells me not to charge them, ensuring that I will not receive a tip. Children have no concept of tipping, and they are loud and all elbows and spit and should not be allowed in public spaces until they are fifteen. The morning parades before me as a chaotic and unrewarding waste of time.

My head hurts.

'Hi, guys! Who wants more syrup? How are the pancakes?'

The chubby girl wearing a sailor outfit points to her brother and says, 'He likes you!'

All of them giggle except for the brother in a navy-blue

blazer who likes me. He throws a sausage link at his sister, saying, '*Eff you!* I do not.'

The sausage link hits the chubby sister in the face and leaves a grease mark, and I decide I like the brother back, waiting with my tray to watch what happens. The chubby sister stands up, hands on hips, and gets right in his face.

'I'm telling Mom you tried to kiss Sara.' She wipes her cheek and sits down, satisfied.

'*Eff* you, if you do,' he says, ominously.

As I set down a pitcher of orange juice on the table, the chubby sister says, 'Oh, I forgot. We won't drink this if it has bits. Does this orange juice have bits?'

I tell her there are no bits, that it is smooth and comes out of a machine.

'Thank you,' the chubby sister says.

I wonder if they have servants at home and what they would do if I curtseyed. By the time their breakfast is finished I have figured out that the quiet sister, the pretty one dressed in yellow, must be Sara, and I hope she has enough sense to ward off her brother's advances.

The twelve o'clock air-raid siren sounds its long, shrill marking of time, and my lunch guests jump in their seats putting hands over hearts and then looking around apologetically, reminding me that my lunch shift does not end until three. Every single customer sits outside in the heat of the sun, wanting to enjoy the view. Setting down cups of gourmet coffee, Zucchini Bread French Toast with Ginger Sorbet, and replacing fallen silverware, I am sweating, smiling, but I am far away. Underneath my uniform I have a bite mark on my thigh. The favor was returned, and it's better than a tattoo. The evidence of a mouth.

57

Bryce tells me things I've always wanted to learn, like how to make an origami cup from a square of paper, how to load a Remington 7600 pump action rifle although I will only watch, and he can sing along to all of John Denver's songs – but not in a way that makes me embarrassed to listen. I despise working when he has time off; everyone else in the restaurant is pale, quiet, and maddeningly boring. He feels the same, which is what matters. We go everywhere together, stealing minutes alone in the walk-in freezer. We eat together and gossip and I feel like this place has a purpose and it is for reminding me that all that out there, all that does not exist on this island, are things I can live without. It's too soon of course to feel this way and it will all be over anyway, but everything has sped up, compact and complete, to fit everything in, all this feeling into one summer season.

I think we deserve one another. Both of us alone for so long in so many ways and now I can see there was a reason for that solitude. I have never been like all the others, how I imagine them to be, armed with long lists of past romances, checklists and ideas of what is right. I've had boyfriends named Andrew and Elliot who worked and loved with satisfying sufficiency, but I never dreamt of weddings. I have never imagined dinner-ware and olive dishes. I have always been okay. I have no stories like the other girls here: 'And then he followed me back to my house, slashed my parents' tires. Not even *my* car. Fucking idiot.'

I have never inspired such hatred or lust or panic. But I am starting to believe in the necessity of these extremes.

At three o'clock, Bryce's sister calls the restaurant. I imagine that someday she and I will be friends.

Stripping everything off, my skin is wet underneath my uniform, the damp black polyester acting as a kind of wet suit, keeping the sweat close. My socks I return to my backpack – constantly recycled they've become crusty cotton balls holding whatever shape they dry into. I hang my tuxedo shirt in the closet for its thrice-a-week cleaning in St. Ignace.

I change into too-long jeans frayed and shit-brown at the bottoms and a white tank top. My feet are free in sandals, the in-between of my toes cooling down. I put my hair up and feel my neck begin to dry. Unlike every other restaurant I've worked in, Velvet demands we wear our hair down around our face. It must be either straightened, or curled with a curling iron in ringlets. No one knows why, but I wonder if it isn't some kind of health violation.

My pockets are crammed with twenties, fives, ones, and heavy quarters. Like everyone else, I throw the pennies into the lake. They shine briefly like fishing lures in the air before plunking beneath the water. Then retrieving my bike from the racks, I wheel it from the grass to the street before swinging my leg over the seat, pedaling leisurely away from the Tippecanoe.

The island post office has hundreds of PO boxes available to summer employees, but there are still not enough for everyone. Mine is awkwardly located in the bottom row and involves getting on my knees to open it. I make sure my pants are hiked up before bending down. Because of the shortage, I share the box with a thirty-year-old man from Jamaica named Sylvester who has twice opened my mail, then returned the letters to their open envelopes. During our last encounter at PO box 367, he shrugged when I questioned him as if there could be some other person responsible for this. A single letter now lies through the glass, but when I turn the key and pull it out it is addressed to him. Resisting the temptation to open it, I join the line in the lobby to buy stamps.

A man walks in wearing a top hat. Standing behind me, his cell phone rings and when he answers he says, 'Hey, Doc, how's the new yacht treating you? Yep, slip number seven, same as always.'

When he returns the phone to his pocket he shakes his linen pants so they hang properly again.

This is why people come here.

I hear Velvet's voice.

You are here for our guests as part of the play. You are here to unobtrusively make their visit to the island perfect because this is a dining experience that they will remember for the rest of their lives.

And don't forget we have new steak knives that need to be washed by hand so they go in this bucket over here that says 'steak knives.'

His phone rings again, and I hear him say, 'Bunny! How was Corsica?', but I'm next in line and I don't hear the rest.

It is forty-seven cents each to mail my postcards, and I don't have exact change because I have no pennies. I chose the cards that say, *Have a Road Apple, Courtesy of Mackinac Island.* The picture is a shit-covered Main Street populated with horses, a road apple being a giant lump of horseshit.

It was hard to write anything to anyone at all. I had sat on my bed with my black ink pen, wondering what to write after *making tons of cash.* I used long drawn-out letters to take up the maximum amount of space and I wonder if the tourist bureau has thought about scratch and sniff postcards. Perhaps the accompanying scent would say it all. My parents receive a more tasteful postcard. The heading reads: *A Reconstruction of an Early Missionary Chapel, Marquette Park, Mackinac Island, Michigan.* The photograph shows both the inside and outside of a domed hut made of bark. The inside looks cool and dark, and in full ceremonial dress a man shakes hands with a black-robed missionary.

Thank you, the man seems to be saying. *And welcome.*

The shops here sell tomahawks, bows and arrows, and moccasins.

The name Mackinac is a mangled Chippewa word, according to Bryce.

Depending on what history book you read or what historical plaque you look at, the name Mackinac means:

Great turtle,

Place of the giant fairies,

Place of the great uplifted bow,

A tribute to the Mishinemackinawgo people, or

Gathering place of the ancient tribe of the Mishinimaki.

I prefer the idea of the island as a great sleeping turtle, on whose back we all live as a matter of privilege. It gives me the same sense of awe as when my babysitter told me that we all lived on the head of a massive green giant, and that the grass was his hair.

Outside the post office I hesitate for a moment, undecided as to my next destination – I have nothing at all to do today, no skim milk to buy or laundry to wash. To my left, at the end of Market Street, is Marquette Park where I can sit and watch the water.

The air is hot, the blue metal of my bike burns, and the seat is soft and warm as I straddle it. Riding a bike that has been left in the sun is a surprising thing, it feels alive. Children have orange and purple faces from popsicles and women wear hats and carry water bottles too big for their purses. Men sweat and turn red. I park my bike under a tree and wander onto the green, away from the football game and away from the man without his shirt on, thick and heavy with hair under the lilac tree. The missionary chapel is a dark and pleasing shape by the edge of the park, but I am not interested enough to go inside. Seated, I breathe out, looking at the marina and the yachts easing into the harbor. This is the sort of place, the sort of summer, where an afternoon sitting on the grass feels like an accomplishment.

Pulling up the leg of my jeans I examine the hair that stands straight and black on my shin. This morning I noticed rust on the blades of my razor and I decided not to use it in case I cut myself and contracted a strange rust-related infection. I think maybe a tan will camouflage the hair until I remember to buy a new one. Rolling up the legs of my jeans I arrange my backpack behind my head. Twenty seconds later a kid stomps past and catches a Frisbee right beside my face. I decide to keep my eyes open. Looking up into the sky I can just see the white wall of the fort looming above me.

A man wearing a yellow button that reads, *Ask me about the Mackinac Island Carriage Tour!* appears above me, casting a short shadow across my body. I sit up and he takes a step back.

'Have you taken the carriage tour yet?' he asks.

He points to his gigantic button and says, 'It's only fifteen dollars today.'

'It's always fifteen dollars,' I say.

'Oh, fuck,' he says. 'Do you work here?'

I nod.

'Fuck,' he says again. 'I'm trying to fill my quota.'

'That sucks.'

He shrugs. 'Better than shoveling shit,' he says. 'Plus I get a tan.'

Lifting up his T-shirt higher than is appropriate, he shows me the white skin underneath and compares it to his brown arm. All of his muscles are flexed. There is no hair on his chest.

'Plus the owners of the tour own the whisky bar, so I drink for free.'

He puts his shirt down slowly and I notice it says, 'Moustache Rides 25 Cents.' We both look out across the water for a moment, silent. The sun is burning the metal on my watch and I move my arm into the shade underneath my legs.

'You know who built that?' he asks, motioning to the hill above us.

The wall of the old fort has been painted, and pretty yellow umbrellas are set up along it. They are part of the café, catering to the tourists who get up there and discover the only thing to do is buy a coffee, as the fort is just a series of reconstructed empty buildings and painfully boring.

'It's the British fort.'

'Right,' he says. 'They built it, but we took it.'

'Didn't we get it in a treaty?'

'What?'

'The treaty of Ghent.'

'Whatever. It's ours now.'

We watch a man cutting across the grass and heading towards the fort dressed as a civil war soldier and holding a long rifle as he chats to a Native American complete with feathers. For the entertainment this provides I think the presence of the fort is worthwhile.

They pass quite close to us and the Native American is saying, 'I swear to God, Rick, both fucking legs right behind her head.'

'No shit,' says Rick, 'do you still have her number?'

The tour guy looks for my reaction, and the cannons go off suddenly, startling me. Loud heavy bursts. I've never gotten used to them, though they fit with my impression of what a fort should be – heavy with the sounds of war and surprise. As the smoke clouds drift across the park and dissipate, he points to the yellow umbrellas and comments, 'They make good cappuccinos up there in that café.'

I shrug, and then make him an offer: 'I'll give you a free appetizer down at the Tippecanoe if you give me a ticket for the carriage ride.'

'Deal,' he says.

He hands me a green ticket with a picture of a horse on it. I put it on the grass beside me and I don't say anything else. He asks anyway.

'You have a boyfriend?'

'Yes,' I say.

'Oh. Okay, well I'll see you around.'

I watch as he approaches a family sitting on a picnic blanket, and a woman wearing a huge white sun visor fans her face with her hand as she looks up at him. She looks at her husband who reaches for his wallet. They have three kids.

I roll down the legs of my jeans and pick up my bag. On the back of the ticket in big letters it says, *See Famous Arch Rock*. As it is the natural wonder of the island I have seen many wooden arrows indicating its whereabouts. I have never actually been there, however, and I've heard the tour takes a good hour, so I'll be learning as well as wasting time before this evening.

The carriage winds from Main Street up to Market Street and I am sitting next to a couple from Cheboygan, which they tell me is a town not too far from the island. They come here every summer at least once, but as he can't ride a bike because of his back problem they always make a point of taking the tour. He used to be a pilot. Their names are Martin and Barb.

The carriage stops by Arch Rock for about ten minutes, allowing us to climb off and take pictures while the horses eat and piss, to the delight of the young school groups. The earthy smell of horseshit doesn't bother me anymore, but the wet sharp smell of urine is still unbearable. The class of ten-year-olds on the carriage tour seem to agree with me. Horse piss does come out with quite a bit of force and I will admit it is an impressive show, the yellow draining quickly to the sides of the road to be easily stepped in if not paid attention to. It is also, I discover, easily sprayed up your back if cycled over without mudguards.

Arch Rock is made of soft limestone and stands on a cliff overlooking the lake. It looks as if an ancient, rocky thumb and forefinger came to pluck away a piece of the cliffside and then never left. A natural formation, the leg of the first arch is planted close to the cliff's edge with brush and grasses growing from its base, while the second half descends over the cliff and ends somewhere further down. On a hot perfect day like today you can take a photograph using the archway as a frame, in which you can capture all the blues and greens of the water. There is a metal fence around the site that's been bolted firmly into the ground, however, so everyone waits to stand in the one spot with the best angle. The fact that I haven't brought my camera separates me from the rest of the group and I stand behind them, as if I've seen it before.

When our ten minutes are up and everyone has taken pictures, used the public restrooms, and bought a Coke from the vending machine, we slide back into the bench seats, the tour guide yelling:

'Carriage four preparing for take-off.'

I make a point of sitting on a different bench as I climb back on, and I hear Martin behind me hoot, 'Take-off! Gets me every time when they say that.'

As we continue through the forest, the tour guide begins to recite the fable of Arch Rock, straining to be heard over the clopping of horses, chattering of tourists, and cries of the children. Eventually he gives up and speaks in a normal voice, so I don't quite catch the last of the story.

★

Bryce cannot believe I didn't pay to take the carriage ride. At the Cock we have claimed the table by the window, and by not sitting at the bar or on the couch we are technically out for dinner, according to him. I wanted to go somewhere else.

'Anything you need to know about this island,' he says over the table, 'I already know it.'

He taps his temple with his index finger as if indicating just how much knowledge is in there. I ignore him and spear an ice cube with my straw.

'Look at these ice cubes,' I tell him.

'What's wrong with them?'

'They're perfect cubes. Big perfect cubes of ice.'

He pulls it off my straw and eats it.

'There's a hole in it,' he says. 'So what did you learn on this carriage ride?' he asks, from around the ice.

I warn him I will be making some of it up, but I suppose the details don't matter when it comes to things like this. The fable is universal and timeless and borderless and this one is for us, here, now.

'A young woman and her lover spent many nights together on the cliffs of the island, wandering, holding hands, and having sex.'

Bryce interrupts me. 'The tour guide did not say *having sex*.'

I ignore him, and he rolls his eyes as my voice takes on the tone of a tour guide.

'They were very much in love because they were young, and young people know that love lasts forever. They enjoyed dreaming about the future and all the things they would do together in that future. It went on like this until one day her lover ventured out into the open water in a canoe, on a day when men should not be out in canoes, and he drowned.'

'Poor kid,' says Bryce.

'Quiet. So when she heard this, she went to the spot where

they had spent so much time together, determined to wait for him there until he came home, convinced that he would. And she cried. Day after day she threw herself against the cold rock and cried. And her tears began to wash away the rock. Soon there was a deep cavity against the rock where she stood, but still she cried. Eventually her tears washed right through the rock to the other side, creating a large gaping archway, that we today call Arch Rock.

'No such thing as a happy ending, I guess.'

That the woman died of a broken heart is something I do not mention. It seems to me like that might be the easy way out.

Bryce is only marginally impressed with the tale, but this is always his reaction to finding out things he didn't know about before.

'Would you cry a hole into a rock if I drowned?' he asks.

'Of course.'

He puts a hand over mine and winks at me. 'That's what they all say.'

John brings over our food, everything in plastic baskets. I've ordered the deep-fried whitefish, which ruins the taste of the fish, but I'm in the mood for something crisp and fat. My drink is an expensive Long Island Iced Tea, and Bryce has a Screwdriver, also unusual for him. We trade sips.

Some days you feel like something different. It's nice to be able to change your mind.

As we begin eating our fish, I remember to tell him that his sister called.

St. Paul, 2:01 p.m.

I have a souvenir from that day of fairytales and deep-fried fish. My mug is not the only thing I have kept from that summer, although it is the most practical. It's a silly thing to speak of now, so trivial it seems.

He bent the straw from my long island into a triangle, fitting the ends into each other so that it kept its shape. 'For you,' he said, flicking it at me. I left it on the table when we got up, and then later, taking off my clothes before bed, I discovered it in the hood of my jacket. It stayed on the dresser there until I left. What makes one keep things like this? But I did, I brought it home with me, and it went into an envelope.

This morning Anna came and put her hand on my shoulder, startling me. I'd been wondering about my breasts and how I wanted them to appear this evening, imagining the encounter both with and without them.

I think I *will* wear them, I told Anna, turning towards her touch.

She nodded and brought me to the bedroom. The thick envelope lay at the bottom of the closet surrounded by men's shoes. Some pairs shiny and hardly worn and others creased across the toe. The mail bag beside Anna was full. She had already discovered the two lavender air fresheners stuck to the back wall and when she pried them off the paint came with them. When she apologized, I was far away, remembering how nice the lavender used to smell, masking the scent of Alan's wet leather running shoes in the morning.

*

Alan's favorite smell was sand. When we played my *What Would You Give Up?* game, he insisted he would trade all the fingers on his left hand for our own private beach. He would not give up any of his toes, as that would upset his balance. I told him sand was just made of rocks and rocks don't smell, and he said for someone raised Catholic I had very little faith in my own senses. *If you just sit still and concentrate long enough, you can smell anything, taste anything.* He sometimes tried moving pencils with his thoughts. Anna with all her meditation and studies about transcendence to different worlds agreed with her father. Anything was possible.

The envelope from my closet was heavy and marked with the word MACKINAC, as if all the contents, all the cards, letters, the one cassette and the triangle straw memento were geographically branded somehow. I imagined my island past as a person, with hair made of dry green grass and a lighthouse beacon for a heart.

'It's full of old papers,' Anna said, reaching a hand into the envelope.

'I know what it's full of,' I told her. 'Just leave it.'

She ignored me. 'You can't keep this, Mom. What is this? A *cassette tape?*'

She held it out reading long-ago handwriting that wasn't mine. '*Sex* Machine?'

There was a brief pause – the song selected, the disk set in place, the music beginning suddenly. The lights of the jukebox turned red, then green.

'Mom?'

The voice was sultry, sweaty.

She sighed, putting the cassette tape back in the envelope and placing it in the round curve of my papasan chair, which I cannot sit in anymore as it's impossible to get out of. The chair was full of things I couldn't yet bring myself to throw away. I wondered if Anna were just anticipating all the subsequent cleaning she would do after I died – if her encouragement for purging was a result of her own selfishness.

This morning's efforts now fill two canvas bags marked *Property of The United States Postal Service*, bulging and lopsided by the front door – the huge bags they use in the warehouse before the mail gets sorted. Funny to think they're full of a dead mailman's shoes instead of birthday cards and bills. He had more shoes than I ever did. *Bought them on sale*, he always said proudly. *For work*.

I wonder if I should attempt to move the bags somewhere else; they look so uninviting, crowding the hallway with the type of past we won't want to remember. But where else could they go? *Welcome*, I will say. *Don't mind my dead husband's shoes*.

Open before me is the story of Arch Rock written faithfully in my red journal, the speech bubble around my old words leading to a young ink woman with feathers in her hair. I put the envelope on top of her. It is bulky at the bottom, some of the items misshapen and the envelope worn thin in places. I touch my tongue briefly to the open flap, but the adhesive has long disappeared along with my taste buds. I decide to begin by chance, and reaching in I'm reminded of the haunted houses at St. Mary's Primary where, with eyes closed, you hoped for something manageable like the peeled grape-witch's eyeball. My mind is certain, however, that this long-ago envelope was carefully filled with only pleasant things. Some memories have no need of a physical reminder.

I pull out the cassette tape that Anna had found so offensive and rattle it beside my ear. The plastic casing is cracked, and there's nowhere to play it now except the old stereo in the basement. We haven't done the basement yet. I make a note to see if the stereo still works; it would be nice to hear again. Setting it down, I notice the brown ribbon running through the bottom of the tape is broken.

Impatient now, I turn the envelope upside down and everything slides out together as if the passing of half a century has enabled each souvenir to attach itself to the next, afraid of being alone.

In the pile, a thin paper rectangle is shiny with the politics of the summer. Though it never occurred to me at the time, I suppose giving out bumper stickers on the island had an air of the ridiculous about it. I try to peel away the waxy paper backing but my fingers won't work and this governor died a long time ago anyway. Still, I think I'll keep it.

I'm reminded of the shows on television, where a professional cleaner will come into someone's house to help them get rid of things. There will be protests, the mother saying, *But it was my grandmother's chair*. And the professional cleaner will say, *Yes, but that chair is not your grandmother*.

It's easy to laugh then. It is easy to laugh, but it is much different when it's your own hand, hovering above the trash, hesitating with memory.

Mackinac

The sun from each day etches itself in progressing shades of brown on my skin and Bryce begins calling me his Little Indian Princess. Trainer says he's sick of the white man appropriating minority culture this way, and Rummy points out that Trainer is white himself and the least politically correct person he knows, and Trainer calls him a lying Canuck. The resulting conversation ends with shots of Jaegermeister, and Trainer giving Rummy a piggyback ride down Main Street, both of them yelling, *The British are coming!* At four in the afternoon tourists stop to take pictures.

These strange incidents are rarely worthy of conversation, each unlikely act obtaining a sort of normalcy and blending together with the last. The schedule hanging in the back of the Tippecanoe runs from Thursday to Thursday and often there are no corresponding dates, or even the month.

Everything is green and the lilacs begin to bloom. Hundreds and hundreds of trees turn purple and white and pink. Bushes that were thin and broken and brown just days ago now reveal their purpose, exploding with breezy trumpets of flowers; the air is full of their scent. Some people come just for this, to take pictures and walk among them. They blossom quickly and stay for weeks. The shops sell sweatshirts and china plates with sprays of lilac on them.

What *else* should we see on the island?

When guests ask, I point to the large white house near the west bluff.

'You can't go in,' I tell them, 'but sometimes she's there. You can see her through the windows.'

The governor of Michigan uses the summerhouse for both business and pleasure. Supposedly when the state flag is raised it means she is in residence, but though the flagpole is tall and visible from atop Fort Hill, the small blue flag is difficult to see. The *Detroit Free Press* is a better indication of the governor's whereabouts. Bryce tells me the flag's crest includes both a moose and an elk, supporting a shield on which a man is waving and holding a gun. 'We don't fuck around here in Michigan,' Bryce told me proudly. Incongruously, the white ribbon at the bottom of the flag reads in Latin: *if you seek a pleasant peninsula, look around.*

The governor's mansion is described as stately, Victorian, picturesque, and also as a tax burden by some Republicans. The current governor is a Democrat, and she points out that when the Republicans were in office and made use of the home the cost of it didn't bother them. It is a nice house for parties. I know this because the groundskeeper employed by the governor lives in the house and loves drinking Shiraz-Cabernet. After a bottle or two he becomes a gracious host, inviting random people he's just met back to the mansion.

We arrive there late one sweltering night after the pubs have closed. No one knows his name, but none of us care as he leads a group of us, stumbling, into the living room which is tasteful and white and open. Trainer keeps wondering aloud where his bellboy is, and Rummy throws up on the governor's couch.

'You guys fucking know how to party,' the groundskeeper says with approval.

Trainer takes in the vases of flowers, the gold candlesticks, the heavy portraits on the walls, and says, 'This place needs a lot of fucking to liven it up.'

The groundskeeper nods and says, 'hell yeah', and then takes a mirror from his pocket.

'You guys need a bump?'

Rummy shakes his head, no, and wanders out the front door wiping his chin, where we hear him continue his dry heaving on the front stoop. Bryce pretends he doesn't indulge, so Trainer sits down to do a line and the two of them discover they have the same dealer. After more drinking someone brings out a deck of cards, and at four in the morning all of us, minus Rummy, play Crazy Eights, a game the groundskeeper punctuates with accusations.

'Cheating motherfuckers,' he says after every hand.

We ignore him.

'You all think this island is some backwater shithole,' he continues, as if defending it from some unspoken insult.

'But, seriously. You know who's stayed here? In that bedroom?' He points to a window. 'George fucking Bush.'

'I told you!' Bryce says to me.

Bryce has already told me the long list of historical figures that have visited the island over the years. Mark Twain is said to have rocked in a chair on the porch of the Grand Hotel, Gerald Ford came here as an Eagle Scout, and George Bush Senior, as the groundskeeper now swears on his life, was here in secret one summer. Bryce's friend Dickweed has corroborated this fact, although I didn't believe him at the time. Dickweed claimed that while he was wandering the streets late one night a few years ago he fell over in front of a carriage. It was forced to stop and two men wearing black searched him. After the men realized Dickweed was merely drunk, they led him by the arm to the roadside and were on their way.

'So I'm by the side of the road and this old guy leans out of the carriage as it speeds up and says, "Have a good night," and it was the *fucking* president.'

So the story may or may not be true.

The groundskeeper gets up abruptly, and he disappears saying something about turning on the sprinklers. I look out the front door to check on Rummy, but he's disappeared. His bike is gone, so maybe he made it home.

We choose the third-floor guest bedroom for the night, listening to the gentle sound of the chugging waterworks and the occasional swearing from our new friend still somewhere outside.

'Rummy says Anna Jameson visited the island back in the day,' I say.

My face is buried in Bryce's armpit, and there is a pause while I wonder if he's asleep.

'I refuse to give you the satisfaction of asking who that is,' he says.

The stately bedroom has thousands of flowers everywhere: the bedspread, the curtains, the wallpaper. We do not notice this until the next morning when the governor's butler asks us to please get the hell out of the house before he calls the police. The house is on a hill, however, and we know that the trek upwards on bicycles will not be one the police make eagerly. We also cannot believe that the governor has a butler.

When we leave the governor's mansion it is cool and raining, and we notice the gardens around the front of the home have been dug up during the night. Strange mounds of dirt and uprooted plants lie in the darkening soil.

Rain is impossible to ignore when you travel by bike, and water saturates my eyebrows and eyelashes. My face is wet and dripping, my fingers cold on the handlebars. The rain

soaks my knees as they bob up and down, and wets two
patches over my breasts, until gradually I'm wet through. The
neglected piles of horseshit become muddy lumps, steaming
and disintegrating before they can be shoveled away. We
swerve expertly around each of these, spraying gravel as we
skid too fast into the lane leading to the Pine Suites. In five
minutes we are home and splash into Bryce's apartment,
taking our clothes off. My jeans weigh thirty pounds – I could
have been swimming in them. We throw everything into the
bathtub and my body is wet and shiny, beads of rainwater
moist in the hollows of my collarbone and elbows.

'Give me a wet hug!' Bryce shouts.

His arms extend towards me, his crotch red and waiting.
I squeal away from him, our bodies bare and uneven in the
morning light. He spins me onto the bed and wraps me in the
white sheet, rubbing me dry.

'You're like my little butterfly in a cotton cocoon,' he says.

My head pokes out from around the sheets I have been
sausage-rolled into.

'I'm telling all your friends you said that.'

He touches my nose to his, a gentle gesture, before bundling
me over his shoulder, still helplessly entangled in the sheets,
and spanking me thoroughly. My shrieks are muted by the
sound of the rain hitting pavement, roofs, and windows, and
there isn't anyone else.

We stay naked, playing with the wooden chessboard he
brought from home. I lose. Both games. I strategize with my
horses, the alphabet L a letter of attack. He plays with his
castles and captures all my pieces, horses first. I find this
particularly demoralizing.

'I don't understand why you don't let me win.'

'It's chess. It's a game. You're not four.'

'You should let me win.'

He chalks up my unsportsmanlike behavior to my spoiled upbringing.

'You'll never go places in life with that attitude,' he tells me.

I refuse to play chess with him again.

St. Paul, 2:30 p.m.

I owe my career to a pair of boots.

Russ Gerhardt was in office for forty-five years, city councillor, mayor. He liked me because he liked my father. They met on Seminary Avenue when Russ rolled down his window for directions to the hair salon and took a liking to my father's cowboy boots. Russ bought them right off his feet for seventy-five dollars after he promised to give my father a ride home. Real leather and made by Minetonka, my dad had worn those boots for years, but figured Russ's offer was a sign from the Virgin that it was time he got himself a new pair. The boots didn't fit Russ, but they had a drink together and my mother served steak and potato salad for dinner, thick mayonnaise-and dill-covered potatoes lit by the flames of her best red tapered candles. Alan and I stopped by for the celebration, her check-up that morning marking five years since her diagnosis, and at that time we were still renting out in Bloomington; Alan's route was not the best and I was tutoring for hardly any money and trying to find it rewarding.

'International politics,' Russ said over the potatoes. 'Hell! I don't know anything about that, but whenever you feel like answering some phone calls come down to city hall anytime.' I started that Monday. He already had a secretary, but he gave me a desk and eventually paid for some trendy business cards printed on Deluxe Victorian Gray Linen that stated I was his assistant, which meant nothing except I was on the payroll and safe, far away from children who didn't understand conjunctions or where India was on a map.

When the press called, I always knew my lines. I was never fooled like Patty often was, getting her name in print beside a damaging quotation.

'Mayor Gerhardt likes having a good time, you know? And he*llo*? All the charges were *dropped*.'

Russ always looked to me for damage control.

'You know people, Bell,' Russ would say with a hand on my shoulder after giving Patty the afternoon off. 'You know what they need, and make them think you've given it to them. In another life, you could have been a politician.'

Russ was a man whose gray hair had been dyed black, his scalp stretched in the operation that spreads the hair you've still got across a larger portion of your skull. From far away he looked young, as he had when I first met him as he tried to walk in my father's too small boots. From up close, his skin was unnaturally tight, tanned. His nails were always manicured, his teeth whitened. His only visible fault was a lazy eye that confounded the doctors; numerous surgeries had been unsuccessful and Russ accepted it finally as his cross to bear. A very lightweight cross.

He was a man in public office, and he needed me – although initially only to fetch his grande double-shot lattes with whipped cream. In the twenty-five years I worked for him, the price of these luxury lattes tripled. When he'd eaten the whipped cream with the plastic spoon, he'd top up his latte with whisky. I'm not sure how many people in the office knew this. I went home and told Alan, of course. Alan hadn't voted for him, but neither had I. My first election was the most exhilarating, after that they became routine.

Bell, Russ would call the night before the municipal vote, *go make some signs disappear, but don't tell me about it.*

When she was old enough I took Anna with me, asking if she wanted to see democracy in action. It was always late at night; she slid sleepily into the passenger seat beside me, waking up as soon as we spotted the first sign.

'*There's one!*'

A different name every election. Bob Anliss. Gerry Carmichael. Sanyika Hassan. Each one went in the trunk. There were hundreds of us all over the city, playing politics. The blue signs were good, everything else the enemy. These silent nights were when I liked Anna best. She and I, headlights off, cruising up to dark-green lawns, the trunk open slightly, engine idling as I waited for her to uproot the metal frame with the plastic sign attached, then leap back into the car so we could slide off towards our next conquest. On a good night we'd get up to a hundred lawn signs, some from public spaces as well. Ours disappeared too, of course – some of the night was spent putting back signs that had disappeared.

'Russ is the team we want to win, right, Mom?'

'Always. That way I keep my job.'

At two or three a.m. we cruised back into the driveway, and I carried the warm body of my daughter back into the house, her palms black from the dirt. When she was in bed I made one last trip to the dump at the east end of the city. I waited until the entrance was empty of other late-night visitors, reversing into the stench through the chainlink gates.

The sky black overhead, that moment was my own small part in history. Surrounded by garbage and plastic bags that would never disappear, I was the center of it all. I loved the surprising cold of the metal frame, the slice of the sign's plastic edge on my fingers – dozens of cuts carved into my skin, thin white marks just deep enough to hint at the blood beneath.

Propping the trunk open I flung the signs by the handful. Victorious, elated, I spun like a discus thrower, letting go and saying,

'Fuck you, Carmichael!'

Or:

'See you later, Sanyika!'

As the trunk emptied, as the sky hinted at gray, I imagined myself: picked up by the ankles, spun and flung into another world where the night was always like this. Always exciting, and better than the day. No labels left but one. Alone.

I returned to my car, loving this secret life.

The next morning I answered the phones, telling Barry from the *Pioneer Press* how Russ was appalled that opponents' signs had gone missing. *Vandals, it happens every year*, I recited carefully, pointing out that many of our own signs were stolen as well.

'Off the record,' Barry said, 'how many'd you get?'

'About a hundred,' I told him. 'It was a good night.'

But these experiences are on a sliding scale, and this will always be the middle of my life. It always *felt* like the middle, even then, when I stopped to think about it. I knew the beginning had ended. The middle was something to fill in the gap before the end. RE-ELECT GOVERNOR GRANHOLM, the bumper sticker from my envelope says.

There are many things I have accomplished since that summer evening, many labels I can tape to my chest, though most have been stripped away again, altered and reaffixed. Mother. Retired. Widow. Beautiful, once.

The last the hardest to wear.

Retired, the easiest to understand.

I return the still-shiny bumper sticker to the envelope.

RE-ELECT GOVERNOR GRANHOLM.

Everyone depending upon everyone else.

RE-ELECT RUSS FOR CONGRESS.

I pick up the small library book instead and open it.

That Mackinac summer there was so much more ahead of me. Sickness. Endings. Death. And everything that comes after these things.

The doorbell is silent still, though the sound of the siren echoes over and over. Thirty seconds on, then silence. Soon it wails again, a warning.

Mackinac

The island streets are busier than I've ever seen them, the first yachts from the Port Huron to Mackinac race expected sometime today. Wives, girlfriends, fiancées, and mistresses drink white wine and lime daiquiris while waiting for their sailors to arrive. Camera crews and journalists from all over Michigan settle themselves on patios with a view of the lake. Velvet is losing her mind, giving me instructions like, *avocados*, before hurrying off again. She told Trainer to come in early today to weed the patio, which earned her at least an hour of imaginative expletives at the Cock last night. I hear St. Mary's church has been noticeably well attended over the past few days, and I wonder if the prayers were for good weather or victory or both.

Bryce and I have the afternoon off, and he refuses to indulge my fascination with his religion beyond our initial conversation last month; he rolls his eyes when I tell him I'm on my way downtown to research the Mormon religion and the history of Salt Lake City.

'Mine's just as bad as the rest of them,' he insists.

'You have pedophile priests?'

'We have everything you have, only we keep quiet about it. No crusades or anything.'

'You don't believe in anything anyway,' I tell him.

He shrugs. 'I believe in doing the right thing.'

'How fantastic for you.'

With a sigh he sits next to me on the bed, lacing up the

worn boots he uses for hunting. 'So. Does this mean you won't ask me any more questions?'

'Does *what* mean I won't ask you any more questions?'

'I *love* that you're so hilarious,' he says.

Standing, he kisses the top of my head and his white T-shirt billows out from his body to touch my face. It smells of long-ago laundry detergent and more recent sweat.

'I'm going to meet some sailors' wives,' he says.

'Not without a platinum credit card you're not,' I tell him. I bite the fabric with my teeth as he tries to pull away.

'There's popcorn in the cupboard if you're hungry,' he says, trying to extricate himself. 'Have fun with your books.'

I let go of his shirt. He smiles and gives me a wave, and leaves the front door wide open. After a moment, the warm draft from the open window slams it shut again.

There are people who believe they are lonely because it suits them and Bryce lives alone in Grayling in a rented room, far away from the Sunday services and organ music and the G-Rated, LDS-produced movies of his childhood. He hasn't spoken to his parents or his sister Odette since he arrived on the island. But I believe everyone is allowed to escape, and to choose what they wish to escape from.

We watched a movie last week where one of the characters had said something about a white horse.

'Do you know what that's from?' Bryce asked.

'Where what's from?'

'The white horse thing.'

'I guess not.'

'It's from Revelations. "I saw heaven standing open and there before me was a white horse, whose rider is called Faithful and True."'

I had to lift my head up from his chest to look at him. 'Holy fuck. Did you just quote from the bible?'

'Everyone knows that JC rides a white horse,' he said.

Bryce looked pleased with himself and told me he was full of surprises.

I am not used to being outshone like this, but I don't intend to read the bible. I've tried before and made it through maybe three pages of Genesis, despite my best intentions. It really is tedious. The history of the Mormon religion however seems a little more manageable. It's newer, more political, and Trainer says he's heard the CIA recruits a lot of Mormons because they're really good at keeping secrets.

'They don't drink,' Trainer explained.

The ride into town is warm and quick, and I park in the dark-green bike rack in front of the library. I consider not locking it, but have no desire to lose another bike this summer, and common sense outweighs my laziness. I take the time to loop the coil through the spokes and around the frame.

The Mackinac public library is one room painted turquoise. It opens at strange hours and never on Mondays or Sundays. I have never been to a library with a fireplace before, but it is huge and calming. Each surrounding tile is a bright and perfect purple. The two doors flanking the fireplace stand open on this warm afternoon, and they lead to a porch with rocking chairs. The cottage-red chairs face the lake, and there is a woman rocking slowly when I arrive; she is still there when I leave.

There is a book-club meeting gathering itself as I browse the stacks. The meeting is led by a tiny man who introduces himself as Father Kim, the priest for Saint Mary's Catholic Church on Main Street. I have seen him around town riding a bizarrely complicated vintage Mongoose, the envy of many young riders. A Korean American, Father Kim exudes a sense of quiet amusement with everything he encounters. He attended seminary school in northern France he tells the group as they are still settling, and warns that when he is in agreement with someone he says, *mais oui*, which he translates to mean, *of course*. The book he has chosen for discussion is Yann Martel's *Life of Pi*. They are not allowed to discuss the end of the book, as it is a three-part discussion. I read the novel a year ago, though I barely remember any of it.

The library has a small section on religious studies, and I find one promotional volume with a seagull on the cover called, *Why I'm a Latter Day Saint*. I wonder if the library bought it or if it was donated.

I sit at a solid oak table alongside the Pi discussion.

My yearbook quote from high school was something about always trying everything once. I'd like to think I keep true to this motto for the most part except when it comes to trying things like coke or threesomes, both of which scare the shit out of me. I guess the saying applies more to life than to reading, but as I'm not converting to Mormonism, reading about it and sleeping with one is as close as I'm going to get. I open the book.

It turns out to be more of a promotional tourism item than a historical account of Mormon history. The city is painted as a shining haven of civilization, which I suppose it might be, never having been there. I think of the plastic tourist magnet on our fridge and smile. Salt Lake City is in a valley surrounded by the Rocky Mountains. It is part of the great American west, although its history is not one of lawlessness and cowboys. Utah is an insular state founded by Brigham Young, the leader of the religion in the 1840s, and his followers, moving across America to escape the persecution they had endured in the east. They brought guns and the Book of Mormon, and a belief in their own religion. The Church officially outlawed polygamy in 1890 as a prerequisite for statehood. The seagull is the state bird. Over seventy percent of Utahans today are members of the Church of Latter Day Saints. The Church owns a large part of the city's downtown core, rendering it free from alcohol. In the one city block that is occupied by the temple, there is no smoking allowed. As insurance against unforeseen global superbugs or nuclear wars, each Mormon family is required to have enough canned food in their basement to last about one year. It is a well-planned and well-executed religion. I think about joining up and how one goes about it. I wonder if it's a sin to join a religion out of curiosity; if there's a kind of test that weeds out people like me: an x-ray that shows my heart is actually made of used condoms and ill intentions.

Flyers artfully arranged into a fan shape cover the table in front of me: *Meet People and Talk Books. Bring Your Discussion Cap.* I am by far the youngest person in the library, and the women in the book club address one another by name, as they are neighbors, friends, islanders.

The woman at the other end of the table begins by putting up her hand, which is manicured. On her gleaming white blouse is a silver brooch in the shape of a potted geranium plant. Father Kim suggests that hand-raising is not necessary, and she begins.

'I was wondering if anyone else was uncomfortable with the narrator's ping-pong approach to religion. You can't just bounce back and forth taking what you like from each. Christianity is a commitment.'

I wonder if I am outnumbered, non-church-going-youth versus room-of-religious-people. As one of her friends nods and says, 'Yes, I found that troublesome as well,' Father Kim responds.

'I think that Gretel, and all of us, should wonder if Martel isn't using his narrator to draw attention to the commonalities between each religion. It seems young Pi is mostly interested in the ways in which love manifests itself universally through each religion.'

Gretel's friend shakes her head. 'I don't see why he can't just pick one then. What does he need them all for?'

My book lies open on the table and I watch them. Father Kim nods as if conceding a point, though I think his eyes betray him. I wonder if he has chosen the book with this controversy in mind.

They then have the inevitable discussion that arises in all book clubs I imagine, as to whether or not the story is true, and I notice some women are taking notes. Geranium-brooch Gretel is sure that in South America a man lived at sea for days on the back of a great snapping turtle. Another woman suggests that she is perhaps thinking of a popular short story by Roald Dahl, and not a news article. The only man in the group, who owns an art gallery on Market Street, points out that comparing Pi's tiger to a snapping turtle is hardly worthwhile, as once you were on the turtle's back he'd be harmless. They decide and agree on nothing, and perhaps that is the point.

The rectangles of blue created by the open doors fill the library with light, and the temperature is perfect. I wonder if I can hear the creak of the one occupied rocking chair, or if I'm just imagining it over the lapping of the lake and the quiet noise of the seagulls.

Father Kim adjourns the meeting. 'Just a reminder to every-one about the Jamaican service tonight at the church. We're also organizing an event to help everyone celebrate Jamaica's Independence Day on August 6th. If you'd like to volunteer and help our workers feel at home, see me after the meeting.'

Father Kim organizes the Jamaican choir for Saturday night service. Tomorrow morning is the traditional Catholic service, and he also delivers a sermon every week in his fourth language, Spanish, on Sunday evenings. The state of Michigan employs people from all over the world, and there is room for everyone's God on this small island it seems. Some of the Mexican workers with their heavy accents – the ones hired to shovel shit or wash dishes – will call out to him on the street. The K from Kim is lost. It sounds like, 'Padre Him.'

Dickweed was born in Flint, but lives on the island year round. His nickname comes from having slept with and subsequently cast off so many women, and from his fondness for smoking pot. He is outside the library as I leave with my one book, and he is walking as he has fallen off his bike so many times that his knee is damaged and will no longer make the proper up and down motion necessary for pedaling. Bryce tells me that when Dickweed has to climb a set of stairs, a group of friends will surround him yelling good-natured insults as he struggles peg-legged up the steps.

Riding a bicycle after drinking is difficult, I will attest to that. Often, while I am sure that I am pedaling at a reasonable speed, I tip over because I have in fact come to a standstill. After making the decision to walk alongside the bike, I might still find myself on my back, too unsteady to manage my feet and the wheels together. It's heavy and awkward to climb out from underneath a bike. Observers either laugh or help – it depends upon the time of day. Drunk at four p.m. will likely get you gawked at by tourists. At two a.m., I am just one of many, lying on the road, waiting for someone to come along and pick me up.

I am always curious as to how my night will end.

*

'Hey, girly girl!' he shouts at me. 'Whatcha doin in the library?'

He says 'library' in a singsong voice, dragging it out so that for a moment I have to reassure myself I am not in fact embarrassed to have been inside.

'Reading, asshole. What are you doing?'

He holds up a white plastic bag from Mackinac Mart, the only grocery store on the island. Everything there is almost double what you would pay on the mainland, but there is only one store so we all shop there.

'Burgers on the BBQ. Bring some of your waitressing friends over. There'll be plenty.'

He waves the bag back and forth, as if tempting me with its contents, his face unshaven and grinning. Dickweed is almost forty, and I have no idea who it is he sleeps with, but I am sure it will not be with anyone that I know. When I return home I mention it to some of the girls, and Brenna decides that she will go. She shrugs and says, 'If it's free why not?' I see her leave with Bailey, both of them wearing skirts.

At home I read the rest of the book, and go through all of Bryce's dresser drawers. In the bathroom I put on his glasses, which he doesn't wear when I'm around. The wire frames are stylish – light brown in some lights and gold in others, like the finish of a car. Taking them off, I notice the congealed grease on the plastic nosepieces and rub them, looking at the shiny mark left on the tip of my index finger. I smell the piece that curves over his ear, and it smells of hair gel and alcohol. Taking the lid off his deodorant, I smell that too.

I wait for Bryce to return from town, but he doesn't and I can't sleep. Placing his pillow over my face, I breathe him in, willing him to come home. It occurs to me to be upset with him, that he has taken so long, but the night makes me more understanding than I would be in daylight. He arrives wet and chaotic, drunk, with scraped hands from where he fell off his bike and then fell asleep on the road.

'Do you have tins of condensed milk in your basement?' I ask him immediately, wide awake.

He licks the side of my face. 'Guess who just won the Port Huron to Mackinac yacht race?'

'A bunch of rich men on a yacht?'

'Bob Seger.'

'The musician?'

'I swear. Me and Trainer were just partying with him.'

We consider this for a moment.

'I learned your religion today,' I say.

The metal from his belt pokes into my flesh as he wraps himself around me.

'Great. Tell me all about it tomorrow.'

'You're stabbing me.'

'I love you too,' he says.

But he takes off his jeans.

Into the far away sanctuary of my sleep comes a low loud melody, and, lying with my eyes closed, I try to decipher the words. Bryce moves restlessly onto his back and then sits up.

'What the fuck is that noise?'

'*Guess I lost my way.*'

'It sounds like Trainer,' I say.

'*There were oh so many roads . . .*'

Joining Bryce at the window I can't see Trainer at first, though I can hear the spattering of puke on bushes. I hear him giggling in between puking. Directly below us in the darkness I can just make out his body lying in the azalea bushes. Velvet will be pissed when she finds out someone crushed her flowers and covered them in vomit. Two nights ago Brenna passed out in the same set of bushes, though no one found her until the morning, and they haven't yet recovered.

'You fucking idiot, Trainer. Go to bed!'

This time in a conversational tone he says, 'I can't get out of the bush.'

There is feeble rustling, then silence.

'Is Bob with you?' Bryce yells.

We look out across the black grass towards the road, but there is no one else outside, and the nearest lamppost burns yellow and alone.

'I puked on my hat,' Trainer says.

We hear '*Still Runnin*' one more time before he falls asleep on the ground.

Bryce puts on his jeans and goes down the stairs to help Trainer to bed.

St. Paul, 3:24 p.m.

It gets harder caring for someone else after that first perfect relationship – so young and free of responsibilities, the first is always better than what comes next. The first time it's Fate and you can really believe it *is*. After that there are lots of reasons why it probably isn't anything more than chance. Even after everything that happened with Bryce, as my school began and life moved on, I missed him. Everyone I met was balanced and measured according to an impossible checklist of spontaneity, alcohol consumption, their honest opinions of backless shirts and ability to procure wine bottles in romantic settings. It never occurred to me that it could happen the way it did. That there *was* no next best thing. That I could not get my prince. Perhaps the problem was thinking of myself as a princess in the first place.

It took years until I loved Alan, really loved him.

When Alan and I first met we were twenty-six, he had his own car, a white Honda Civic. We met through my friend Meredith, who received a human rights degree at St. Kat's – we took *Europe and the Individual* together, and she told me her upstairs neighbor just got into the postal workers union and was what she called 'lickable.'

Have you tasted him? I wanted to know.

I also wanted to know if he'd ever murdered anyone.

She said no, and gave me his number.

On our way to the restaurant for our first lunch date together, I lit up a cigarette, an occasional habit of mine when I'm nervous. I tried to ash out of the window, but a bright ember flew back in unnoticed. It singed the leather seat, smoking so much he had to pull over while I said something like, 'Well, it was nice to meet you, Alan. You can drop me off right here.'

He smiled at me, and his teeth looked straight.

'I knew you were trouble when I first met you,' he said. 'Meredith should have warned me.'

I'd never looked like trouble to anyone before. But I understood why it was attractive. We didn't get back on the road right away; we had to aerate the car.

That summer was wet and humid, so the grass was damp against our calves as we waded into the deep sloping ditch away from the road, into the Queen Anne's lace and milkweed, and the naked brown beer bottles whose labels had long since washed away. In front of us was an abandoned house with green siding – so old there was no sign of a driveway anymore; the roof had fallen in and the windows were boarded. On one of the boards someone had spray-painted HELP, in white capital letters.

'Wonder if it's haunted,' Alan said, motioning towards it.

I walked closer to him, waving the bugs away, the sound of crickets humming in the wet air.

'I hope so,' I said. 'Looks like it should be.'

'You ever seen a ghost?' he asked.

'Once,' I said. 'Maybe.'

He nodded, and we went closer to look at the tiny roadside home that had nothing around the back of it, but privacy from the road.

What I remember clearly about that moment lying in the long grass as I pulled his navy collared shirt up above his head was the birthmark by his left nipple – dark red and shaped like Lake Superior, slightly raised from the white skin. Something

I took to be a sign even though I wasn't sure I believed in them.

It only lasted about three minutes and was far from romantic, a sodden coffee cup stuck to my ass when I got up. It was a surprising demonstration of Alan's spontaneity, something I learned to relish later in our relationship.

So I was the wild one, and that's the way I wanted it, I thought.

Alan never had stocks or bonds though he was always careful with money. He bought the cheapest chardonnays and insisted there was no difference. He never threw anything when he was angry. Once when I was furious with him I threw a copy of the *TV Guide* at his head. It slapped against the side of his face and he looked so sad it made me even angrier. He never said a thing. In silence, he took Anna from her crib and went for a drive, just the two of them. I willed him not to come home, *willed* him to keep driving, imagining what I would do with my freedom. When he finally pulled into the driveway, I got up from the couch where I'd been waiting and quickly went upstairs to pretend I was asleep.

Anna always asked for her father to put her to bed. I used to feel left out.

You don't even *like* putting her to bed, he would reason.

He always had a peculiar sense of logic, of facts and so-called 'evidence.' He embraced the idea of ghost sightings and extra-terrestrial autopsies, documented telekinesis and unlikely photographs of prehistoric sea-creatures – but while the stories of the Virgin Mary's image appearing on someone's breakfast bagel did arouse his interest somewhat, there simply wasn't enough *good evidence* to convince him of a need for worship. The books of the bible were too old, too remote, and he couldn't be bothered to examine them in any detail.

You don't even know who really wrote them, he would say. Matthew *who*?

Alan preferred the *modern* mysteries of the secular world. He was an atheist, just like so many other people who claim to be atheists, until they start to pray. That's why what happened to me left him so helpless, reading the brochures and the Internet statistics. He even asked about *keeping* it, like it was my appendix from grade four in a jar, and underneath my revulsion I was oddly flattered. He wanted the evidence. Ironic in the end, I suppose, considering how it all turned out.

As an adult I only ever went to church for Christmas mass, classifying me as a PIPP – prayer-in-private-person. The terminology was developed by the Catholic Church as an effort to inflate the number of its members worldwide – a necessary step in its ongoing public relations battle with the Church of Latter Day Saints. The propaganda is so fierce now there's no telling which church is expanding more rapidly.

Being inside the church never did me any good. I might as well say my prayers when I need them – on icy highways or in the hospital room. The last time I prayed in church was the day before leaving the island, but no one heard me.

I admit to taking great delight in the symbols and commercial trinkets of Catholicism. Looking up at the kitchen clock, the famous virgin is pointing to three and half past with her blue-robed arms. I look at it again, not remembering what it said the first time.

Sifting through the rest of the envelope's contents, I come across my small day calendar of the Pope. A gift from my Aunt Lydia, a woman partial to hand-crocheted lace doilies and flea-market rosary beads. Every year Rome would see fit to bestow upon her some new trinket to pass on to me. Bryce had hung the calendar above his bed, and I suddenly remember the evening we defaced it – perhaps that's why my summer prayers were never answered and everything came undone. I flip the pages and, yes, the July pope has a moustache. The August pope has a penis.

Anna fancies herself a Buddhist. It's better than most religions, I guess, preaching peace and acceptance. Anna has always been even and balanced, on the outside. Even now that Michael has gone and her father is dead, she will never admit to loneliness or wish things different. Everything is a lesson to be turned over and tasted, then *accepted*. She only looks forward. Seems a waste to me sometimes.

I myself have always found a sort of spiritual comfort in candles and light, because these are things I take on faith, even though they make no sense: fire and electricity. When your big questions go unanswered, you have to take comfort in the little things, I suppose. Maybe if that summer had ended differently, I'd be a different person now. Better, or more hopeful.

One evening, soon after we had bought the house, I came home with a Jesus nightlight for the hallway between our bedroom and the bathroom, and Alan refused to let me plug it in.

'It's creepy,' he said, 'and disrespectful.'

'What do you care anyway?' I asked.

'Just because I'm not religious, doesn't mean I need to make fun of people who are.'

I held the nightlight up to his face.

'Jesus says you're boring,' I told him.

'Well, Alan says you're being a bitch,' he replied.

Alan hardly ever swore, so I knew he was serious. I plugged it in anyway. Anna enjoyed it when she was younger, often sitting in front of the plastic figure as if she were praying, running her hands over his robe and enjoying the warmth.

We moved it into her bedroom, and years later she took it with her to college.

'Thank God,' Alan said when he noticed its absence.

We were a divided family then, and not just on our opinions of the CIA's involvement in the selection of the papacy when the news was revealed in the early thirties.

'*The LDS and the CIA*,' the papers said. '*Who's really in control of the Catholic Church?*' The smaller headlines were about six RWPs hitting Indiana in the space of just over a month.

'I hear the CIA *is* all Mormon,' Alan said to me, loving the idea of a conspiracy theory. A secret religious takeover, a hostile bid. His favorite book from his youth was *The Da Vinci Code*. While I believed the church of my childhood would survive this media frenzy, I optimistically imagined the aftermath to involve a systematic utopian deconstruction of the world's religions, everyone shrugging and saying: I guess we really did get it wrong and the otter with the dirt in its mouth and the breath of Vishnu and the endless wheel of misery and the Great Mother Goddess and the cosmic egg of opposites are all one and the same and it's all about the individual journey and it's nothing about power so everything is okay.

As long as I could still get my *His Essence* candles that smelled like Jesus – myrrh, aloe, and cassia.

But no one who ever believed had any problem *still* believing, the way it should be I suppose. It was the system that was perhaps at fault, but the white-columned arms of the Vatican still embraced the world ready to forgive the political ambitions of its followers. After a few days of violence anyway.

'Good riddance,' Alan said, watching the riots in St. Peter's Square.

Russ Gerhardt shook his head when I delivered the morning papers to his desk along with his whipped cream latte.

'I hear Italy's got some real nice paintings,' was all he said.

One of Anna's friends brought her a shell casing as a souvenir from the Via della Conciliazione, where the Italian military opened fire on the crowd.

'You can't separate the two, can you?' she asked, as she held the gold casing up to the light. 'Religion and politics, I mean.'

I looked over to where she sat at the table, as she tried to have some kind of Zen moment.

'The Mormons never hurt anyone,' I pointed out.

I close the calendar. Something to throw away.

I pick up the letter.

Mackinac

When my mother's breasts wash up on the shore heavy with cancer, I cast them out again with the tide. I have been expecting them for years, but I am not ready for them yet.

I walk down to the beach to read the letter again. After the mile of shops on either side of Main Street the shore opens up, and beside the narrow road everything tumbles down slowly towards the water. The beach is made of stones the size of my fist. In colors of slate and sand and brick, the ground shifts under my feet as I pick down the incline to the shore. I've been daring enough to go swimming in the lake only once, and that was around the other side of the island, where it's shallower.

I sit on a flat piece of driftwood looking out at the water. From here I can watch all the ferries slide across the short dark horizon, as well as the traffic as it arcs along the Mackinac Bridge. The sun is a hazy bulb behind gray clouds, the light soft and muted. Families on bicycles pass along the road behind me, their voices full of idleness and air.

Stewart stay with us, don't ride so far ahead, STEWART!

Where's the Evian? Did you bring the Evian?

They come and go in waves, and soon there is nothing.

Finally, reluctantly, I drag my mother's disease aground to examine it closely.

When my grandmother died after living her last years in a special bed in our basement, I had gone outside to smoke a cigarette. It was late at night and the highway in front of my house was silent. With the cigarette still in my mouth, I lay down along the double yellow line in the middle of the road. The pavement was dry and still warm from the heat of day. I lay there for maybe a minute, but probably not that long. I wanted the moment to mean something, but I think it meant nothing at all.

Dear Bell. The letter has a border of yellow pansies. The wind folds the top of the paper over, and I hold it open like a scroll. *Everything is fine*, she says.

I notice a fat ladybug, one with not too many spots, moving along the driftwood towards me. I put my index finger down to tempt it. Changing direction when it meets my skin, it continues down towards the underside of the log and disappears.

Everything is fine.

They wheeled my grandmother out the next morning, upright on the gurney because she couldn't fit around the corners. My last image is of her strapped down and dead, a grotesque Frankenstein's monster. I was on my way to the bathroom, and you'd think someone would have warned me she was coming.

She is the only person close to me who has died. Bryce's best friend died when he was fourteen after being hit by a school bus, and another of his friends has a bullet in his knee from a drive-by. No one in my high school even suffered a serious illness, apart from alcohol poisoning. It's left me unprepared. I've been too long without tragedy, and I have no learned response, no instincts. Maybe I'm overreacting. But I cry anyway.

Everything's fine, she writes, *no need to come home.*

I make the long walk to the other end of Main Street, not riding my bike, not wanting to get there too fast. Saint Mary's church is white and impermanent looking – its severe, square shape and high wooden stairs a testament to its preparedness for snow and isolation. Whenever I pass by, its doors are always open.

Inside the ceiling is higher than seems possible from the outside. It is white inside as well, the pews warm and made of wood. Above the altar is a strange mural – the Virgin Mary arriving on Mackinac Island via ferryboat, her arms outstretched. There aren't too many ornaments, just red carnations on either side of the altar, crimson hymnbooks in place, everything functional. The church is busy with visitors, the click of cameras echoes about the space. I have a massive painful splinter from the driftwood log, and it reminds me of when I used to get pencil lead jammed into my skin at school.

At the back of the church are the candles where I expect them to be, and for a dollar donation I light one with a long match.

Burning in its metal cup I put my candle beside the others. It strikes me that two tea lights together look like waxy white breasts with flaming nipples. I move my candle so it sits alone, but then I wonder if it was some sort of sign. I move it back.

The skin around my eyes feels wet, and I wish I'd brought my sunglasses.

A man enters the church with his two sons, all three of them eating ice cream, and they stop near the back as he points out the mural.

'I told you God was everywhere,' he says. 'Even here, look.'

He points to the Virgin Mary arriving on the island.

'He's like Santa, he sees everything.'

The family stands, licking and staring.

'I thought God was a man,' says the youngest son finally.

I wonder if his wife is dead, or left him. I put my head down, like I'm praying. There is a two-year waiting list to get married on Mackinac. Each church and public space is booked at ridiculously high prices, years in advance. Some churches hold as many as three weddings a day. At least once a day on my way to work, a slick black carriage slides by pulled by high-stepping horses, carrying a woman in white and her new husband. They wave like royalty, the carriage full of flowers and ribbons. And why not? They have paid for their perfect fairytale, one that I get to live every day. I wave back.

My mother was married in a turquoise dress, my father in a cream suit with raised texture like paper towel. The ceremony was held at Holy Trinity in Cheyenne in 1978, and the reception was at my grandparents' house – the wide brown prairies and too much sky waiting for them out each window as they ate potato salad and downed champagne. Their wedding photographs are small and square with a white border, only wide enough for the important things, everything else left out.

'I never knew what to do next,' my mother confided to me. She had thought maybe they would buy a farm.

Sometimes Bryce will ask me to take a nap with him. Like cats we pick a piece of grass in Marquette Park and lie together, on the back of this great turtle called Mackinac. The grass is sometimes damp, or sometimes it's so hot and sharp it burns my skin and we have to leave. Lately, however, the weather has been perfect, and we can lie for an hour or more. When older couples or families walk by looking for a place to picnic with their Mackinac T-shirts and ice-cream cones, Bryce will put his hand on my breast, and they will keep walking.

'I wonder if people wish they were us,' Bryce said once.

Bryce and I love having sex outside. On an island full of tradition and other people's weddings, it feels good to do something daring. Sometimes in between a lunch shift and a dinner shift Bryce and I will have sex in the forest. With half of the island designated a national park, there are endless opportunities to go naked without worrying about wandering families becoming unwilling observers. There is a clearing we discover where the ground is covered with leafy plants and grasses. Five minutes later, Bryce is drying off his wet penis before putting his shorts back on, and I'm placing my palms together, trying to press away the grassy imprints that itch long after the marks have disappeared.

I watch my candle burn until it is time to go, needing to leave before it burns out; needing to believe it won't. When I leave Blue is at the end of a wooden pew near the door, her hands covering her face, her head bent. Her shoulders move up and down beneath her T-shirt. I look around, but there is no one waiting for her. I guess happiness isn't guaranteed just because you're on vacation. Maybe that's why the island has so many churches. I want to sit next to her, put my hands over my face and not be alone when I do it, but I decide to leave St. Mary's, seeing no one else, not even Father Kim.

I tell only Bryce about my mother.

'That's awful,' he says.

And that's all he needs to say.

St. Paul, 4:00 p.m.

I fold up my mother's letter from so long ago, the familiar handwriting tight and small. Something to keep.

The heating comes on softly, the hum of the furnace sweeping up through the floor which means the temperature outside has dropped at least five degrees. I imagine Althea will call soon to tell me it's a 6.5, to remind me where she hides her good jewelry, her platinum wedding ring, to make sure I remember the key to her front door is in the birdfeeder. When she calls I will not talk about the weather though, I will tell her about my visitor, how I have been waiting, but it's not too much longer now. The weather is a few degrees cooler but that is all and I might even tell her a story or two to make her understand. I look up at Mary, counting the minutes. My prescriptions are delivered tomorrow. There is no mail today, I checked twice. The phone doesn't ring.

Yesterday after Anna left for her Thursday yoga class, someone called asking for Alan. A marketing company. I told them he wasn't in at the moment, feeling confused, embarrassed. When I hung up, I stood for maybe a minute before collapsing slowly. I don't know how I managed it; I can barely sit on my own toilet anymore, let alone the floor. But there I was. I had to crawl all the way across the kitchen and use a chair to help myself up again. *What a fucking joke*, I thought while on my hands and knees, crying, then laughing, then crying again, *to have such a useless body*. I had only a few moments to recover, sitting upright on the chair that saved me, before I had to leave for my appointment. Dr. Trevor was expecting me.

I went to him yesterday because I was lonely. He's a male doctor, it doesn't matter to me one way or the other, but I think men doctors are softer. All through my twenties and thirties I had a woman, feeling that pap smears and breast exams were less awkward this way, but she was the sort of woman who would stand up before she asked, 'Is that all?' – daring me not to have anything else wrong with me. Dr. Trevor has been my doctor for the last fifteen years, taking the practice over from his father. There are almost no men left in family practice anymore, but this man is warm and kind with no interest in surgery or brains – the areas of medicine that would bring him serious money. I got my hair done downtown at Scissors before my appointment.

I stopped being embarrassed ages ago. My graying pubic hair sprouts everywhere, untamed; I used to keep it trim when I could still get my leg on to the toilet seat to shave properly. My armpits I can still manage, but they are sweaty by the time I get to his office. My stomach has crease marks from the skin hanging over skin; I no longer apply the scented shimmering lotion that used to shine when my body caught the light. The thin slivers of scar travel across where my breasts used to be; the Victoria's Secret catalogues still come years and years too late. Alan used to read them in bed; Anna takes them home now to flip through. All of this I am used to now. He's just a doctor. A man doing his job. I am nothing to him, an aging body.

I told him my stomach was hurting and he pressed a hand to my belly and asked, 'Do you feel any tenderness here?'

His hand was dry and warm and all at once I imagined him sliding his hand lower, sliding his fingers into me asking, 'How does this feel? Down here?'

I imagined this and my body was younger, my thighs smooth and taut, my toenails painted red, my underwear black and made of lace, and I remembered my perfect body lost somewhere inside the one I have now. He pressed the other side of my stomach. 'What about here?'

I nodded as if that's where it hurt.

Lying there so sexless and bare, I wondered if there were some instances where despite ethics and codes of conduct and society, the doctor and patient could not control themselves – if somewhere, it must have happened, they were both too wild to resist. I wondered if the doctor, a man of course, became hard underneath his white coat as he returned to the room where his female patient had undressed, if it came as a surprise, if the woman knew her effect on him, if it was calculated. I wondered if, while giving her a breast exam, he brushed her nipple ever so slightly and she gasped, involuntarily perhaps, at the sensation, if he would return to it, questioningly at first, and then encouraged by her breathing and the crinkle of the clean white paper underneath her body as she arched her back, with more certainty. I wondered if he would massage her breasts while she rubbed the front of his khaki pants, grabbing and pulling at him until he lay down on top of her. There wouldn't be time to laugh at the ridiculousness of the situation, because everything would be wet, erect, urgent. The condoms would be in his desk drawer. He would be married, or they both would, and despite the circumstances the sex would be routine – quick, but satisfying, absent of any kinky additions like tongue depressors or stethoscopes. She would think about switching doctors but wouldn't, because secretly she enjoyed this complication in her life.

Is it absurd to fantasize such things?

I surprised myself, how quickly my feelings turned like that, not realizing they were so near the surface, waiting.

'It's your posture,' he said.

He'd determined that my imaginary stomach complaint was the result of my leaning over when I walked, cramping my insides.

'When you walk imagine a string pulling you straight up towards the ceiling.'

'Am I going to get a hunchback?' I asked.

He laughed. 'If you were going to have a hunchback,' he said, 'you'd surely have it by now.'

I collected my things quickly and left. I bought a coffee from the drive-through on the way home, but the young woman didn't let me get a proper hold of the cup before she let go, and it dropped. It splattered on the pavement between us and the young woman said, 'Oh, fuck, just a minute,' but I drove away. I didn't know where to go and didn't want to go home – back to the memories I had no place for.

I drove around the familiar city streets slowly, looking too often in the rear-view mirror, wondering where I had gone. My hair did look nice, and driving past the post office where Alan used to work I hoped to see one of the men or women leaving on their route so I could pull over and say hello, but it was too late in the day. There was no one. Looking at my reflection again, I remembered something Bryce told me long ago about the *Salt Lake Tribune*. The obituary section, he said, had 'before' and 'after' pictures. Not after death, but after youth. It was like a Where's Waldo he had said, staring into the second face and trying to match up the bone structure, the shape of the eyes, to determine if this was indeed the same person.

I drove around for a while, still not wanting to return home. But in the end I did.

Now I am sitting up straight in my kitchen chair, still watching the clock. I can't decide whether or not I can still hear the warning siren, it seems a part of the atmosphere now, the sound registering unconsciously perhaps, but not really there like the chirping of birds or the sound of waves after a day at the beach. Perhaps I should have asked Dr. Trevor about my hearing.

I remember the invisible string, and concentrate, sitting straight in my kitchen chair because I can't believe it's ever too late in life to worry about getting a hunchback.

Mackinac

This morning Velvet sends me to pick up a prescription arriving on the first ferry from St. Ignace and the dock is busy with cigarette-smoking porters and ferry workers sorting out the morning's orders. On my left are four boxes of tomatoes, eight boxes of black straws (Bryce says all the restaurants use the same straws so they can borrow from each other if they run out), and a bag of mail in a canvas sack marked PROPERTY OF THE UNITED STATES POSTAL SERVICE. On my right is a case of maple syrup and a ready-to-be-assembled oak dresser in a cardboard box. At the end of the dock Rummy stands alone, watching the departing ferry move slowly out into the lake towards the lighthouse. As it disappears around the edge of the island, he flicks a coin into the water, but he doesn't turn around.

Velvet's prescription is not at the dock, and one of the porters tells me to try the island's medical center.

The center is impressive: pink granite and tinted glass with metal bike racks out front. There are no wooden shutters, tubs of geraniums, or wind chimes hanging from the eaves. It is functional, set back from Market Street so its modernity doesn't offend the landscape. Community flyers on the door advertise Mackinac High School's Italy fundraiser, Maureen's Art Exhibition at Old Warren House, the book club led by Father Kim, and a community meeting about the proposed bike helmet legislation. I return to the Tippecanoe with two thousand milligrams of muscle relaxant.

Yesterday Brenna came to work complaining the center

doesn't offer abortions. Blue had followed behind her into the change room, looking horrified.

'On this fucking island? They'd make a killing,' Brenna said.

'Why are you corrupting Blue with all your ungodly sin?' Trainer yelled through the closed door.

Blue quit this morning, and she must have packed last night as she apparently left on the first ferry. She was a small silent girl from somewhere outside Chicago, and Bryce says she drank the vanilla latte syrup when she thought no one was looking, so maybe she's better off at home.

Rummy finally arrives late for work and carrying his newspaper and Brenna pounces on him, pulling him into the walk-in cooler impatiently, her Tiffany bracelet shiny against her tanned forearm. He emerges after a few minutes, still carrying the paper and looking upset.

His parents send him the *Sunday Star* via overnight delivery every week, and he retreats with it to the Voodoo Altar – the ornate walnut end table decorated with carved faces is a Velvet family heirloom which also serves as the staff break table. I join him quietly, both of us sipping Velvet's gourmet coffee thick with cream and sweet with sugar. Sitting across from him it feels like our own kitchen table, our own home, fresh with the smell of coffee and the Tippecanoe's famous chocolate croissants; I imagine we are married, as Rummy fits the sort of imaginings I have about husbands, which aren't many.

We sit together every Monday; no one else is interested in his current events, and no one ever asks to read the paper when he is finished with it, although someone usually manages to start the crossword. 'Hemingway's paper,' he calls it. He is in his second year of journalism at a place called Ryerson, and usually when he reads he says things like, 'Now *this* is news' and, 'This Siddiqui guy, his column is really something.'

Today he says nothing.

'What do you think about Blue quitting?' I ask.

He lowers his paper, and stares over at Brenna who is arguing with Chef Walter about a blonde hair he found in the ice machine. Waiting for Rummy's answer I add more sugar cubes to my coffee, using my pen as a stir stick.

'I liked her,' he says finally.

While sucking coffee from the end of my pen, I remember Rummy at the end of the dock this morning and suddenly connect.

'Is she okay?' I ask.

He shrugs.

'And Brenna knows?'

He nods. I've secretly always assumed that Rummy was a virgin, but I don't ask him about it anymore.

'What did you wish for?' I ask him.

Rummy stares at me.

'With your coin. In the lake.'

'World peace,' he says, and goes back to his paper.

I realize in spending all my time with Bryce, my relationship with Rummy has suffered.

'So what's going on in that great country of yours?'

He straightens the paper and turns the front page towards me so I can see the photo of a black and brown dog. 'The pit bulls are eating the children. They're thinking of banning the dogs.'

'The dogs? What about the owners?'

Skimming the column he shakes his head.

'Well, that's the debate. Four people have been killed in just the last month. A five-year-old girl was mauled to death in front of her mother by a trained attack dog.' He looks up and winks at me. 'And you thought Canadian culture wasn't violent.'

I roll my eyes at him. 'What else?'

'Global warming, religion . . . horoscopes?' he asks, and I nod. *'Keep your eye on the prize, Virgo,'* he reads. *'Don't get caught up in the small details. Things will soon become clear and your path will unfold itself before you. Avoid travel on the 17th.'*

'Great.' I drink my coffee.

He looks up. 'Mine says I'm handsome.'

After my morning shift I call my mother using the pay phone furthest away from the restaurant. Located on one of the ferry docks, it is noisy as people load and disembark, their feet pounding along the wooden planks. I wait until the boat sounds its horn briefly and begins to back out and turn around. I put a pocket full of quarters into the slot and the receiver is hot and wet, the humidity suggesting a storm later on this evening. I pray for rain so the restaurant won't be busy. My mother picks up quietly at the other end, happy to hear from me. To use the library's internet is costly, and without a phone in my apartment there is little way to get a hold of me besides sending letters.

'I got your letter, Mom.'

'Oh, well. It's fine, I was going to call, but I thought a letter, maybe.'

She tells me there are appointments to keep, and my dad has rearranged his work schedule so they can drive into the city together.

'We'll make a day of it,' she says. 'A little day trip. We still haven't tried that Thai place you recommended to us.'

'The Friendly Thai,' I say. 'Make sure you get the pineapple-fried rice.'

'It's a long way from plucking chickens,' she says.

This is a saying she uses sometimes, referring to her child-hood farm chore of plucking the feathers off the dead chickens her brother killed. The family chores were divided evenly along gender lines: her brother would kill the chickens, and she would pluck them while her mother, my grandmother, cooked the chickens for dinner with potatoes and corn and carrots. Whatever was left over would go into a soup.

She repeats this saying when she's trying new things or visiting new places to remind herself of just how far she's come. It reminds me of just how far I've gone.

'So tell me about your day,' she says.

When I hang up the phone I observe a man wearing a twenty-five dollar novelty foam cowboy hat on his head, walking towards the docks to wait for the next ferry. His hat is neon orange, although you can get them in pink or green as well. His friends follow close behind him, all of them drunk.

'Barry, you shithead!' one of them is yelling. 'You still owe me twenty bucks for eating that burger off the floor.'

The group pounds past me, the wooden dock shuddering with their heavy feet, the space filling with masculinity, sports teams supported on various T-shirts and one man smacking a miniature basketball against the planks.

'Fuck off!' Barry in the neon orange cowboy hat yells at him. 'You threw up afterwards. It doesn't fucking count.'

I return to work thinking of pit bulls and abortions and malignant growths, all wearing novelty hats atop their heads.

The chef special this evening is Horseradish Crusted Michigan Whitefish with Caramelized Onion, Seared in a Bacon Emulsion. With a different special every day, I sometimes get the adjectives mixed up, sometimes the meat as well. I had an entire table order veal chops once when the special was actually pork. Depending on the amount of French included in my descriptions, eyes will either glaze over as they hurriedly order the lobster fettucini, or there might be a knowing nod to the rest of the table. 'I love mascarpone,' they'll say, or, 'the BC salmon has been particularly nice this year.' I have three tables tonight, two with water and pastas, one with wine (Château Grand Traverse Late Harvest Riesling, 1998), Scotch (Laphroaig), and two chef specials.

The air outside is slightly damp with mist and the sky is gray with clouds. An older woman with beautiful white hair waves me over.

'Do you know the weather report for this evening?'

'I think it's supposed to rain later on,' I say, having no idea.

Her tanned husband with cufflinks in the shape of anchors wants to know which bars will be good tonight. I list a number of them, telling him whether or not they have live music, and which bar supposedly makes the best Manhattan – his drink of choice. This earns me a wink. I avoid mentioning the Cock.

'So are you from the island, Bell?' he asks, reading my nametag.

'Actually I'm from St. Paul.'

'St. *Paul*.'

They look at one another, smiling.

'Dina *loves A Prairie Home Companion*,' he says.

All across the restaurant everyone carries on the same conversations.

The evening drags, and outside the sky gets darker. Waves with rough whitecaps roll towards the shore. I gravitate towards the window and watch the light change. Rummy stands beside me and we stare at the lake, though we are always alert for Velvet's quick ponytailed figure. I am holding a crystal water pitcher, and he has a tray of carefully balanced dirty dishes, both of us able within seconds to appear busy.

The air in the restaurant changes slightly, cools, becomes heavy. Small sailboats and yachts gather together, heading for the safety of the marina which fills quickly. The black clouds advance and lightning blazes down to meet the water, splitting and cracking with bright silver light. The storm swoops in. The sky is lit every few seconds with sharp lines of electricity, and the wind hurls sheets of rain into the windows. Thunder invades the pleasant tinkling of the Tippecanoe.

'It never gives up its dead,' Rummy says, looking out the window.

'What doesn't?'

'The lake.'

'What?'

'Gordon Lightfoot,' he says.

'What?'

'Gordon Lightfoot lyrics. Look it up.'

Rummy likes to lord his useless knowledge over me. I go and find Bryce, forgetting that he does the same. He is in the back polishing silverware with a muslin cloth. Velvet gets these cloths from a supplier in Ann Arbor who imports them directly from India. 'The best muslin,' she says with a sigh, 'is from Mosul of course, but it's impossible to get.'

'Who's Gordon Lightfoot?' I ask him.

'He sang "The Wreck of the Edmund Fitzgerald",' Bryce says immediately. 'But it sank in Lake Superior, not here.'

'What?'

He sighs and puts down the knife he was rubbing.

'Gordon Lightfoot is the folksinger that sang "The Wreck of the Edmund Fitzgerald", about the ship that sank in Superior. Twenty-nine people died. Famous song.'

'Why have I not heard about it?'

'Because,' he says, smacking my ass with the flat part of the knife then putting it in the pile of clean cutlery, 'you're adorable.'

I go back and find Rummy.

'He's a folksinger,' I say.

'A *Canadian* folksinger,' he corrects me. 'Like Stan Rogers.'

I sigh. The rain runs gray and streaming down the windows, distorting the view, and someone motions me towards their table to ask when the storm is going to stop.

'Not tonight,' I tell them.

St. Paul, 4:07 p.m.

Hearing the sound of a car door, I go quickly to the living-room window. The sky to the north is dark now, almost black above the rooftops and a small V of Canadian geese flies overhead and disappears. I look to see if, perhaps, because of the weather warning and my guest's subsequent determination to ensure an arrival, he has come early.

Across the road and the fading green lawn, Alison and her teenage daughter Amy are getting into their van, quickly, both wearing winter jackets. I lift my hand to wave, even though the van is already backing out and I'm sure they can't see me anyway. Lowering my hand I cross my arms, leaning slowly forward until my forehead rests on the glass.

Anna used to baby-sit for Amy; the two of them spent all their time outside, throwing baseballs at one another, rollerblading, biking. Amy loved Anna, the two of them so alike. Now I never see her without a short skirt, jewelry flashing from across the street. Anna didn't approve of this transformation, her sporting protégée transfigured from tomboy to tart. I loved it. One night a few years ago when I couldn't sleep I saw Amy, maybe fifteen, spread-eagled on the front lawn of her house, her body covered by a man wearing a bright-blue shirt. I watched, fascinated, wondering if my white face in the window was bright and visible from where they were lying. An hour they were there, fully clothed, first him on top, then the other way round. I watched to make sure she was okay, the neighborly thing. I felt proud of her. This secret we now shared was important; she was unknowingly connected to me. To her I was just the woman across the street who picked the gravel from her hands so long ago when she fell off her bicycle. In fact it was Anna's old bike, stuck in the garage for years, offered to our young neighbors just starting out with new jobs and struggling with money. An old BMX, smooth and quiet with a bit of grease.

The first bicycle was invented in Scotland, in 1840 I think it was. I've seen pictures, a big monstrous thing made of wood and metal, the seat curved way up in the back like a chair. Not the penny-farthing, not the one with the giant wheel in front, that came later. After this came a version with no pedals, everyone just scooted around using their feet. Aristocrats in Germany and France snapped these up, using them to coast along almost as quickly as a horse and carriage. Everyone was able to go places faster than they had before. Women were free to self-propel themselves wherever they liked. They wore bloomers; the bicycle *forced the invention of women's pants*. Though I never thought about it back then, I think the bicycle deserves more credit as an integral part of the women's movement.

After leaving the island that summer, I was determined to ride my bike more often. But that feeling of wild alive-ness was impossible to recreate. Without the place that made it all real a bicycle is boring, useless on the streets of a modern city except for bike messengers and women that don't mind wearing helmets or taping one pant leg so it won't catch in the chain. I never rode one again. Not once. When Anna learned to ride I ran behind her with my hand on the seat of that purple BMX, waiting until the wobbles had stopped, letting go. Does anyone after the age of ten look at a bike as anything other than a toy? They are impractical really. Cars are affordable and gas is plentiful again. The vast Athabascan oil sands at twice the size of Lake Ontario are the largest

in the world, and our northern neighbors have been gener-
ous if only because of NAFTA. The massive RWPs and
violent weather patterns are everything we were warned of,
I suppose.

Do I get nostalgic when I look at bicycles? Of course. I am
a stupid old woman that stares misty-eyed at children as they
rush past, feet pedaling furiously. I am especially moved by
the older models, the ones with baskets, like my own taken
from the airport so long ago. As I watch the children getting
smaller, disappearing from me, I imagine these bicycles as
metaphors, and pretend I'm the only woman wise enough to
have ever thought of this.

But there are no bicycles today; the children are kept at
home using websites for lessons. Anna did a safety unit once
on what to do in case of an RWP. 'Duck and cover,' she
explained, the instructions never going out of style. Smoke
rises from every chimney except my own in anticipation of a
disruption in electricity.

Alan used to stop and chat with everyone on his daily walk.
Once around the neighborhood every day after he retired, I
think it reminded him of work. Even in winter when it was
icy, I think he took pleasure in everyone saying, 'Alan, what
the hell are you doing out today in this weather, you'll kill
yourself.'

'Been out in worse than this,' he'd say cheerfully, always
cheerfully. 'Neither rain nor sleet nor snow!'

Then he'd come up to the front porch and stomp the snow
from his boots, always two hard stomps for each foot. It
annoyed me one day, that he was so predictable.

'Why can't you switch it up a little?' I asked.

The next day he waded into the house with all the snow
still stuck to his boots. 'No stomps today, your highness,' he
said. The white mounds became tiny lakes filled with bits of

gravel, cold and isolated on the carpet and tile. We stepped in wet puddles for the rest of the afternoon.

Sometimes I laugh when I remember these things, but not today.

I can feel the draft standing close to the window, but there won't be snow yet for ages. That reminds me we've still got the garage to do, with the snow blower, the lawn mower, lengths of wire, patio furniture, sheets of wood, the tools and tins of paint, it's too much. There are too many things collected, waiting. I look down at the beige sofa covered in boxes, no room on the cushions for sitting. Anna's marked one of the boxes MINE, and it's too much for me, to wonder what's in it.

Through the window the street is still quiet, and though I wait, and watch, no one comes.

Mackinac

My time is divided into shifts. Every day I fold swan napkins and break glasses and try to remember my orders correctly as we are not allowed to write anything down. When asked, I always recommend the most expensive bottle of wine and offer everyone dessert to ensure the bill is as high as possible. Every day I work, watch the waves, complain about the heat and sometimes have a table of guests worth talking to. These guests will be interested in where I live during the summer or where I'm from or where I got such an unusual name. They will *not* ask if the Tippecanoe's arugula is organic.

Outside the streets are filled with men in suits wearing badges and smiling at everyone, as the Republican convention is in town. Rumor has it that last night a senator from out west was beat up on Main Street. (The man had propositioned Neil's wife; Neil owns the Whisky Bar and like most locals has no tolerance for tourists who get loud after a few drinks, regardless of their rank in the outside world.) The Democrats come next month for more of the same. The grass on the island is dark green even though it hardly ever rains anymore and the clouds move across the vast expanse of sky while more arrive to take their place. The flow of people is constant, and last night outside our apartments someone hung Brenna's pink bike from the lowest branch of a pine tree, making her late for work this morning. It is August.

Bryce appears in the doorway of our bedroom with a box of Q-tips in his hand. I look up from my place on the bed, waiting for an explanation.

'Guess what time it is?' he asks.

'What are you doing?'

'Operation Earwax!'

He shakes the box beside his ear like there's candy in it.

'No way,' I say.

'Here, you sit on this.' He pulls up a chair and stands behind it, motioning me into it.

'Fuck off. What's wrong with my eardrums?'

He opens the package, and patiently motions to the chair again. 'They're dirty,' he says.

'They are not.' But I sit in the chair. I tilt my head to offer him the best access to my ear canal. 'Don't burst my eardrum,' I warn.

'Don't worry,' he says.

Holding the opposite side of my head gently with one hand, he starts in the large ridge where the top of my ear is pierced. The cotton is dry and sounds loud. He sweeps down and around the outer ridges, around all the parts that probably have names, but I don't know them. He switches to the clean end before going in all the way, twisting the Q-tip as it plunges into my ear.

'Not too far in,' I say.

He doesn't answer. After a moment he pulls the swab out and holds it up for me to see. 'Look at your disgusting earwax.'

The swab is yellow at the end.

'Gross.'

'Next ear,' he announces.

'I only have two.'

He switches sides and begins again. 'Any news about your mom?'

The hand holding my head begins to feel hot, making my hair damp. I can't move away.

'Can we open a window?'

'I take it that means no?'

I don't say anything. I'd rather be here than there. Where I would know instantly, how everything was, when something new happened. Where my whole life would be that. But I'd rather be here. And so I know nothing.

Closing my eyes I practice the relaxation technique of pushing out my stomach when I breathe, forcing my muscles to relax, and I think of shrimp cocktails in crystal goblets and clean linen. I think of order and organization, of setting tables and lining the bottom edge of the fork and knife and spoon with the folded beak of the swan so there is a clean line one inch from the rounded curve of the tabletop.

'Would you love me if I had no breasts?' I ask.

He thinks for a moment. 'Of course,' he says.

And then, 'Not as much, obviously.'

I grab his probing Q-tip and throw it across the room. He laughs and pats the top of my head.

'I'd love you even without any arms and legs,' he says.

'Ha.'

He retrieves the swab from the floor. 'Would you love me if I were a superhero that killed bad guys to avenge the innocent?'

'Only if you wore tights.'

There's a knock on our apartment door, and someone has their hand over the peephole.

'I know it's you, asshole,' I say loudly. 'You're the only one who does that.'

'Open the door,' the voice demands.

'Who is it?' Bryce wants to know.

'Trainer,' I say.

'Let him in.'

'I'm going to.'

I open the door and he's barefoot.

'Come see the caterpillar I stepped on,' Trainer says.

'You stepped on it in your bare feet?'

He shrugs. 'It was an accident. Come see.'

I follow him down the wooden steps. The grounds are quiet today as it's Friday and most people are working; no music and no voices. There is hardly any wind.

I'm not wearing shoes either and the ground is hard and uneven under my feet. Trainer pulls up the legs of his jeans before crouching down over a patch of gravel. I get on my knees beside him, and notice the tops of his toes and feet are hairy.

'You have hobbit feet,' I say.

He touches the splattered remains of the caterpillar.

'Honey, if you want to talk about hair we can talk about your eyebrows,' he says absently.

We keep looking at the ground. The watery yellow innards wet the sharp stones, the skin no longer visible.

'I wonder where its family is?' I say.

We look up at the surrounding trees as if it had fallen from them like a pine cone. Nothing moves, not even the highest branches.

'Everything dies alone anyway,' says Trainer. He keeps looking up, looking out above the trees.

'Thank you, Zen master.' I bow my head towards him, but he's not in the mood.

'You're alone right now,' he says. He adjusts his baseball cap and stands up. 'But you just don't know it.'

He kicks a foot full of gravel over the caterpillar's remains. In the sunlight the tops of his feet are gray with dust, and the hair looks silver. I'm about to ask him a question when Bryce opens the window above our heads and leans out.

'I'm not done de-waxing you yet,' he shouts down at me.

Trainer raises an eyebrow at me, and shrugs. 'Wax on,'

he says. 'I'm going to go throw rocks at some Republicans.'

He shuffles off towards the bike rack.

'*Liberal!*' I yell after him. '*I'm telling Velvet.*'

He swings a leg over the seat of his red Schwinn, the one with Spice Girls playing cards stuck in the spokes.

'Not really,' he shrugs. 'I hate everyone equally.'

He gives me a salute before pedaling off down the gravel path, yelling behind him as an afterthought:

'*Except for the governor though. Her shit is all right!*'

The flapping and flipping of the cards recedes until I can't hear anything any more.

Back in our room Bryce finishes my ears and we both want sex afterwards, the plunging of cotton into certain orifices not quite satisfying enough, and this week it is particularly messy.

'At least my sheets are dark blue,' he says.

'They're green. I told you that already,' I say from beneath him.

After ten minutes he withdraws, only half-heartedly hard. I immediately wonder if there's something wrong with him. Kneeling on the bed, he flaps his penis back and forth with his left hand while we look at it, concerned. Wet, pink and slightly bloody, he massages it with no result. There are so many things to learn about our bodies – liquids and plasma, hormones, cells containing codes not under our control. Add in the body of another and it seems there are infinite things likely to go wrong. Bryce loses interest in his dick and announces he's going to buy some beer. Getting off the bed he pulls on a pair of wrinkled khakis, then checks his wallet and withdraws a bunch of notes, tips from his breakfast shift this morning.

'Can I see that?' I point to his driver's license.

'What for?' He doesn't hand it over immediately.

'Don't be difficult,' I say.

I take his wallet from him, the brown leather turned almost white with wear. On the outside is a round sticker of a pot leaf with the word 'Heidelberg' above it, a souvenir from his class trip to Germany.

I examine the picture on his license, taken almost three years ago: Bryce with much longer hair and rounder features.

Date of Birth, November 30th, 1978. We have already discussed how Virgo and Sagittarius go well together.

Address, 45 Old Lake Drive, Grayling, Michigan. Grayling is located about midway up the index finger of Bryce's right hand, only a few hours south of the island. Home of the world's longest canoe marathon, he tells me.

I stop and read the name a second time.

'Lehi B. Russo. Lehi?'

'Yep.'

I look up at him and back down again at the license.

'What?'

'It's my first name. I don't use it, everyone calls me Bryce.'

'You never told me your real name?'

'Bryce is my real name. My middle name.'

He takes the license from my hand and casually scratches the end of his nose with it, before returning it to his wallet. We stare at each other.

'I think you enjoy surprising me,' I say.

'I'm proud of my name,' he says crossing his arms. 'You just never asked.'

I cross my arms back. 'Fine, *Lehi*. I'll tell Velvet to change your nametag.'

He thinks for a moment and sits beside me on the bed, putting his hand on my knee. 'Fine. Here. Ask me anything.'

'That's not the point. You're missing the point.'

'Take it or leave it.'

I think for a moment, wondering what I don't know about

him that I need to ask. Who is the blonde woman in your photo album, the one wearing overalls that came before me in more ways than one? Why is your favorite color so predictable? Why did your sister Odette throw her ice skate at you when you were ten? Why did she call you at the restaurant on Tuesday? Why do you want to be an electrical engineer? Why do you keep telling me about the intricacies of testing an electrical current and how the brown wire is always the live wire and the blue wire is always neutral and how easy it is to forget to dry your hands when I don't give a shit? How can you do all of this work with colored wires when you're color blind? Why are we both going back to community college in October instead of buying a yacht and living off the coast of Portugal drinking Spanish sangria and imported beers with limes in them and suntanning naked while you bite my skin with your crooked teeth just to make sure I'm real, it's all real?

'Who's your favorite author?' I say.

He rolls his eyes. 'Lame question. People with favorite authors are assholes.'

'*I* have a favorite author. Asshole.'

He claps his hands and bounces on the bed with sarcastic expectancy. 'Thrilling! Tell me.'

I ignore him, and think for a moment. 'Well, when I was little, it was John Bellairs.'

'Bel Air, like California?'

'No.'

I don't explain and he doesn't ask.

Instead he says, 'Books are boring. New question.'

'Fine. What's your worst secret?'

He looks out the window and seems unusually serious. 'You're not interested in my worst secret.'

'Tell me,' I insist, squeezing his knee.

'Let me think.'

'And kicking cats doesn't count,' I add.

Bryce looks at me as if he's not sure I'm ready. I raise my eyebrows, waiting. Suddenly, I'm nervous and everything feels sad somehow, sitting together on a bed that doesn't belong to us on an island we cannot, will *never* afford, and I don't want to know what he's done that didn't happen here.

Putting his hand over mine, he tells me the worst thing he's ever done –

'When I was fourteen, for an entire year I saved all my semen in a two-liter pop bottle.'

'You're joking.'

He shakes his head. 'I'm not.'

'What for?'

'I don't know. One day I looked at it, on my stomach or whatever, and it was like, potential halves of babies. I wanted to keep them. It was like my own little aquarium.'

I imagine a cloudy white bottle in the back of his teenaged closet, the contents wet and creamy like hand soap.

'Didn't it smell after a while?' I ask.

'Semen doesn't smell.'

'Says you.'

He shrugs.

'It's not the easiest substance to work with though,' he admits. 'The lid of the bottle got all crusty. And then my mom found it.'

'Oh my God.'

He pats my knee again. 'She freaked. So does this make up for the name thing?'

'No.'

'Your turn. Worst thing.'

I shake my head. 'I have no worst thing.'

But I know he doesn't believe me.

'We're sharing, Bell,' he insists. 'We're having a moment. It's your turn.'

He waits, and I wait, both of us wondering what I will say. Until I know what it is.

'My worst secret is knowing that if my mother dies, I'll be okay.'

My sentence sounds too loud, echoes in the air so I can't take it back. I wonder if it's true.

Bryce leans over and bites my earlobe softly.

'Nice clean ears you've got,' he says.

He leaves the door open on his way out.

In the bathroom I use wet toilet paper to wipe the brown smears dried like finger-paint to the tops of my thighs, then I peel away the soft yellow wrapper of a new 'pearlized' tampon hidden in my purse – knowing I should buy the unbleached organic type with no applicator, the ones good for the environment, but also knowing I'll never be bothered to spend the money. The plastic sparkles in the light.

When I'm finished I pray, like I always do, that the toilet won't get clogged.

As the water sinks and disappears smoothly I breathe out, closing the lid and sitting on top of it, while the word Lehi swirls round and round, its weight unfamiliar, its edges soft and fluid in my skull.

St. Paul, 4:55 p.m.

Not that I've ever told anyone this, but the next person I slept with after Bryce had his daughter's name tattooed across his abdomen. Old English script like a declaration.

'Anna.'

I told Alan it was my grandmother's middle name. He liked it because it was a palindrome.

On my own back is a small blue letter B, the first letter of my name scratched into me professionally with a needle and ink. A letter was the most obvious choice, a part of the alphabet I wanted to be labeled with. A letter I could lie about. This twenty-five dollar investment has since stood for baseball, Bannockburn, breath, Baileys, a canyon in Utah that 'moved me beyond words,' and the nickname of my non-existent dog Brady.

Something for everyone; that's what politics has done to me.

Russ's office had overlooked West Kellogg. It had a wide view, of a city that for me has always felt quiet, alone, and cool even in the heat of summer. We Minnesotans have come to understand the necessity of pace, and the streets are always busy with slow determination and common sense and the right amount of coffee. Among other things the long boulevard held the archdiocese of St. Paul, the science museum, the Minnesota Museum of American Art (Russ would pronounce it M-a-a like the bleating of a sheep), seven independent bookstores and one small publisher. My favorite bookstore was the

Dog Ear as it was the last stop on Alan's route. At eleven, just as my lunch break started I would whip down to street level and give myself high-heeled blisters, walking quickly to where we would meet amongst the towering stacks of used up words – to discuss the Hanovers' Rottweiler, the still untrimmed hedge at number eighty-four, and the affairs at city hall. Alan's ergonomically designed mailbag fitted over both his shoulders and had pockets in the sides, so if he found a book he liked while waiting for me, he'd buy it and slip it in his mail pouch.

The building where I worked for over twenty-five years was designed in the nineteen thirties and looked like an art-deco train station where women should be wearing hats with feathers and saying passionate goodbyes to men while standing in the rain. The men would have lipstick on their clean-shaven faces as they said things like, 'I love you, kid.'

It was thirty stories tall and I knew every floor intimately.

An unexpected space, the name *city hall* didn't fit with its perfect interior. Visitors speaking loudly as they entered would immediately start to whisper. Dark, exact, beautiful, even the elevator doors and stairway railings were thoughtful. According to the Historical Society of St. Paul's PLACES OF INTEREST plaque, the style of the interior was called Zigzag Moderne, inspired by a Parisian art exhibition in the twenties.

In Memorial Hall rising tall and straight like a giant stone erection from the smoke of five peace pipes, was the God of Peace. The sort of statue one can't believe the government spent its own money on – thirty-six feet high and made of Mexican onyx. When Russ was feeling sentimental he'd make me stop in front of it, touch its base for about four seconds, then we'd be off again. Russ made up for his lack of any kind of minority status by taking an obsessive but superficial interest in many cultures. Apart from attending every cultural festival in the city, and also to feed his interest in the Other, Russ worked closely with the Dakota and their lobbyists to ensure funding for the Minnesota Coalition for Native American Economic Development. He was sorely disappointed he hadn't been invited to any special ceremonies as a result. We hadn't visited the statue for almost a week after that. Then, just before the press conference when he announced his intention to run for office again, he'd gone to touch his God of Peace.

'Hey, old boy. Tell them to go easy on me.'

In the mornings as I crossed the wide lobby with Russ's latte, the whipped cream foaming out the top of the plastic lid, the *Pioneer Press* and *Washington Post* under my arm, my heels echoing on the waxed floor, I'd take a detour to Memorial Hall. I would look up at the Native American God of Peace, and wink. Sometimes I imagined a giant mouth giving the statue a blowjob. Other times, gold and white with morning, the names of Minnesota's war dead etched on the walls around me, it seemed to be a gift.

I was slightly disappointed to discover the artist was from Sweden.

On reaching my office I'd be trusted with recent gossip from Russ's secretary. Patty had large breasts and red hair, and though we shared the same office space I was paid much more. I was Russ's confidant, charged with making important bookings, arranging flights, accompanying him to important events and scheduling everything from public appearances to his dentist appointments. I was a personal assistant, public relations officer, and designated driver. Patty answered the phones and chattered charmingly to the office visitors. He didn't need two of us, but there we were – Patty was beautiful, and Russ was in politics. Patty's boyfriend reduced me to wishful fantasies when he came to take her to lunch; he wore heavy boots and jeans that looked as if he'd done something exciting in them, worn and faded. Patty said he never wore underwear. 'The skin of his cock is like *velvet*,' she confided.

Our desks were made of walnut; hers covered in sayings like, 'to enjoy the flavor of life, you have to take big bites.'

'Russ adores you,' she complained. 'I don't understand why.'

'Thank you.'

'Well, I *do* know why. I mean, you *get* him. I don't *get* him, you know. I think he *feels* that I don't get him.'

'No one gets Russ, Patty. He's an *enigma*.'

Russ appeared in his doorway and indicated that I should follow him into the hall. Patty mouthed 'sorry' as I left, in case I was in trouble. In the dim corridor I waited while Russ slapped the wall with a manicured hand. He held up the city council-issued pamphlet about the history of city hall that had circulated earlier that week.

'You see this, Bell,' he said.

'I've read it, Russ. I gave it to *you* to read.'

He slapped the wall again.

'Real Wisconsin Rosetta granite. Indiana limestone too. This was built by people who knew about *art* and *livable* space. They had *vision*. Have you *seen* the hardwood in my office?'

'You just turned down the grant application for the Minnesota State Theater renovation,' I pointed out.

'I'm a politician, Bell,' he said waving a hand at me. 'Not a saint.'

Bell. He said my name in every sentence.

'Also, Bell. Do you think Patty's skirt is too short today?'

'Does the length of her skirt inhibit her job performance, Russ?' I asked.

'Blah, blah, feminist, blah. Please. What do you think?'

'It is a bit short,' I admitted. 'Cute though. New designer from Minneapolis apparently.'

'Great. Find out their name, we'll look into a business grant.'

Russ was careful in our interactions and never inappropriate. Our relationship depended upon the knowledge that everything could have been more, perhaps. This understanding made it difficult for us to function without one another. The one year I spent in the Civil Liberties department on the fourteenth floor, he still phoned my house from Stravagin's Piano Bar at three in the morning after his keys had been confiscated.

So while the spotlight that shone for Russ was never focused on me, sometimes it would catch my foot, or my shoulder as I turned. This instance of light reflected reaffirmed my choices, ensuring that my single blue thread was integral to the tapestry, woven, unbroken, part of the whole. Alan might have credited the moon's pull on the water in our bodies at birth, a cosmic imprint of how our lives would unfold. A kind of Fate independent from God. Anna would call it karma.

However my life has been lived in the past, it's up to me now to get it back. To resurrect the ghosts. Though to this day I still don't know for sure why he did it, and why he never wrote.

I registered certain moments of my past with a website dedicated to bringing people together. Schools, jobs, military service, kickboxing classes, everyone there waiting to be reconnected. But living longer doesn't necessarily make you interesting, and I stopped checking in – turns out I don't know any astronauts or sex trade workers or anyone who became ultimately surprising. A few profiles claimed old classmates of mine to be communists, anarchists, happily married or something else equally unlikely, but it seemed the probable destinations of our graduate yearbook predictions – the starving artists and 'sleeping in a ditch wearing TK's bra' – have opted for the security of a normal life after all. The tragedy is how average we've become. I'm not the exception.

But someone did find me.

This email correspondence isn't something I chose. I was found, and neither of us ever let go. It's a nice feeling when your past catches up with you, not in a *here's a subpoena for your four unpaid speeding tickets in Florida* kind of way, but in a way that confirms when you were alive and twenty you were important to someone else at the same time. Someone who might remember the night you started a small brush fire at Turtle Park with a dropped match you were using to find the path. Someone who might remember you both looking up at the same time that evening it was too hot in August after ten or so pints while you could still hear that song playing on the jukebox even though you were outside and saying with conviction, *This is our sky, you know? This is for us, and fuck everything that isn't here, right now.*

Or maybe they'd remember it differently.

Soon though, we will begin. The project I am to be part of, my past on offer to the historians, needs only my voice. I have trouble with my fingers now, and since Anna's been back I've often thought of asking her to type the messages while I dictate over her shoulder. Funny how my veins have become bigger while seemingly less efficient.

Before my doctor's appointment yesterday I put on an old brown corduroy jacket, loose but flattering. The buttons are large so I have never had a problem with them before, but this time they wouldn't fit into the opening, as if the buttonhole had gotten smaller somehow over the last few months. I struggled, first trying one side of the button and then the other. I tried to do it looking down at my hands and then standing in front of the mirror, and finally, tears streaming down my face as my fingers fumbled, I just sat down on the bed, my shoulders bent forward, saying *fuck fuck fuck*.

And it's not fair, none of it is.

I take my green inhaler from the cupboard and breathe once, the sharp chemical wind at the back of my throat barely registering, the one long, unending blast of the air-raid siren indicating the threat is immediate, even if the storm remains something I cannot see.

Mackinac

'Hey, Rummy!' Trainer shouts from across the restaurant.

Velvet whips around to glare at him, ponytail snapping against her perfectly blushed cheek, golden bangles clanking along her white forearms. He slinks into the kitchen, motioning for Rummy to follow. I follow both of them because I'm bored. The kitchen is hot and Chef Walter is swearing because he's run out of basil.

'I've got some of your countrymen at table fourteen,' Trainer says to Rummy.

'Oh ya? Where from?' Rummy asks.

'I don't know, Gelf, or Golf or something.'

'Guelph?'

Trainer claps him on the back. 'Anyway, be a darling and remind them the going rate for tips is *eighteen percent* no matter what the exchange rate.'

Rummy shrugs off Trainer's arm. 'We give you shitty tips on purpose,' he says. 'It's all part of our master plan. Starve the waiters, then send in the troops. Isn't that right, Bell?'

He looks at me and I'm laughing. Trainer says something snotty about the Canadian army or the lack thereof and goes back into the dining room.

'Can I get some goddamn basil over here?' Chef Walter is shouting.

In the dining room Rummy goes over to chat with Trainer's table. Bryce is watching his patio table through the window by the canoe bar and talking to Brenna, whose tongue, for some reason, is running slowly around her top lip. This is okay because Bryce knows the guy from the marina she's sleeping with and has been told she cries in bed. This fact makes her less threatening. Then I remember that *I've* cried in bed, but it was about my mother and that's different.

Straightening my bow tie I stare out of the window while trying to look busy. I do this by shifting my weight and moving my head from side to side as if scanning the restaurant for guests that need my help. A woman at table four uses her long acrylic nail to scrape Caesar salad from her daughter's chin. The daughter is wearing white platform sandals and has her hair done in ringlets. Her mother is wearing expensive slacks and I can see the diamond from here.

'Honestly, Mackenzie Ray,' the mother says. 'This dressing is bad for your skin.'

When I was much younger my mother would talk to me about ethics, without using the word exactly. On cross-country trips to Disneyland or Memphis we often made ourselves comfortable in small cities that looked nothing like St. Paul, but somehow felt familiar. Gas stations, pickup trucks, pavement, and bricks. Small parks with shit-covered statues of men in the center. Motels called Maple Lanes, Parkview, the Buena Vista, and the American Bed. Inside every motel was the same brown vending machine, with the standard selection of pork puffs and cheese bits and roast-beef sandwiches and gum. From one of these machines in South Carolina I once received two packages of Jelly Worms instead of one.

'You can't keep that one, Bell,' my mother told me. 'God will know you didn't pay for it.'

She made me return it to the front desk of our motel, and I'm sure the person I returned it to became the benefactor of my honesty, promptly eating it as soon as we left. But the point was made. I was not allowed something for nothing. I was to pay for what I wanted.

The sun is now setting and outside the marina is full with end-of-August visitors, white yachts turning pink with diminishing light, flags flapping atop their masts. The lighthouse is bright. I've already made seventy dollars and it's not even eight o'clock. Bryce washed my bike this morning and it's shiny. Everything I could ever want has happened today. I don't even need a yesterday or a tomorrow when the island is so complete in each hour of its own perfection. Maybe after work I'll buy myself an ice cream. Or a pint.

A man arrives in deck shoes and a white linen shirt looking for his wife and daughter, his nose pink from sun or alcohol. I show him to table four and he slips me a bill which I slide into my apron, wondering at its denomination while he tells me he shot a seventy-two on the links this afternoon.

When I last spoke to my father, he answered the phone from his gardening shed. I could hear the sounds of birds.

'Scorcher today,' he said.

'What did they say?'

He paused, and the sound of a chickadee came down the wire.

'Well, it's your mother versus the doctors and God,' he said. 'I've no doubt who'll win.'

I imagined his large palms turned upwards as he shrugged.

'No doubt at all,' he said.

Table thirteen calls me over. They would like a fresh white pillar candle; the woman raises her eyebrows disapprovingly as she points to a huge bluebottle struggling in the wax. I take the tainted candle into the back room where I use a knife engraved with the words THE TIPPECANOE to lift the fly out. I try and wipe the poor thing clean, but soon the clear wax turns into a cloudy cocoon and I think how expensive hot wax treatments are at the salon on the island.

The fly dies, and I bring the woman a new candle.

I tell Rummy about it as we polish silverware later that night. I dip my muslin cloth gently into the hot vinegar and water solution, and pick up a knife.

'A bluebottle?' he says.

'I guess so, the big ones. Kind of shiny.'

'*Calliphora Vomitoria*,' he says.

I sigh, while eliminating the water spots efficiently from the bowl of a spoon. We've got it down to one piece of silverware every three seconds.

'What?'

'It's their Latin name,' he says. 'Vomitoria. Appropriate, eh?'

Trainer comes up behind Rummy holding a bucket of silverware still needing to be polished and says, 'Jesus Christ, *Latin*? This is why you don't get laid.'

Rummy laughs and I can see the gums above his top teeth, but I wonder if he's thinking of Blue. He hasn't mentioned her since she left, but Rummy doesn't forget things easily. She was so tiny too, an entire person and spirit caught up in such a small amount of skin, holding the possibilities of babies within her when she left and making men remember her long after she was gone.

Trainer sets the bucket of silverware down with a crash.

'*Arbeit Macht Frei*,' he says. 'Let's hurry up and get to the bar.'

Trainer's ancestors were German and his grandmother won't let him wear his pink triangle button in her house. She is immune to his explanations of *the movement of marginalized groups to reclaim negative symbols and language in order to subvert their original meanings.*

'*Allons-nous* then,' Rummy says, picking up a fork.

'Jesus Christ,' Trainer says again.

I wonder how I'll ever be able to leave this place.

Leaving the Cock after last call, I stand outside alone, preparing myself for the ping-pong tournament scheduled to begin in one hour. The dark expanse of the park to my left is quiet and filled with bare lilac bushes and the hollow black form of Jacques Marquette, the Jesuit priest. Standing alone on a concrete base in the center of the park, he is often found supervising Christian rallies, football games, locals, kids with cans of beer, Ultimate Frisbee matches, BMX competitions, late-night lovers – all this he does solemn and steadfast, covered in the thick white mess of seagulls. The guidebooks say he discovered the Mississippi river – after the Spanish, and after the two million or so Sioux, Algonquin and Ojibwa who lived along its banks I suppose.

At home the river flows brown and polluted.

Bryce told me Marquette went on missions as far away as Montréal, where the diaries of his extensive travels were lost after his canoe overturned in the rapids of the St. Lawrence. Therefore, he told me, little is known of his personal life except that he had an ear for languages and spoke exceptional Huron.

'And you want to be an *electrician?*' I said.

Bryce joins me now on the front step of the Cock. Across from us, the two stories of the Tippecanoe are luminous and white with moonlight. A taxi clips by with harnesses jangling, one black horse, one brown, heading down Main Street filled with dock porters, servers, and housekeepers from other restaurants and hotels, everyone loud and paired with their respective late-night conquests. An islander named Richard or

Roy rides past confidently on his battered Schwinn at a pace that suggests he is out for a leisurely bike ride, despite the fact that it's three a.m. A regular for lunch at the Tippecanoe, he always orders three lemons with his mineral water and tips twenty dollars, regardless of the bill.

Bryce gives him a wave.

'Roy was in Korea,' he says.

Roy's figure recedes into the night – his slow pedaling carrying him away, although it seems to me now the shadows are behind him, and not in front.

'When he can't sleep he rides around the island,' Bryce tells me. 'On late-night patrol.'

Bryce then mentions he'd like to join the army maybe, be a soldier himself. I don't respond. Our own bikes parked around the corner on Fort Street have been knocked down in a twisted show of turned wheels and scraped handlebars, pedals from one bike stuck in the spokes of another.

'Drunk driver,' nods Trainer, joining us. 'Disgusting.'

He swings a leg over a bicycle which is not his own, and continues:

'You'd think the police would do something.'

We begin to separate them. I pull mine upright and flip the kickstand down while everyone else files out the front door, discussing the upcoming event at Mackinac Pines.

'Judgment day,' someone says.

Bryce points at Rummy as he stumbles out the door:

'We'll show you how it's done here in the U S of A.'

'Wait,' says Tom. 'Are we allowing girls?'

Despite Tom's generosity in giving me his old bike earlier this summer, he is the sort of person I have subsequently avoided talking to as much as possible: thirty-two years old, a rumored dishonorable discharge from the Marines, and nothing but plaid flannel shirts and odd comments. Tom has a photograph in his apartment of his aunt who passed away a year ago. She is posed and graying in a gold frame, and when he has had too much whisky he will bring the photo with him on late-night walks. *She was my aunt Ava.* He will talk about his aunt and show the picture and apparently everyone has seen it. We have all agreed that while Tom may be from Iowa and close with his family, this habit is still strange, and he has taken to drinking in his room by himself a lot.

'Of course girls are allowed,' Bryce says, patting my head condescendingly. 'So long as they're topless.'

He moves to reach his hand up my shirt and I drop my bike, wrestling with him, trying to stomp on his instep until I manage to pull him over. We smack painfully onto the pavement, laughing.

'She's crushing me!' he yells.

'Lovely,' says Trainer, from astride his locked bike. 'Mature love, what an inspiration.'

'I'll see you all at the tournament,' John says from the door of the Cock.

Tom looks suddenly bored. 'I wish the island had a strip club,' he says.

An employee games room has been created out of the old Pine Suites office. It is a small awkward space, the standard pink carpet etched with golden beer stains. The room is just large enough for a faded dartboard hanging above the front desk, eight board games, and a ping-pong table, which has become the center of a never-ending tournament among the few male wait staff. Tonight and every other night, behind the door that still says 'office', they make bets, drink, and engage in the sort of behavior they have probably read about in magazines or senators' biographies; one night involved Cuban cigars, and has been rated one of the top three island evenings thus far. The winners are recorded on a wall chalkboard, and only the designated scorekeeper is allowed to touch the chalk.

Bryce and Rummy face one another across the table, which has been duct-taped in the middle. I'm not sure how exactly it broke, as no one will own up to being a participant in the *how many people will the table hold* experiment. Tom holds the chalk, Trainer throws the only dart supplied with the dartboard, and Brenna sits on the edge of the office desk, leaning forward, looking like she's ready to start waving pom-poms. John's lanky form arrives with more beer, the evil clown tattoo on his calf always surprising when I see him outside of work. He and Trainer take turns throwing the dart. I stand near the door, smelling the wet sweat of competition and hot beer and wondering how the month of August can seem so long and contain so much.

Bryce gives the ball a practice bounce, blows on it, then rubs it on his polo shirt.

'It's okay, Rummy,' he says. 'I'll start off slow so you can get the hang of it. Don't feel bad when you lose.'

Bryce's first serve misses the table.

'Let's go, Bryce,' Brenna calls, clapping her hands.

Cheerleading is a sport involving dedication and fitness, and our high-school trophy case was full of golden figures in tights balancing atop wooden pillars – but whatever female genetic code may be responsible for instigating excitement at men's physical competition is not one I am in possession of.

My own family, apart from my father's 1974 bowling trophy, is sadly lacking in golden statues, the kind of sporting legacy one leaves to their children. There was never anyone cheering us on from the sidelines and so it seems we are losing the competition slowly, to everyone else – the object to be the lucky ones without tragedy.

Needing space, I step outside and there is the island moon again, making the pine trees look black. Outside my apartment, number eight, I notice someone has left flowers as they occasionally do. A tribute by the island tourists who are not interested in fudge and romance, but axe-murderers and the real history of the human race that doesn't involve the noble discovery of land or rivers. The bouquet, upon closer investigation, is made up of pink carnations and some baby's breath. Sold by Mackinac Mart for eighteen dollars. I have never seen anyone delivering their offering, and upon discovery I usually put them in water. I might still tomorrow morning. Standing above the dampening cone of paper, I wonder when they come out – the ghosts – the remnants of the vacationing family chopped up by their father. It's easy to suppose they're here, wanting to remind everyone left to never feel safe, not even when you're surrounded by water. I wonder where exactly he swung first, if he aimed for the head or neck or if the first blow had been buried into abdomens, if there had been any second thoughts.

A moth hits the back of my head, its thick body heavy and its wings loud.

'Hey, ding-dong, show some support for your man in here!' Tom yells out of the office door.

I hear Trainer's voice over the shouting and the hollow smack of the ball hitting the paddles.

'I've been meaning to ask you, Tom, where *do* you get all your great flannel?'

Stepping away from the light I walk out into the trees. Eyes closed, I keep my arms before me in a cross, flexed against the branches. Pine needles touch my legs and skin, my arms held out in protection, my weight breaking the undergrowth beneath me. An animal crashes away from my approach, and after three steps I start to squint but pretend it still counts. I do not run into anything.

Dropping my arms, I stand in the dark, wanting a ghost, deserving one. There are crickets, there is wind, and possibility. But they won't come because I don't know their names. Perhaps they were called something thoughtful like Edward or Lily, after grandparents. Or something modern and genderless – Taylor, Alex. Their last name was Mc something. Something Scottish sounding. Bryce said they were sleeping. I imagine the axe thunking into the flesh of them, all the effort of learning proper manners and shoelace tying come to nothing, just a body full of blood let out all over the sheets.

It seems the closer I come to leaving here, the more registration letters and residence information from St. Kat's I receive, the more history and the past descend upon me, undeterred by my island hideaway. For now, the letters are folded, and ignored. I will return soon, to learn about the world and examine the blood stains on the soil of each country, but the island comes first.

It is four a.m., and my shift begins at seven. The island gives everyone the gift of irresponsibility, and the game moves outside.

'Bell, what the fuck are you doing?' Trainer yells as he comes out to the front porch. 'You on a nature hike?'

The next morning the cement pathway is a sea of ping-pong ball carcasses, stepped on and broken, the half orbs scattered like moons. Only one paddle, the red one, can be found again, despite searches throughout the brush and flower gardens.

'Serves all of you right,' I tell Bryce.

'Speaking of serves,' he says. 'Dickweed is bringing over his volleyball net tonight.'

St. Paul, 4:26 p.m.

We sent Anna to private school.

The Tate Academy had white columns out front, a security guard, cameras, and well-groomed teachers with masters' degrees. Miss Fedora Hall had impossibly long dark hair which she pinned and curled in complicated twists, and she wore long skirts that made me want to take a vacation.

One June afternoon, the sky hazy with pollution, she motioned gracefully to the granite bench positioned just inside the school gates, and invited me to sit. *In Memoriam* the bench said. It was placed in memory of the young Dakota boy, Hinto, who drowned in the school's ornamental pond three years earlier. They found him floating, Anna told us solemnly, arms and legs spread like a star, drifting. From the Prairie Island reservation, Hinto had been one of the thirty-two children on a government scholarship to the Tate after Minnesota's first RWP and the subsequent flooding of the Mississippi river eight years previous. His reservation had been just south of St. Paul, located on a floodplain, and the rising waters had destroyed the island's two nuclear reactors and damaged the seventeen dry cask containers used for storing spent fuel rods. Hinto's elders had been warning the federal and state governments of this possibility for years. Now twelve people were dead, the land contaminated along with the Mississippi river, all the way down to Louisiana. The compensation from the Minnesota government involved new homes, new schools, and new land.

Hinto had developed a fascination with tree climbing, teaching Anna how to distribute her weight near the crook of each branch so as to reach the highest possible point before retreat.

His granite memorial bench carries an engraving of a sailboat.

'Please will you sit?' Fedora asked me again.

Smiling at her, I sat. The cherry blossoms smelled musky and thick and I tried not to breathe deeply. A local judge strode past on his way up to the school, nodding as he spoke into his headset. In casual but expensive denims, he had an American eagle on his belt buckle.

The Tate Academy was a favorite dumping ground for St. Paul's political offspring – Benjamin Gerhardt confided in me solemnly one day after Russ had locked him out of the inner office, that he had *eight* friends in his Tate kindergarten class, and they all had swimming pools. Four-year-old Benjamin was enrolled at the academy until Russ's not-yet-ex wife transferred him to a different school because his teacher kept referring to him as Ben.

'If I'd *wanted* to call him Ben, I would have *named* him Ben,' she explained to me the night of my dinner party.

Sitting awkwardly with Fedora, I wished Alan had come in my place, though this personal attention was what we paid for. We wanted Anna to be safe, not stabbed or shot or kidnapped – all the things you worry about happening to your child. Who knew this extension of yourself could be so painful? The pain of delivery can't possibly compare to the torture of having something from inside you suddenly outside, walking about, alone.

'Your Alan is always walking,' Fedora commented, as she arranged her skirt. 'That is how he has legs so big and strong.'

'He does a lot of walking,' I agreed.

Her skirt was orange, the colour of popsicles. I was wearing all black, but my purse was beige.

'He even walks in the rain,' I added.

She nodded and her long earrings were made of warm gold, almost touching her shoulders. Her neck was much longer than mine.

'Now your Anna,' she began.

I waited. Other women always seemed better informed about my daughter than I was.

'She knows very well what she wants from her life.'

Anna was eight.

'Yes.'

I looked for Anna, walking down the paved path with her pink backpack in the shape of a ladybug, but she wasn't there. I became slightly more nervous.

'Just today she has made a wall hanging of the sea turtle. From hemp. Do you know this material?'

'Yes,' I said. 'She wants to be a marine biologist.'

Fedora looked to the sky for a moment, and then back at me. I was suspicious of being prayed for, and of not having all the information. Checking the time on the Tate's clock tower just visible above the gray-green pine trees, I remembered the clock was broken – the time was always noon. I waited for her to continue.

'I am from an island,' she said. 'Majorca, you have heard of this, yes?'

I nodded. Russ and his new wife had gone to Magaluf for a week's holiday last year.

'The sea, it is very important to us there. I would like to encourage your daughter in this interest.'

'I lived on an island once,' I said, surprising myself.

'You know what I say then,' she said enthusiastically. 'To

be alone surrounded by water, dependent on boats. It does an important thing to a person.'

'What made you come to America?' I wondered.

'I have left a man there,' she said, waving a hand. 'Is this not why every woman travels?'

We laughed together. A brown petal landed on my knee, and though she said nothing else about Anna she still seemed to want to talk. Giving a quiet sigh, she looked upwards again.

'We are all islands,' she said thoughtfully.

I decided not to comment. The cherry blossom scent was now overwhelming, the sky burning yellow with the suspended particles of car fumes and cigarettes and skin.

'It must be hard for you here,' I said finally.

I wanted suddenly to smoke – to be alone with the God of Peace and his onyx pipe, surrounded only by the dead.

'It is very cold,' she admitted.

Anna finally arrived, and I stood abruptly, my black kitten heels sinking into the lawn. Reaching the paved pathway, I turned with relief to say goodbye.

'Say to your father I said hello,' she called after us.

That evening I ordered in from the Friendly Thai and changed into a dark-green sweater for dinner. Our house seemed huge, white, and empty, and I remembered wondering what it would look like with the walls blackened, paint cracked and bubbled, everything destroyed by fire.

Alan insisted over our bowls of soup that Miss Hall was too young for him, wore too much make-up, investing in juicy lip gloss that made her mouth look wet. I pointed out at least she had good taste in men.

When Anna brought Michael home for the first time they had already been dating for a year. It was July and too hot to be sitting outside, but we were trying to make the most of our expensive new patio furniture. The shapes of the metal and oak chairs were inspired by the praying mantis, an endangered insect which a local artist had immortalized in an admittedly abstract way with his new line of *outside installation* pieces. Alan and I were drinking a new Slovenian beer, and the spindly-legged table was wet with condensation.

We didn't hear the doorbell, and suddenly there they were. He had a Florida tan, a native of the Sunshine State. Wearing long shorts that came past his knees, a gray T-shirt and black hoops that stretched his earlobes from the inside out, I was impressed that he hadn't made an effort before meeting us, and I thought I might like him. Anna had met him on an alligator hunt in the Everglades.

'This is Michael. These are my parents.'

She said it quickly.

I sat, rolling my shoulders forward, feeling, like I still do, that he must look at my chest first. He didn't look, smiled, and shook our hands while Alan offered, 'Beer or wine?'

'Just a lemonade or juice is fine,' he said.

'Michael doesn't drink either,' she explained, looking at me.

He talked about going to the gym, I remember. His diet included canned tuna every two hours, something about body-building and protein. Judging him solely by his wardrobe I'd thought at first he might be lazy enough to dampen her ambitions, keep her from her environmental crusading and everything she enjoyed in life. But it seems he had his own holy war to be fought – against loss of muscle mass and carbohydrates. I wasn't sure what to say.

'We're only staying in St. Paul a week or two,' Anna said. 'We're looking at houses out in the bay area.'

We. She spoke with such an assurance of their future. Such confidence in things to come. A feeling I had forgotten long ago. But seeing them together, with his legs wide so that his knee touched hers, drinking his orange juice, I remembered how it felt to have all the possibilities ahead of me. And even though I couldn't help but wonder if he was boring, even though he swallowed noisily and only drank juice, I envied Anna for being at the beginning of something.

'Michael competed in the X-games,' Anna told us.

Alan and I smiled.

'That's fantastic,' Alan said, and I knew he thought it was.

As evening descended I lit a citronella candle and Michael said the scent reminded him of his days scrubbing toilets at a resort in Banff. One winter he'd worked in exchange for the privilege of as much snowboarding as he could handle. 'Work five days, board for two,' he said, grinning, drinking his juice. I leaned forward.

'I used to do resort work when I was younger. In Michigan.'

He nodded. 'Not too much boarding in Michigan,' he said. 'Too flat.'

I sat back in my chair.

'Those toilets though,' Michael said, waving a hand in front of his nose. 'Whew.'

We weren't invited to the wedding. Spur of the moment they said. It was in California, some kind of Buddhist ceremony. I wondered what her journals contained at the time, what colour ink she chose, if she was carefully recording her 'union' or if everything happening at each new moment was more important than the anticipation of a need for remembering.

After three years of them both teaching in the public school system on the West coast, it was a surprise to all of us when they moved back to St. Paul.

*

'Where is Michael?' I asked Anna this morning.

She shook her head. 'It doesn't matter anymore does it?'

I wondered when I'd last seen him. 'Is he coming over?'

Anna looked at me and took my hand. Her gesture gave me an awful feeling, panic, because it meant I didn't remember.

'He's gone, Mother. He's in California.'

I took my hand away from hers. 'Of course,' I said. 'And you're getting a divorce. Good.'

Confused, I wanted her to leave so that I wouldn't make such mistakes anymore. She looked sad and I felt somehow it was my fault; she reached for a picture on my dresser. In it, Michael was wearing an infuriating woolen hat that said *Board 4 Life* on it, even though he must have been at least thirty, while Anna had on some kind of hand-woven sweater that was probably made from yak fur. Michael was giving the peace sign. It was their wedding day at the Odiyan Temple, the one they helped build in Sonoma County.

I waited, and finally she put the picture in the garbage bag on her left, the one for things we weren't keeping or giving away. Anna didn't ask if she could throw it out, but I didn't object. It was a present from years ago, and it was dusty. For years I'd managed to keep it obscured behind a square glass vase filled with bamboo. Alan kept the same picture in his wallet.

She tied the plastic in a quick knot and hefted the bag, testing its weight. I followed her down into the front hall where she placed it with the others, waiting for the Amity pick-up tomorrow morning. Whole rooms have been cleared out. I was worried at first there would be nothing left. Then I began to welcome the thought.

'Mother, stop following me.'

'I'm tidying,' I insisted.

I took the small framed picture of a red stiletto heel off the wall and awkwardly leaned it against the garbage bags. What did it mean, this bright red shoe? I couldn't remember anything about it, couldn't even speculate as to where it came from.

'See?'

'You love that picture.'

'I don't. I'm getting rid of it.'

She sighed. 'Fine. What are you going to do with all dad's CDs?'

Alan's music, endless disks of digital voices conjured into the air by technology. The singers were mostly dead now.

'I don't listen to music anymore,' I said.

She went into the family room to pick out the ones she wanted. I sat in my reclining chair to watch her, her efficient fingers pink and nourished from my own wet insides. Opening a book of song lyrics, she flipped its pages. I closed my eyes and when she spoke she was talking to herself, as if I wasn't there, or couldn't listen.

'I miss you,' she said.

But I was right in front of her.

All that living, all those places visited, the pins on the map and still – her skin and insides so vulnerable to pain. It must be Michael's fault, he had done something awful to my daughter and I imagined blood bubbling out of him from a wound cleaved into his chest, staining the bed sheets of a young girl, the student he'd been sleeping with, who would wake up to find him dead. Perhaps the fine sharpened edge of a snowboard would do it. In the Buddhist tradition he would have to live life again, his soul unable to move on until he stopped being such an asshole. Until he wanted a woman with creases by her eyelids – whose favorite drink was no longer vodka and cranberry juice, and whose experiences inside her skin revealed themselves on the outside. Until he got rid of that woolly hat.

I imagined all these things and then opened my eyes in a

panic, but she was still there, only a moment had passed, and as the CD pile got bigger, she stopped having to wipe her eyes with the back of her hand. She held out a CD to show me.

'James Brown? I didn't think Dad listened to this sort of stuff.'

'That one's mine,' I said. 'I think I'd like to hear it.'

Mackinac

The heat inside the Cock is oppressive. The air conditioning is broken again, so the bar feels cramped and louder than usual. Slow, muggy jazz plays on the jukebox and sweat from my thighs seeps through my jeans, leaving a mark on the vinyl top of the barstool. The pint glasses lining the bar are wet, the paper coasters soggy underneath. I press my beer against my neck. Another letter from my mother, stamped with a far away postscript, is folded, unread, in my back pocket.

Rummy walks back into the bar after trying to cool down outside, though his face is still red with liquor and heat.

'I think you might want to go out there,' he says. 'Or maybe not.'

'Why, what's wrong?'

He shrugs, and I already know. When I came to the bar this evening Bryce could barely stand. Even though the bar is non-smoking, he had lit up a cigarette, ashing into an empty glass, his sweaty armpits staining rings on his shirt. He had been here all day.

When I tried to join him he said, 'You shouldn't be around when I'm this drunk.'

Surprised, I simply nodded and went to sit with Rummy. After Bryce stumbled out without saying goodbye, John cleared away his empty glass – the bottom black and wet with cigarettes and beer – telling me not to worry.

'Guy needs his space.' He shrugged.

I glared at him. John is not a bartender that cuts people off.

As long as you can stand, you can drink. If John knows you and likes you, you don't even have to be able to stand, just sitting upright on a barstool or a couch is good enough.

I wonder why Rummy didn't alert me when the fight started, and why he didn't go out to help. When I leave the bar it is slightly cooler outside from the breeze off the lake, the moon a white hole in the sky. Under the streetlights are smartly dressed tourists, people staying overnight. Tipsy women in black high heels and expensive blonde highlights clutch the arms of men in suit jackets, crossing to the other side of Main Street to avoid Bryce, whose face is covered in blood. It is smeared all over his hands, and the front of his shirt is dark. The window behind him, the front of the store that sells all the Indian moccasins, is splattered with a fine red spray.

I start towards him before noticing Brenna, holding his arm saying, 'Come on, I'll take you back to my place to get cleaned up.' Some of his friends stand around, not so much interested in his busted lip as wanting to fight someone.

Bryce shrugs away from her and says, 'You're not my girlfriend.'

Brenna looks up at me and raises her eyebrows, saying nothing. I shrug, and she grabs his arm again.

'I *know* that, *asshole*, but your face is bleeding.'

I wonder what she would have said in my absence.

'Guys' night out!' Bryce yells, and someone cheers.

I watch as Brenna marches away, before turning back inside the Cock to finish my beer. Tomorrow he won't remember fighting. He won't remember me trying to help, when I tell him I did. One of his friends who works down at the marina calls after me, 'Don't worry, we'll take care of him.'

I don't turn around. It is the same suntanned guy who, one night last week, put an arm around me at the Cock while

Bryce was in the washroom and said, 'Your nose is so fucking awesome.' Then he'd asked if he could touch it.

'Is he all right?' Rummy asks me as I sit down.

'I guess so.'

'You're just going to leave him out there?'

'I'm not his babysitter, Rummy. What the fuck am I supposed to do?'

I feel I am sliding into something that I didn't expect, but what the hell. The safety of bachelor degrees and shiny shoes and never too much of anything is something that's never appealed to me anyway.

Because I cannot escape the constructs of the island, built around liquor and violence and endings, because the stage was set when I arrived and I must simply learn my cue, I raise my empty glass at John and order another beer. Being drunk is easy, it's weak, and it's comforting.

After two more drinks the heat seems less oppressive. My skin is still clammy, but I've stopped noticing this; I'm thinking of Bryce, and of today's unopened letter from home turning damp in my pocket. Rummy is telling me how he can't get in touch with Blue, the number she gave him by the docks that long ago morning is out of service. He is worried, but I'm not really listening. Motioning to John at my empty glass, I get up unsteadily from the bar, telling Rummy I'll be right back.

Someone has stolen the sign for the women's bathroom, and just a patch of adhesive glue is left behind. It occurs to me the sign might turn up in Bryce's bedroom. Locking myself in the second stall, I turn and sit down to read the new graffiti scratched in the turquoise paint:

Cameron L. has herpes

I love God

SPANK ME ANY DAY

WHITE RIVER ROX!!

I am no terrorist

Brenna S. is a whore

The last entry has been scribbled over and below it,

Fuck you bitch if I find who wrote this I'll slit your throat

The bathroom is cool compared to the rest of the bar, my fingertips turn clumsy. I open my letter, putting the empty envelope in the sanitary bin, the swinging door sweeping it cleanly away. Unfolding the yellow stationery, I read quickly.

Sometimes if I'm lucky, my grief seems like a heart attack, a constricting of the chest until I'm not sure my heart is beating anymore. Before my grandmother died, when the cancer was in her bones, blood, and brain, she used to confuse apples and oranges for her grandchildren, calling out to the fruit baskets in her room. Afterwards, I was sure I would also die in my sleep – I would often lie awake to ensure my breath remained constant. When the feeling finally went away, I trod carefully in the cavities of my brain, knowing the grief was there, that it was perhaps just giving me a break for a while.

Scanning the letter quickly, I leap over sentences, impatient for information. My cousin Laura is pregnant, although her boyfriend has been serving overseas for the last year. My parents have bought a new stove. My father thinks he might be allergic to milk. I skip to the end.

There was frost and my mother is worried about the tulip bulbs she planted. Did she plant them deep enough? A girl I'd gone to high school with has been killed in a car accident, she'd hit a deer late at night and there is nothing new to report nothing growing nothing getting bigger everything contained just tired is all.

And the letter is finished. I breathe out. The panic deep in my throat grips and releases, and I start to cry. Nothing has changed; there is no news.

When my tears have stopped, I blow my nose with toilet

paper, but it's too thin and the wet tissue rips in my hand. I stare at the turquoise walls defaced with markers and imagine the bright blue watering can my mother uses for gardening. Then, taking my key to Bryce's apartment out of my purse, I lean hard into the task, scraping the paint away in clean straight lines. Thin curls fall to the floor, and I smooth the words with my palm.

Pausing on my way out of the bathroom, I notice how bare and red my skin looks in the mirror, and a horrible red lipstick kiss hovers where my nose should be. I lift up my shirt. My breasts feel hotter than the rest of my body and I wipe the sweat from beneath them, turning to examine myself from the side. It's hard to believe they could ever betray me. I wonder at the perfume I wear everyday, if the chemicals aren't somehow collecting, plotting against me; if my sunburns, deodorants, extra fat and dislike of free radical fighting broccoli are slowly killing me from the inside out. Hard to say when everything looks so perfectly ordinary. I put my shirt down and leave, remembering there's a beer waiting for me at the bar.

Rummy puts his hand on my shoulder, but doesn't ask me what's wrong or if I am okay. He orders us both a shot of Jameson. Remembering the bare face in the bathroom mirror I pull my Bollywood Beige lip gloss from my back pocket, and my hands are almost steady.

'Did you know women ingest over two pounds of lipstick in their lifetimes?' Rummy asks.

I roll my eyes and put a thick smear of gloss across my lips.

'You are literally a beauty consumer,' he says.

Licking some gloss from the end of the applicator I smile at him. 'My stomach must be really shiny then.'

When I say this I sound like myself. We raise our shot

glasses to each other, and before we drink I look right at him.

'Thanks,' I tell him.

Trainer appears suddenly in the doorway of the Cock, not wearing a shirt, his chest a blanket of hair.

'Hey, Bell,' he says loudly. 'Your boyfriend's got himself arrested.'

Then, as an afterthought,

'And he looks like shit.'

Bryce spends the night in the drunk tank, and I imagine him holding one of his bottom teeth in his hand, the blood on his face crusting, flaking, and black.

When he comes home the next morning, he's exhausted, his lip swollen and cracked. He has a ninety-dollar fine for drunken disorderly conduct, but instead of being pissed off, he seems pleased. He falls into bed, telling me about his wild evening. He doesn't remember seeing me, and he doesn't remember who he was fighting except that whoever it was had drunkenly grabbed the breast of a young receptionist from the hotel down the street.

'My hero,' I tell him.

'Did Rummy take care of you then?' he wants to know.

As I tell Bryce about the letter, he puts his head on my chest, resting his cheek against my collarbone, listening. He tells me next time I'm overwhelmed to think about a beach. He claims beaches are relaxing, like looking into a fish tank.

'Think about our honeymoon in Maui,' he says.

'I think I have sunburn,' I say, stroking his greasy hair that smells of smoke.

He rolls away from me, offended that I won't join in his make-believe. He reaches for the picture of us sitting on the bedside table, taped over the glassed photo of his dog Milo, and pretends to talk to it instead of addressing me directly.

From where I am lying, the space inside the frame looks like an empty gray square.

'I'm not going to marry you after all,' he says to my photograph.

I make him kiss the picture and he obliges, wincing as his lip touches the glass.

St. Paul, 4:37 p.m.

In my brown envelope I find a scab. A dry, yellowed brown bit of long ago blood and skin. He is missing a part of himself and so am I: shedding, extracting, stealing, it's all the same.

I once spent an hour in front of my bathroom mirror, sweeping the drooping skin of my eyelids up in different directions, trying to see what I'd look like with a bit of a lift. Everyone's had it done; I think I'm in the minority. But Alan would roll his eyes when I brought it up. Too expensive, although it wasn't really. And then he'd trace a finger along a crack, a crevice, and tell me not to change a thing. The last time he did that he had the cough, a heaving bark that made his whole body convulse. It ruined the moment for me, this tender attempt to placate my insecurities ruined by his hacking. I left and went to another room. That was in the beginning of his illness though, just a cough. We were only worried about me.

I lived my entire life paying no attention to genetically modified ingredients, mono-saturates, sodium content (0.1 per 100 grams is acceptable) and recommended alcohol intake (14 units a week). What happens *inside* us all is luck, despite what Anna insists as she eats her granola. The possible effects of cigarettes, dark rum, blackouts, bacon, and unprotected sex don't scare you when you're young, and if you live long enough with all these vices you think, well, what the hell, I've lived this long. And you keep going. Believing in luck.

*

It felt like a hard edge of flesh buried underneath my skin. Panic implanted in my body. Part of me felt relieved. Something to reward my searching. I made Alan feel it to be sure. I even thought about asking Russ, to have a third opinion. But I knew, and I made the appointment the same day. The doctor would tell me it was a cyst, or something else that didn't need worrying about and I'd drive home feeling proud that I'd dealt with it right away. I'd stop to get a thin crust avocado pizza from Roma's on Queen Street as a celebration.

So when the last doctor of five finally told me weeks later: this is what's happening, in your body, at this exact moment, I still couldn't believe they hadn't figured it all out by now. How to cure me. What were they doing, I wondered, these last few decades in universities, in government labs, eating sandwiches and taking lunch breaks while my body was getting ready to die. Why the fuck had I been giving my money away to charities all those years? My mother had breast cancer, I'd say as I opened my purse.

I got pizza on the way home, like I'd planned to weeks before. Thin crust avocado. I wanted to tell the smooth-faced teenager behind the counter, wanted to mention something about the hospital, about how that morning I'd rubbed the waxed and polished stone on my dresser for good luck, telling myself there was nothing inside me because nothing hurt, but at the same time knowing this was my last chance, this must be it, I must be dying. How I rubbed the stone fiercely until it became warm, how I put it in my purse. How four hours ago I was normal, but as I stood before her ordering extra cheese and commenting on the new vintage cuckoo clock they'd hung above the drinks cooler, I was no longer like her.

She shrugged when I mentioned the clock.

'The little guy chopping wood is broken,' she said. 'Only the dancing maids come out when it chimes.'

Seated in my car, the leather was hot, the summer air was stifling, and I started the engine and drove home having nowhere else to go. I told Alan when I handed him the pizza box, Luck had fucked us over. We'd lost the competition.

After that hot, impossible Thursday, my weeks were divided into *how much, how long, how likely?* I'd already surpassed the Stage One Designation because my body had been busy, my tumor already the size of a grape. I imagined a green grape. Watery and off color like phlegm turned hard. Edible, perhaps. Would the cancer spread if I ingested it? Or would my stomach acids destroy it? Would digesting my cancer grape create antibodies, tiny cells to live in my bloodstream, not to be fooled again by anything? I imagined them draining me, filling me up again with someone else, someone healthy. A transplant of my insides to keep me normal.

What I got was A Modified Radical Mastectomy.

The night before the operation Alan was in our bedroom, reading for the nineteenth time all the information we had been given. 'A Buddy is a Good Idea,' the leaflet said. On the front of it was a young woman, looking reassuringly at an older woman wearing purple shoes, seated on a park bench.

He read aloud: *Even if you are an independent woman, it is nice to have someone with you before and after surgery.*

Sitting beside him on the bed I lifted his shirt and fingered his Lake Superior birthmark, pressing it firmly with my thumb. My fingers sunk more deeply into his flesh each year, his chest softer, lower. I wanted someone to ask *me* to be in a leaflet photograph. When I was finished and healed, I wanted to be dressed in reassuring clothing, ready to offer other women what those women had offered me.

'You okay, buddy?' he asked me.

I never answered him, feeling the red ridges of his skin, the uneven shoreline.

Anna was at college in Wyoming. Thinking of her, I remembered that Mackinac summer. How the island's invincible isolation made me feel as if everything would always be okay.

Now it's Anna who might be left behind while I've taken my mother's place, and it doesn't seem fair – this cycle of daughters losing, and learning to be alone. I wondered if my mother had felt the same.

'I'm going to say goodbye,' I told Alan.

'Wait,' he said. 'Let me pee first.'

With the door closed off from the rest of the house, I sat on our *quiet flush* toilet and looked at myself in our mirrored shower doors, imagining how much liquid I'd pissed out in that position over two decades.

Lifting off Alan's Minnesota Twins T-shirt, I carefully unhooked my expensive uplifting bra – a vanity purchase from when Patty had her breasts done and kept wearing low-cut shirts to work. I put the bra on the tile floor, next to the T-shirt. I was cold in there, naked, feet on white tile, the first snow of the year sticking to the window screen outside. Naked, fifty and I'd made it this far, but already I felt so far away from my past life.

I turned out the light, but still looked ahead – I knew what was there by touch. Flat and thin with years, nipples slightly dejected, but still mine. For one more night. I examined the place on my breast, feeling what my body was growing beneath the skin. I kneaded it hard, painfully hard with my cold fingers.

I'm winning, I told it.

The part of me being removed tomorrow.

Because tomorrow, you'll have no place to go.

My fingers warmed up as they dug into the tissue, then out and around in an unnecessary exam – what more could my fingers find? Then massaging my nipples, pulling at them *hard* and hoping to bruise them, I wanted the promise of that feeling forever, but knew I was shit out of luck.

'Fuck you,' I told the mirror.

When I came out twenty minutes later, Alan was kneeling by our bed, his twenty-five-year-old rainbow house slippers knitted by his grandmother showing their worn bottoms to the ceiling. He didn't offer an explanation, but I didn't ask for one.

'Who'd you pick to pray to?' I wondered, curious.

He shrugged.

'It was kind of a general address.'

My wind chimes clatter together outside, making it difficult to concentrate. There's always something, an uninvited force trying to interfere when it should leave well enough alone. The door begins to make noise, but it's not my guest, just the weather intruding. The outer edge of the storm as it passes, I suppose. The siren wails and I sit, flipping the front cover of my blue journal open and closed, trying to channel my ghosts, but I know what happened next. There in blue ink on the first of September, it says *Sinking*.

I am wild with the thought of the wind breaking the door and sweeping away the treasures I have earned and kept safe all these years. I put the scab in my mouth. It will be safe inside me, and keeping it on my tongue like a pill, I let it get wet and hot. I won't let the weather take anything from me, not tonight. My souvenir is tasteless, hard, and I nibble on the tiny bit of dried flesh – part of a body that loved me. And left.

What else is there left to remember, but that everything slowly went wrong?

Mackinac

September has been a bit cool so far, our clientele changing as residents from local towns like Cheboygan, Traverse City, Marquette and Cedar Springs plan their visits after the school year has begun. I haven't given out a children's menu in weeks. The wind off the lake is strong. Seagulls hover in the sky, riding air currents above the water. I spend the early morning hosing their shit off the slate patio; the white yellow gobs are bright against the black. It takes only minutes to dry, the sun heating everything quickly. Opening the umbrellas next, I stay for a moment under the white canvas, watching the one big seagull with the broken wing stagger around the rocks by the water. The dark creases of the waves are sharp, the sun illuminating the crest and shadowing the valleys.

Bryce joins me as we watch the first ferryboat angle into the harbor, its top deck empty except for an elderly couple.

'There's you and me someday,' he says.

'Can we have a dog too?'

He pats me on the head. 'A bunch of fish maybe.'

The ferry docks and the couple get off.

'I'd like to meet your mom and dad,' I tell him.

He spits onto the slate patio, and after a moment he says, 'You'll like my sister.'

Odette is in her second year at Grayling High School. Bryce tells me she plays softball and is an excellent swimmer. The picture in his wallet reveals her shiny blonde hair and small frame, her eyes looking down and not at the camera.

'Does she have a boyfriend?' I wonder.

He shakes his head, frowning. 'She never has.'

He says nothing else, watching the seagull stumble over wet rocks towards the marina, dragging its wing awkwardly.

'You haven't talked about your family much,' I say.

Rummy appears at the French doors behind us. 'Phone's for you, Bryce. Your sister.'

Bryce turns to me.

'That's because I'm not a boring asshole.'

He leaves me alone on the patio, and Rummy says nothing.

Trainer puts his arm around me later as Velvet reprimands Bryce for his poor performance this evening. A table of four middle-aged men has complained about his attitude, and his refusal to substitute organic asparagus for a baked potato.

'The Tippecanoe *always* accommodates its guests,' she tells him fiercely.

Trainer looks at Velvet swanning off, and whispers in my ear –

'I just ate fifteen jumbo shrimp from the walk-in freezer.'

I don't answer, and he gives a big sigh.

'Let's let Uncle Trainer analyze your boyfriend, shall we? While *handsome* and *quite* charming, your ex-Mormon sweetheart has a problem with authority, especially of the male variety. He is also very protective of his female relationships, and often sees himself as a martyr.'

'As a *what?*'

Trainer examines a fingernail and looks bored again.

'*Newsflash*, cupcake – your boyfriend is a moody bitch. Vodka's the best thing for it.'

I take his advice.

We leave the Cock at three in the morning – everything feels close, even the sky. I can feel the evening sweat of bodies on my skin. The walk home is slow and stumbling, our bikes veering off in directions uncontrolled. The street is wet and shit-free from its midnight cleaning, the water slapping from my flip-flops up the back of my jeans, but at least it's clean. A carriage clips past us, the driver yelling, 'Up, Gerald, get up. Come on, Frances.' The two horses clatter off into the night ahead of us, hooves clopping, the sound of the carriage creaking and fading. In the grass by the side of the road are dead oak leaves, even though it's too early for them to be falling.

This is not a walk when Bryce and I hold hands while he points out Orion's belt. When he makes me find the Big Dipper and then kisses my face like it means something that I know where the stars are in the sky. We don't look up at all. Tonight he is concentrating on walking, drinking a can of beer smuggled from the bar. The pockets of his jeans are deep and wide enough to slide a whole can inside, which necessitates a kind of straight-legged gait so as to ensure the beer doesn't spill. I'm pretty sure John saw him take the beer anyway.

'Is your sister upset? Is that why she called?'

Bryce drinks his beer and continues to ignore me. I feel something in him, something tipping and not in my direction. He has been quiet all evening. I try and remember the parts of that book I read about how men are like elastics and need to stretch out as far as they can before snapping back.

Near the horse barn, the chain falls off his bike. There is a clanking sound as it drags on the ground.

'Fucking Christ,' he says.

He abruptly throws his beer can into the night, the amber spray twirling as the can spins. It hits a tree somewhere, the sound of impact high up, far away. The metallic sound of it hitting branches on the way down. A soft thunk as it hits the grass.

'Motherfucker.'

Shoving the handlebars violently, his BMX hits the pavement, pedal first, spinning. We both stare at the bike and Bryce's breath sounds hot and fast. He's beyond me now – his face is hard and closed. How can so much violence come so quickly?

'Just go,' he tells me.

He flips the bike upside-down and tries to spin the front wheel.

At home when my mother says, 'We are not discussing this further because you're being difficult,' my father retreats to his gardening shed to cut new wooden shapes for the birdhouse of the week, or to smear a pine cone in peanut butter and roll it round in a pile of shelled sunflower seeds for stringing up in the fir trees. I imagine he dreams of horses and the sky and how far away they are, waiting for him in Montana. I imagine my mother standing alone on our front porch, irritated, flicking her earlobe with her middle finger, and wondering if this is it – if the landscape never gets any larger.

'I'll wait,' I say.

'Just go,' he says again.

'Bryce.'

'Bell. Jesus Christ, please, fuck off.'

I turn immediately, yanking my bike and pointing it straight, leaning into the hill and shoving it ahead of me. I walk at a normal pace so he won't have to run to catch up, but he doesn't start fixing the chain until I am almost out of sight. He never catches up.

At the Pine Suites I ignore the lights and voices coming from Brenna's apartment, and leave the bike by my apartment door. There are no flowers here tonight.

Unslept in for months, my bedroom is cold and the sheets unfriendly, the pillow soon wet as well. The world has shifted slightly, outside of its frame. The sharp picture I'd begun with is bleeding colors everywhere. Bryce's sister is fifteen and lonely and calls Bryce too often, but I like this about him, this loyalty to his family, but he won't tell me more. As long as we are here, he doesn't need to. On the mainland, the world will become large again, and there's always the worry that it could be too big.

There are hooting noises outside followed by a crash and then laughter.

'Give me back the tomatoes,' someone says.

We are lucky we are here, where none of the difficult things seem real. The family things. I blow my nose into my hand and wipe it on the bed sheets.

It is only alcohol, this one evening, and maybe he won't remember his words. If I make an effort to forget them as well, this entire day will evaporate into island air.

Still – as I hear his bike crunch slowly up the gravel path, as I hear Brenna's voice calling out, his rebuttal, and the drunken banging on my window, I almost wonder – filled with this much alcohol, where else can he go but down? Sinking, blood vessels bursting, attached to his own self-made anchor. What would it be like, to be alone now? But he is so beautiful. We all make exceptions.

St. Paul, 4:51 p.m.

They call it breast reconstruction, as if my body were a building.

Something explodes outside, a transformer. I hear the crackling sound of a fire beginning.

As if there's a secret medical blueprint with angles marked and measured and locations indicated for electrical outlets and suggested federal standards for earthquake proofing. As if all the muscle and flaps of skin and pulled apart fat will become production materials, efficient, put to proper use.

I could make them bigger if I wanted.

But I didn't trust the meat of my body anymore. I didn't want anything there waiting, heavy with the possibilities of an irregular reading.

So I came out of the hospital with nothing, and went home feeling lighter.

I didn't leave the house for eight weeks.

Russ gave me six months leave after the operation, a formal gesture. In practice I never left. He couldn't swim without me, and I needed to know that his life continued and depended upon my memory for all those trivial things, from birthdays to political scandals. For each woman, the cancer books told me, it was different. There were support groups, fitness classes, vacations, religion. My salvation was simple, the city saved me – I read the *Pioneer Press*, checked my eight daily blogs, and talked to Russ and Patty on the phone – suggesting restaurants, reminding him of his son's birthday, giving opinions about the new governor of Wisconsin's moustache. All of this I could do in my decades-old college of St. Catherine's sweatshirt, stretched over my knees and gray so it never needed washing. I wondered why I ever bothered going into the office, but I suppose thirty phone calls a day might become draining after an extended period of time.

'Bell. It's Russ Gerhardt.'

'I know, Russ. What do you need?'

'Are you crying? Bell, you were fine ten minutes ago, are you crying?'

I could hear Patty in the background, 'Russ, why is she crying?' and then whispering, 'Did it come back, you know, is *it* back? *You* know?'

'*Quiet*, Patty, this is a business call. Where's my latte? Goddamn it, Bell, we need you here. Just *take* the money and get my latte. Wait, use my city hall Amex. *Whipped cream.*'

He returns to the phone.

'Bell, what's wrong?'

'I have no breasts, Russ, otherwise I'm fine.'

If I'd been able to feel anything it would have hurt to say this, but I was empty.

There are sirens now, military sirens not civilian ones. There are no helicopters yet, this means the roads are still clear. It's windy and I worry I won't hear the doorbell.

Patty handed me a box when I returned to the office. The box was pink, the ribbon too. Inside were two knitted breasts trimmed with faux-fur and red buttons for nipples.

'They're expensive, but I thought what the hell. They're *Tit-Bits*! Knitted tits, aren't they a hoot?'

'Is this fur?'

I turned them over in my hand, both of them even, weighted down with tiny beads.

'If they're not the right size I have the receipt,' she said quickly. 'I just thought, you know, might as well get the big ones.'

I promised her I'd try them as soon as the scars healed, my chest still weeping fluid beneath my clothes.

In the first few weeks after they'd taken my breasts, I would lie in our expensive sleigh bed, the white down comforter protecting me from winter and the unexpected – waiting for the thought of something that required leaving my bed. Some days I'd wonder if I'd received any letters. Some days Alan brought home Roma's pizza for lunch. Some days I smoked Anna's leftover pot. Or I just wondered what I looked like, how I'd changed from the night before. In front of our bedroom mirror with the *Russ for Congress* stickers on it, one hovering just above my right temple, I'd stand the way they teach you to when being photographed so as to emphasize the narrowness of your waist. I'd place my hand way up on my ribcage to make me look slimmer, and I'd look at the leftovers. Not enough of a body to make a whole anymore. And I'd squint. Sometimes I'd wear sunglasses so the pink scars were dark and tanned.

I had hips all out of proportion in a way I never really noticed until the top part of me was gone, the part which kept my figure looking like it was supposed to. Over the years I had acquired large thighs from somewhere, and it's odd because your calves don't change much – above the knees age sneaks up on you.

I had nice feet.

The day I smashed the mirror I used the corner of our

pewter snow globe/picture frame that Russ had given us for our fifteenth anniversary. He'd bought us his standard bottle of Dewar's as well, and he'd thought the snow globe was particularly funny. Celebrating St. Paul's Bicentennial, it said. It smashed the mirror in an unsatisfying way. The shards were supposed to explode outwards, cutting me, giving me gashes that would need stitches. But instead, after a few dull swings, my reflection just kind of cracked, and then fell apart.

Cleaning up, I got a sliver of glass in my foot. I wanted to think something romantic and meaningful about how all glass used to be sand and how in each grain of sand there is a universe, but it was too exhausting, so I just sat on the cream sheets of our unmade bed with my heel awkwardly in my hand, letting the too small shard of glass work its way out in a wet ooze of blood.

Mackinac

During a break from work Trainer and I get ice-cream cones and sit in Marquette Park. He has heavenly hash, I choose chocolate mint, and our tongues are working quickly because of the heat.

We talk about how Tom never brews more coffee after he has used the last of it, and how Brenna wears so much mascara that clumps of it fall into the food she serves, and then we talk about Cedar Point, the massive amusement park in his hometown.

'That's where all my hats are from,' he tells me. 'Assholes would lose their hats on the upside-down rollercoasters – like at ninety miles an hour it's going to stay on your head? Brand new baseball caps. I must have at least thirteen that I still wear.'

I nod, using my tongue to mash the ice cream further into its cone.

'I was there four summers,' he says.

'Where'd you stay?'

'Cedar dorms,' he says nostalgically. 'All male.'

He changes the subject.

'Did I tell you about the fucking woman at lunch today that ordered her Merlot straight up?'

'Like a Martini?'

He thinks some people should not be allowed to drink wine.

'And that's twice in two days, yesterday a woman asked me for her Zinfandel on the rocks.'

I try and match him. 'I had a guest on the patio ask me if there were any sharks in the ocean.'

'Well, *I* had some dick point at a seagull and ask me what sort of bird it was.'

He pauses. 'A fucking seagull.'

We sit in silence.

'You've got to lick faster than that, darling.'

My chocolate mint is running down my wrist.

From where we are sitting we can see a massive freighter making its way through the straits. This happens maybe once a week. I've heard they are filled with iron ore going up through the Sault locks to Canada, or coming down and around to Wisconsin or Minnesota or Detroit. Appearing at least half a mile long, the boats slide through the water quickly, even in deep fog, their horns low and strange to the ear. There has never been a collision in these straits, although locals still talk about that one close call: two steamers lumbering towards each other blaring their horns, both moving too quickly to stop. The spectators had gathered at the shoreline, watching the watery game of chicken to see who won. That they missed each other by a quarter of a mile is told with a hint of regret. Something spectacular had been so close at hand.

Trainer reads out the name of the steamer as it slides past, an intrusion among the ferries and holiday yachts.

'I wonder where it's going?' I ask.

'Pittsburgh.'

I look at Trainer and he shrugs. 'You can tell by the number of funnels,' he says.

We look back out at the steamer negotiating the narrow straits and numerous yachts.

'You're lying,' I venture.

'Of course.'

There is just one famous ship that sank in these Great Lakes. Broke in two, like a heart, and was lost. Living near the straits, it is hard to imagine how there is enough open water nearby to swallow anything. There is land everywhere, two lighthouses, and each port awaits ships patiently. I suppose some ships are too far from safety and have to weather the storms on their own. I guess it's the water that always wins.

HOMES, is how I remember all the lakes. It is how we were all taught in school: Huron Ontario Michigan Erie Superior. The last, the deepest.

Trainer thinks it's funny that he lives on Lake Erie, Rummy lives on Lake Ontario and now we are all here in the straits between two others.

'Get it?' Trainer asks me. 'Without Superior, we're HOME.'

He waits, looking at me.

'You've been hanging around Rummy too much,' I say.

At four forty-five we cross Main Street to start our shifts at the Tippecanoe. There is talk that Velvet will fire Trainer.

She's called him into her office. I think she's heard about his water bottles at work. Everyone agrees that he is fucked. Staff have been fired for much less. One unsuspecting kid showed up for work at the beginning of the summer with dreadlocks, his lip pierced, and a T-shirt that read, 'How did our oil get under their sand?' Velvet had told him that there'd been a mistake, and in fact she'd meant to contact him sooner, but there was no longer a place for him at the restaurant. He had to catch the next ferry home, taking his canvas duffel bags with him.

Trainer has been in her office for about ten minutes when he emerges, then leaves the restaurant with his bag containing his work clothes. I am sick. The pattern we have woven together here is too intricate to become unraveled now. We work the entire evening shift, each of us speculating on what has happened. There is nothing else to talk about.

Taking a tray of lobster in a *beurre blanc* sauce out to the dining room, someone comments, 'I just can't believe she fired him.'

Bringing dirty plates back to the dish pit someone else wonders, 'Will he stay for tonight to say goodbye?'

'Keep your mind on your work, shitheads,' Chef Walter tells us absently. 'You're not in Kansas anymore.'

Bryce finds me alone near the broom closet, as I search for a dustpan to sweep up the wine glasses I've dropped. Loud and hard, they had smashed on the hardwood floor, scattering shards under tables, making the woman next to me pull her daughter's chair closer, as if worried I'd leap up and slash her with a leftover wine stem.

'He's not fired, I promise,' Bryce says. 'She doesn't fire people that she likes.'

He takes the broom and dustpan from me and heads off towards my accident, and in the face of such logic I have to believe him.

At the Cockpit Club that evening Trainer is absolutely bombed, and gives us the thumbs up as we all walk in.

'She gave me the night off!' he yells at us.

Then lower, and with a wink, 'She's a bit of a drinker herself, you know.'

'Alcoholism is like a club,' he tells me later, after a few beers. 'We all look out for our own.' He tells me that once he was in Velvet's office she'd offered him a glass tumbler full of water, poured from a carafe on her desk. He had declined, too nervous, too uncertain for such pleasantries. She'd set the glass before him anyway, and as she talked he'd taken a sip.

'Belvedere,' he says. 'The good stuff.'

'Fuck off!' I say.

He nods.

'She's a fucking drunk, and it takes a drunk to know a drunk.

The night I dropped three trays in a row, she wondered what the hell was wrong with me.'

It doesn't take too much to figure it out, I guess. Not on this island. The night he dropped the trays is one that I remember. Trainer had gone to the bar after his morning shift ended and left just before his evening shift began, several shots of vodka and several pints of beer heavier.

'I didn't even need my water bottle that night,' he remembers. 'But,' he adds, with just a hint of embarrassment, 'that lady was pissed about her jacket. Daiquiris are hard to get out of suede.'

I can't wait to tell Bryce about Velvet, though when I tell him he will no doubt nod as if he suspected all along. When Bryce arrives, he claps Trainer on the back and buys him a beer saying,

'I knew you'd pull through.'

He stands behind me, wrapping both arms around my neck and licking my eyebrow. In my ear he says, 'Your mole is delicious.'

We chat for a bit and then he challenges Dickweed to a late-night game of volleyball, leaving Trainer and me to drink ourselves into oblivion. When he leaves he gives a salute, and Trainer turns to me and asks:

'Are you in love with Bryce?'

'Why?'

'Because I'm making conversation.'

'I don't know.' But I'm lying.

He nods wisely. 'Mackinac fever,' he says.

Behind us, Chef Walter feeds a bill into the Pac Man machine, ignoring our presence. His body presses against my back as he shifts with the movements of the game.

'Fuck you,' he tells the ghosts.

Changing the topic, I ask Trainer, 'Did you think she'd fire you?'

Trainer assumes a sober expression with difficulty. 'You're a good girl, Bell.'

'What does that mean?'

'It means whatever you want it to mean.'

I feel oddly comforted, and he decides to answer my question.

'I thought I was gone,' he says. 'And the thought of going back to Sandusky. Well. Jesus.' He pauses. 'What a place.'

But I'm not entirely sure which place he is referring to.

When we finally decide to leave, Trainer puts an arm around my shoulders and says, 'Stick with me, kiddo. Today's my lucky day.'

We grab our bikes and I follow him unsteadily up the road away from the town. Trainer pedals quickly to the side of a carriage heading in the same direction we are.

'Mind if we grab a lift?' he asks.

The carriage driver nods and I am surprised. The drivers usually rebuff the drunken island workers saying, 'Sorry, not allowed,' and urge the horses to go faster. I have done this only once before, with Bryce, and the initial tug when you grab the metal frame, stop pedaling, and let the force of the carriage take you, is surprisingly strong. Trainer picks the left side of the carriage just behind the driver and I the right; two people can't grab a hold of the same side in case the person in front was to let go.

With his right hand holding onto the carriage Trainer steers the bike with his left hand, and I mirror him, concentrating on keeping my bike pointed uphill. The driver sits on his raised seat directly behind the horses, and ignores us. We yell across the empty seats at each other.

'What's your favorite thing about cock?' he shouts at me.

184

I think for a moment. 'Besides getting rammed with it?'

'You stole my fucking answer. Fuck! That's so my answer, you bitch!'

We both start laughing, and my bike starts to wobble and I have to concentrate – though my thoughts are swimming with the lake and the ice cream in the park and my relief that we're still here. Our voices echo up and out into the black of night where they die, with no one but the driver to hear. He snaps the reins, and the horses give a jerk. My hand cramps a bit as the speed increases, the metal pulling at my fingers. We fall silent as the carriage continues upwards towards the Pine Suites, the hooves clopping on the pavement, the metal of the harnesses jangling, the weight of the wheels crunching wayward stones with sharp cracking sounds, and the landscape moving by us in silence.

Trainer says, 'Hey,' and I look over, but he's not looking at me, he's looking down at his handlebars.

'Fuck,' he says, and lets go his hold on the taxi, sliding from my view.

The bike scrapes the pavement, the carriage jostles and he's down.

'Shit, Trainer!' I'm laughing. 'Are you okay?'

I pedal a bit to pick up some momentum, so I can let go of the carriage.

'Trainer, are you okay?'

I grab my left handlebar and press the brakes, but he still hasn't answered. I stop and look back. He is lying in the road with both legs still twisted in his bike and the back wheels of the carriage have run over his chest.

St. Paul, 5:00 p.m.

When Alan died, it was not a surprise. He had the flu; such a simple thing and it made him sweat. So *hot*. All the time I asked for water to cool him and the one nurse, the one who understood, she always brought him water.

The house is cold now, very cold, but I'm sure the furnace is on and must remember to check. I don't want my guest to be uncomfortable.

I was next to Alan when he went. Safe at United Hospital, his room was light purple with a window that overlooked the summer landscape of St. Paul. The weather was fine that summer, it didn't give me any problems, it was predictable. They were repaving the main entrance to emergency and the air smelled of tar, even inside.

There was a green and waxy plant on his windowsill that kept growing even when I didn't remember to water it. I forget who sent that one now. Russ's Foundation sent lilies, and Patty signed the card.

She's doing well for herself now. Or has she retired?

But she didn't *know* Russ. He never would have sent flowers.

Send them cash, he always said. Cash and a bottle of Dewar's. Instant cure.

The cut flowers went on Alan's bedside table – carnations

and other arrangements that sick people get – though he stopped noticing them after a while.

If only the floor had been carpeted the whole thing might have been bearable. If only they had thought to make the room warmer, more like a bedroom, I could have stood it. Sometimes after it rained my shoes would still be wet by the time I got to his door. I would try to plant my feet flat on the linoleum as I walked, so I wouldn't squeak as I entered. If only there'd been a carpet, maybe I could have imagined more easily that I was at home.

The food was fine, when he was still eating. He was on a soft food diet, because of his difficulty swallowing. The dietician said it was the best thing for him, eating being as painful as it was. Apple sauce, puddings, Jello, along with some vitamin supplements. Baby food. He could never eat enough, his body drifting into nothingness.

Alan joked in the beginning – when it was just a cough, when they thought he'd be part of the 75 percent that recover after a week or two – how he'd had to go into hospital to have someone cook for him. We'd laughed, because in all our years of being married he had always done the cooking. Once in a while I'd try to make something, a fried egg or some just-add-water cookies or pancakes, but they were always burned or hard or salty. My kitchen always upset me.

I visited him every day. I watched him go from the hamburgers to the chocolate pudding to the feed tubes. Once, when he was asleep, too weak to be awake for long, I told him how we'd met, hoping he might dream about it.

I prayed, because Alan had prayed for me and I was still alive.

*

Jesus, Lord, Dear Mary, not yet, *just leave him be a while longer,* Lord, keep the roads clear, please, *I have my story yet. I just want the chance to tell it.*

I lost weight as well, and I was proud of myself for losing it. I ordered take-out meals at night, but the cartons full of spring rolls or sushi or hamburgers sat greasy, uneaten on the kitchen counter. The piles of mail soon took up the whole kitchen table. The grass grew. If we'd had a dog, it would have run away, taking charge of its own survival. I left the house alone; it began to look like no one really lived there. Anna had no idea how bad it was until she came to pick me up the afternoon my transmission failed.

'Jesus Christ, Mother,' she said.

Covering her nose with her shirt, Anna examined the kitchen. There were maggots in my refrigerator.

That was when she left the school indefinitely.

I'd find strange tasks for myself during this time, taking Alan's shirts out of the closet and ironing them, or scrubbing the floor of the shower at two in the morning until my hands couldn't hold the brush. I started sleeping on the recliner in the living room, watching television until I fell asleep. This turned into a habit I couldn't break and I sleep there still. Our bedroom is a foreign place to me now, thick with the scent of nothing and no one.

'Why does he have to die from such a stupid disease?' I asked Anna.

But he did. All those years I'd been sure it would be me first.

Soon after this, we began organizing my house. *Packing,* Anna calls it sometimes, which worries me.

*

So much death, and I don't understand where everyone goes. I had looked up, wondering if he could see me looking up, imagining he was there above me taking a last look. Isn't that what they say happens, the people that have died but come back? They don't immediately go anywhere, they get to hang around and watch. The room was quiet, with nothing to announce that there was now one less person in it. I think I waved. I waved at the empty white ceiling because I couldn't think of anything else to do.

Mackinac

I know instantly. I know from the way he is lying there, twisted, jerking, head on the pavement, arms out. He will die. The weight of the wheel has crushed everything inside him that he needs to breathe. Blood is running from his mouth and ears and he is choking violently and I am already there, beside him, my bike abandoned up the road. He cannot speak and the blood is spurting out of his mouth like an explosion, as if his insides have erupted and I am screaming after the taxi driver, 'You fucking ran him over, you fucking killed him, holy fuck.' The carriage stops and radios for an ambulance; the black horses are bucking and straining, panicking in their harnesses, knowing something is wrong, and now the driver is beside me and I notice briefly he is my age. He is crying, sobbing, so I can barely understand him: 'He fell, he fell I didn't see him there was nothing I could do is he okay, oh, fuck, fuck.' The front of Trainer's shirt is drenched and everything is coming out of him, but all I can do is kneel above him, stroking the side of his face, trying to keep his head from bashing against the pavement as he struggles for air, but his eyes are too wide, and he sees me and we both know he cannot breathe, he cannot take a breath and I am watching him die.

It is too late, it's too late, and by the time I find out there are in fact cars on the island, his eyes have stopped rolling and his chest has stopped jerking and heaving, but nothing can stop all the blood.

One ambulance and one fire truck and one police car scream up with sirens and lights to where I am sitting on the pavement with my hands over my face, snot running into my mouth and everything inside me breaking, while my body heaves, shudders, and grows cold. I don't know whether to touch him or not. I don't know whether to stand up and move away. I just sit with my hands over my face so I don't have to look.

By now a huge crowd of people, drunk and on their way home – just like we had been – have stopped to ask what happened, who was it, where does he work? I don't answer, hating them for not knowing who he is.

The ambulance men work quickly, wearing gloves, and when they cover his body in white, they murmur and nod in agreement, saying things like, *perforated lung, windpipe full of blood, never seen anything like it*. I look up. The emergency lights flash and illuminate the people, the carriage, the bikes, the body, but the sky is black and there are no stars. The heavens are covered by unseen clouds.

I remember the next day – and it is the same in all my dreams at the moment just before he gets up again – how he looked surprised, as if something shitty had happened that he wasn't expecting. How the wet black blood had stained his lips so they were bright in the moonlight, and how it had run into the stiff bristle of his beard. I remember how it looked fake – so dark and precise the way it spread – and how I was covered in it, although I don't remember touching him much at the time.

I remember thinking how pissed off he'd be that he had died like that. Something so ridiculous that if it had happened to someone else we would have made fun of them. Killed by a carriage. 'What an asshole,' Trainer would have said dismissively, and he would have ordered another Belvedere and soda.

*

With Trainer dead and thirty days until the Tippecanoe closes for business, it is not the same summer any longer. Rummy spotted the body bag early this morning, loaded onto a waiting Coast Guard boat, accompanied by two police officers. I can't imagine the island having a handy supply of body bags, but maybe the Coast Guard brought one on loan. From the mainland Trainer's body will be flown back to Ohio, back to the town he hated, to be buried there.

I ask Bryce why the flags on the island aren't at half-mast today.

'Only for the islanders,' he says.

There is a long pause as we consider this – death necessitating a kind of class system, ensuring that those being mourned are at least familiar.

'I guess otherwise they'd have to lower them for every tourist that has a heart attack,' he muses.

I shake my head. Velvet has taken down the work schedule with all of our names on it and made a new one, each of us getting more shifts. I look for his name when she puts it back up but of course it's not there. I wonder if she's worried about bad publicity. *This is the restaurant where that guy worked. The guy that died.*

The restaurant feels empty and large and I don't want to be here.

I am serving the executive members of the Consolidated Coalition of Michigan Hunters and Gun Owners tonight. Their party of sixteen has reserved most of the second floor of the restaurant, setting up displays and covering tables with brochures. Everyone seems more interested in drinking however, and I am running up and down the stairs, not caring, fetching Manhattans and then more bottles of wine with dinner. Outside, the lighthouse is obscured by wisps of fog, although its light blinks constantly.

It's getting darker earlier nowadays, and at seven o'clock the light outside is hazy and muted. This eerie time in between day and dusk makes me feel there will never be daylight again. A seagull drifts past the window, then turns towards the water.

I'm not concentrating and I make mistakes. The man who ordered the wine swirls it in his glass, holds it up to the light, sniffs it, sips and then nods. I want to bash him over the head with the bottle.

'This is an excellent wine,' he says to the table.

'Didn't you order the Cabernet?' one of the men asks.

We all look at the bottle, a Pinot Noir, and it is wrong. I have to bring them another one and if I'm lucky the bartender will void the first bottle without Velvet finding out. Fuck. *Pretentious gun-toting assholes*, I think, as I smile and present the Cabernet.

When they all close their menus, I return to the table once more. A large man, who reminds me of my dead uncle Manny, asks loudly what the vegetarian options are. As the men laugh he orders the one-pound Elk Pepper Steak with Water Chestnuts and Morel Mushrooms.

Bryce has offered to help me take drinks back and forth as his section is slow tonight, but what this has amounted to is him waiting by the bar so that once I've loaded the drinks onto my tray he can grab my ass. This is accompanied by a leer and a raising of his eyebrows, as if to ensure there will be more of this later on. I have to laugh, and it's strange how things can still be funny even after so much pain. After the fifth time he does this, Velvet appears at the bar and tells Bryce that as his section is slow tonight he might be interested in ironing some tablecloths for tomorrow's breakfast. He blows me a kiss and follows her clicking heels towards the kitchen.

The men upstairs are loud in the way that men are when they think they are alone with each other, when they've got credit cards in their pockets, when they think the night is theirs. The conversation revolves around guns, ammunition, and hunting.

The table is long, half of the men sitting with their backs to the window and half of them facing it, and I am forced to reach awkwardly in between the men facing the window to pass drinks and food across. As I'm setting down their main course of elk steaks and filets and roast potatoes, some extra-rare and some well-done, one of the men with his back to me says to the group, 'I bet this lady here's done some hunting in her day.'

Some of the men turn and look up at me, others continue looking at the man who has spoken. I smile and shake my head and he continues:

'Sad state of affairs when these women don't know what it feels like to bag their first buck. Shit, when my daughter was twelve . . .'

He continues talking, picking up his fork and steak knife and sawing into the meat without looking at it. I back away from the table, sickened that these men can behave like this, eating steak, talking to me without bothering to read my nametag.

'Hey, where'd she go? Where's the waitress?' He turns in his seat and calls me back to the table. 'I'll have some more wine.'

Picking up the almost empty bottle from the table I pour too quickly, spilling a drop on the white tablecloth and some of the red runs down the stem. He makes a show of using his napkin to wipe his glass.

When they finally leave, they leave behind their brochures and pamphlets and their low-budget magazines. In the quiet of the upstairs, with the men gone and the table cleared except for the tablecloth and the square glass vase with the orchid in it, with the lights dimmed and the night outside softened by the large white moon, I take a chance and sit down, out of sight of the swinging door leading downstairs. I feel that the word 'waitress' is carved into the flesh of my forehead and even when this heals there will be a scar.

The magazine cover is a glossy collage of beasts, all of them behind a cross hairs. The deer are the most prominently featured, followed by bears, rabbits, coyotes, and raccoons. Everything is a target. The name of the organization is in an army green, and the Contents Page lists people who have written in about the benefits of one gun versus another, sharing personal hunting stories, and articles about the progress the NRA is making with its various lobbying initiatives. Someone has circled with red pen an ad for a gun show in Detroit this fall, and Derek from the town of Battlecreek writes:

There's nothing like the feeling you get when you see your first five-point buck dead in the snow with the white ground staining red as you approach, the steam rising from the bullet holes into the cold winter air.

Nothing is spelled 'nthing' and the magazine is littered with grammatical errors.

The swinging door snaps open and inwards as Velvet arrives to ensure the room has been tidied properly. I stand up so quickly I become light headed, and realize I am about to cry. Upon seeing the mess left behind by their literature, she rolls her eyes and fetches a garbage bag. With one arm she efficiently sweeps everything off of the tables and into the trash.

'Garbage,' she announces. 'And I'd like to see you in my office before you leave tonight.'

She leaves the bag on the floor for me to carry down the stairs.

★

I am smiling at Velvet, sitting in her leather chair, waiting while she pours herself a glass of Belvedere from the carafe on her desk. I wonder if she keeps her vodka bottles hidden in the main freezer with the almond ice cream and frozen 'fresh squeezed' juice. She takes a sip and places the tumbler on a black leather coaster. Her lipstick is minimal, leaving no mark on the glass. She doesn't offer me a drink.

'I have something for you,' she says.

'Oh?'

'Have you heard of Petoskey?'

I want desperately to have heard of Petoskey, to appear intelligent and well-informed.

'No, I don't think so.'

She expertly slides open a desk drawer, and leans over, looking for something. I look at the black leather picture frame on her desk that matches her coasters, but the picture is facing her and I can't see who it is. I can't think who it could be. The carpet beneath my feet is white.

She hands me a rock.

'Petoskey stones are common in this area,' she says. 'Look at it.'

I look immediately at the stone not wanting to appear uninterested, which I'm not as I really want to know what's going on. It's the size a stone should be, curved and round in the palm of my hand. It's been polished, all of it glossy as if it's been waxed.

'Look at the pattern,' she instructs.

The dark gray is laced with fossil, thin slivers of line and tiny patterns like honeycomb. An intricate web, the stone is covered in these perfect shapes; it seems impossible there is so much organization within such a small surface. The colours look like explosions, dark black mouths in the center and then brown and creamy out towards the edge.

'That's amazing,' I say.

Velvet nods.

'It's fossilized coral. Michigan used to be an ocean.'

'Thank you,' I say. 'Where's it from?'

She smiles and rises from her chair.

'Petoskey,' she says. 'About an hour from here. Remember the orchid before you leave. You left it in the vase upstairs.'

I stand, leaving the office quickly.

'And one more thing,' she calls, raising her voice after me.

I appear back in the doorway and she is still standing.

'You might as well have this.'

She hands me the sixty-dollar bottle of Pinot Noir that I opened accidentally at dinner. The cork sits dark with sediment, upside down in the neck of the bottle.

'I suggest you don't mention where it came from,' she says.

In the hall, my hands cold, I arrange the bottle carefully in my backpack making sure it's upright. On my way out of the restaurant I meet Rummy. He is indignant.

'What the fuck? Why is she giving you things?'

'Rummy, you fuck nut. I saw Trainer die.'

He is quiet for a moment.

'So she gave you a rock?'

I have no explanation for him and when he asks to see it I refuse to show him.

Bryce and I follow the bottle of Pinot Noir with a case of Miller, and when I throw up everything comes out red like blood.

St. Paul, 6:00 p.m.

Anna's voice comes to me over the answer phone, projecting into space, suspended and intruding. I didn't hear the phone ringing.

Mother? Please pick up, it's Anna. I'm on my way, Mother, please don't worry. It's going to take a while, I've been interlodged at the Sushi Palace until it passes. I know your roof is okay but stay away from the windows, and remember your blue pills.

She tells me to turn on the television, that the weather is getting worse, drifts of a couple feet reported north of the city, rain, then hail.

'He'll come,' I say confidently to her. 'Don't worry.'

The machine clicks.

Outside the living-room window the sky is heavy, and if the weather concerned me I would stand and watch the thick yellowish clouds building and swirling, my oak tree bending in the wind. *This too shall pass*, I say with satisfaction.

It's time for my blue pills, and I take them with cold tea, six hours old.

The day after Alan's funeral I arranged to rewrite my will. The Rising Cross Memorial Home is an unhealthy environment and I refused to become another customer of theirs, drained and refilled and carved up, unnatural slices in my skin releasing the gassy leftovers in my lungs, stomach, and bloodstream – unused air escaped and waiting around to be sucked up by the relatives who lasted longer than me. No. I will die with the scars I have now, and be burned with them as well.

Cremated, half of me will be spread thin over the top of Alan's grave, the other half dropped into a lonely, sacred place I have visited only once, but thought of many times since. Where my ashes will never touch the ground. Always falling, the legend says, towards the earth's center and the spirit that resides there. I'll always have direction, even in death.

Mother, the phone networks are cutting in and out now, I'd really feel better if I could talk to you before they go down. Can you hear me?

I'm sorry I'm talking to my mother, she's alone, yes. Just a minute.

Then louder.

Shit, Mother, the windshields on all the cars are going. They're taking us back into the kitchen.

She is shouting now.

Okay, please be careful. It's Anna.

The meeting with Father Aldo about the funeral arrangements had been tedious, involving questions about Alan's faith, my confirmation, Anna's upbringing. He had black hair and was younger than I thought he should be, thin, with black dress pants – lacking any sort of robe to give him the authority I wanted.

Knowing him only by sight from Christmas Mass, his old-fashioned conservatism was something I admired. His straight-from-the-scripture sermons reminded me of my youth – all those Sundays I spent learning bible verses and drawing eyelashes on my pet, Peter the Rock. Fundamentalism was nothing new for Catholicism, or any other religion for that matter – but to Father Aldo's frustration it seemed that given the choice, an increasing number of people were *choosing the right*, making the Mormon church the fastest growing religion in the world in unexpected places like Brazil, Samoa, Tonga, Chile, Uruguay, and Mexico. Their membership records were disputed of course, how can you keep track of faith? I'd never seriously considered joining – when I prayed it was to Mary, and I told Father Aldo so. I didn't mention that she never listened.

'Our church has had trouble,' he acknowledged. 'Trouble with the government, trouble with *religious sects*. Some people have been set adrift. Especially after Hadley Guard.'

He shrugged.

When the LDS governor of Arizona ascended to the presidency in the late thirties, the church as a whole gained an even higher profile – the Catholics hadn't had a president of their own faith since JFK. Hadley Guard had run under the slogan: *Guard-American Religion, America's Way.*

I'd voted for him on a whim, maybe because Russ told me Hadley Guard swore like a sailor at a Phoenix charity golf tournament.

To Father Aldo, I said nothing – I needed what he had to offer.

Because Alan didn't believe in anything anyway, and Anna believed all religions were essentially the same, the idea of a traditional Catholic funeral appealed to me. I wanted rules and ceremony, my grief organized and given meaning, the responsibility shared.

I wanted to see Alan again.

My family, with its three separate religions of Catholicism, Atheism and Buddhism, would be together in death, I was determined. From the peaks of our individual mountaintops we would descend, to meet together in a common valley in the afterlife, where Alan would have his beach, Anna her tranquility and I could float forever in the clean waters of my heavenly lake. There would be a rowboat.

After an hour Father Aldo was satisfied, and I was triumphant. I would have the ceremony I wanted, Mass and all. Anna had refused to attend the meeting, insisting she would not be an active participant.

'In some countries,' she said, 'death isn't the industry it is here. You die and get to be buried on a windy hillside somewhere overlooking crofts and cattle, your body marked above the ground with rocks. People *sing*.

'I bet Dad would have loved something like that.'

'Funerals are for the living,' I told her.

Flags lowered, expensive gravestones, eulogies, tears, wakes, pilgrimages, candles, the flowers are only for us, the ones left behind. They've already set sail.

Anna took my hand in the hours before her father's funeral service; I kept wondering why Michael hadn't returned from his boarding trip to Lake Tahoe. Her face looked older than I remembered – her pores large, her face damaged from the sun. She had her hair clipped back with some kind of coconut shell and as she collected our water glasses from the table, scrubbed my countertops and organized my pills, I thought the tears were for her father.

'Did Michael say he'd be back for the burial? Is he flying into Minneapolis-St. Paul?'

Anna wiped her eyes with a dishrag and sat across from me.

'I'm going to take care of you, Mom,' she told me.

I had one of Alan's unwashed socks in my pocket. My index finger poking through the hole in the heel, I was thinking of how his foot used to be inside it.

'Where is he?' I wanted to know.

Anna told me at last.

'Michael left me for her. For his student, I mean. Back in California.'

Then she really began to cry.

'Things weren't supposed to turn out this way,' she said to me.

And I knew exactly what she meant. It had been many years since we had shared anything like we did in that moment.

Checking the hands of the Virgin Mary, he is late and I think of a beach to relax myself. An open sky with clouds like scales. A sky empty of Rapid Weather Patterns and government helicopters and rockets and other man-made entities riding the air currents alone above me. A lake where, suspended in water, you can move in circles and never get to the end because there isn't one and you can start over and over again and you can always return to the place you've just left. It is twenty after six and I can't remember taking my blue pills.

I'm certain he will come. There are stories he wants to hear.

The sound of the doorbell comes, finally – the tone echoing in my head so I wonder if I ever heard it at all.

I answer the call.

Mackinac

A tree is burning. I can smell wood smoke through the rain as I open the door, along with the electric odor of ozone and wet leaves. Water clatters continuously from the roof and eaves, while lightning cracks its eerie fluorescence over the two figures on my doorstep. The rain is heavy, disorienting. I can't tell who the second figure is, I was expecting only one.

'Rummy?'

The figure on the left waves her slender fingers at me.

'Hi, Bell. Nice fucking night for a memorial service.'

'Brenna wanted to come too!' Rummy shouts.

She is wearing pink rubber boots. Her presence is sharp, irritating, and not what tonight is meant for. Rummy and I discussed how it should be done, the two of us. Bryce is at Dickweed's birthday party tonight.

'Great,' I say.

'Have you got the hat?' he asks.

I hold up the plastic bag from Mackinac Mart. The three of us are dressed in identical yellow rain suits – the hood with an extended brim that looks like a duckbill, which Velvet made us purchase from The Island Sweat Shop. Moving quickly towards the bike racks, not speaking, I imagine we are ducklings in a too big pond, the storm come to wash us all away.

There are two weeks left until the Tippecanoe closes for the season. The entire island is slowing down, getting colder. With fewer tourists there are fewer carriages, and the sidewalks have long expanses with no people on them at all. The bike rental shops close down, one by one. Seagulls huddle against the wind. Hotels lower their prices. The Tippecanoe offers soups made from acorn squash and cranberries, pumpkin and maple syrup. Some hotels are already empty, the water pipes drained in preparation for the Michigan winter. Each morning more suitcases and bicycles line the dock, workers throwing bits of their breakfast to the gulls, waiting to return home. Today, on Velvet's instructions, Bryce spent three hours polishing the canoe bar with Tecumseh's All American Wood Protector. With its large windows, the restaurant has become draughty and uncomfortable; the cold weather version of our uniforms is a knitted black vest to wear over our tuxedo shirts. I imagine what Trainer's comments would have been.

- Rummy pointed out the vests were made in Burma.

'We have a trade embargo with Burma,' he explained.

We have two weeks, but tonight is when it ends. I'm already nostalgic in anticipation of what I'm about to lose.

As we begin our journey to the Crack in the Island, the rain falls with more intensity, the severity of the storm increasing as the wet sky descends, smacking rooftops, drenching leaves and pavement. Thunder explodes from the dark space between each tree trunk, the sound vibrating up through my handlebars, and I imagine with each crack of electricity that lightning has struck the metal of my bike, and my heart has stopped.

I try holding my breath, to get closer to death, and I hope that Rummy's backpack contains all the things we discussed.

In single file we follow Rummy, his one headlight spotlighting the rain and giving him an odd appearance, glowing, as if he isn't really there. When he takes the corner into the State Park, he disappears altogether and in the darkness I miss the sharp turn, veering into the trees. Brenna waits as I turn around. With difficulty I return to the path, boots sinking in the muddy undergrowth, branches sliding across my body.

'I brought a zebra!' she yells, or that's what it sounds like.

I can't hear properly over the storm. 'A what?'

'How's your mother by the way?' she asks as I mount my bike.

She speaks clearly this time, and shaking my head I begin to pedal away, towards the real purpose of our wet evening.

Last night, I went to the dock after my shift and someone had stuck chewing gum on the listening part of the telephone.

My mother asked me what I would like to eat.

'Your first meal back,' she said. 'What would you like? Potato salad?'

I told her corn on the cob would be nice, but she said it was out of season. Later when my mother hung up the phone for her nap, my father said he'd been doing all the cooking anyway.

'She needs her energy to get well,' he said.

The gum softened and stuck to my ear, the smell of mint making me nauseous.

'Your Aunt Lydia's back from Rome again, by the way. She's brought you a clock.'

Before hanging up the phone my father promised corn, if only from the freezer.

On Garrison Road the pavement is covered in water and where the ground dips we ride through dark puddles pelted with rain, our tires spraying plumes behind us. My thigh muscles begin to cramp, and I'm sure we've gone in the wrong direction. Rummy missed a turn, the path we are looking for is unmarked, a small dirt trail. Turning back, we pass the entrance to Saint Anne's cemetery for the second time, the stone archway black with rain. 'ALCOHOLIC BEVERAGES PRO-HIBITED', a sign reads.

I wondered about the cemetery as a possible location, but Bryce told me it was haunted – photographs taken at night were developed with mist and distortions among the grave markers. 'The Post Cemetery is worse,' he warned, 'the ghost of a young soldier killed in the War of 1812 walks behind the white picket fence after dark, holding his lost lover's handkerchief in his fist.'

I accused him of lying, and he shrugged.

'Whatever you want to believe,' he said.

The long grassy field of the airport opens before us, the wind hurling itself across the wide runways and I wonder if Velvet's orchid shipment will be late tomorrow. Soon the forest consumes us again, dark and blurred with water. My fingers burn numb on the handlebars, the wet collar of my sweatshirt cold beneath my rain jacket. The trail becomes narrow, covered in dark leaves. The trees are close, branches arcing above the pathway as if this ancient spirit forest will arrange itself behind us, leaving no escape. The light ahead stops moving and I brake lightly, sliding on wet leaves under my wheels.

'Is that it?' Rummy asks.

He angles the handlebars of his bike, shining the headlight into the forest. Through the rain and wet undergrowth are four slender elm trees, their trunks white in the light. Between the elms is a dark crevice, splitting the rocky ground as the land rises away from us. The Crack in the Island.

'That's it?' Brenna asks. 'I thought it'd be bigger.'

'Let's go,' Rummy says.

Unwrapping the Mackinac Mart bag from around my right handlebar, we leave our bikes on the trail; except for the gods and ghosts we are the only ones here tonight. We ascend a muddy incline, following along the crack into the dark. The rain echoes inside the forest, sounding as if we're inside a cathedral. Long streams of water plummet from the canopy above, and Rummy takes a flashlight from his backpack. Standing above the dark limestone fracture, it looks as if it descends for miles. Too narrow to climb down into, it is barely wide enough for an arm, but I can understand why people come here to search it out. It looks as if it breathes, a part of the forest's ecosystem.

'Tourists are so fucking dumb,' Brenna says. 'Why would anyone hike all the way out here for this?'

'At least Trainer won't be bothered,' Rummy points out.

The break in the earth continues, surprisingly straight and even, as if the ground was broken by the descent of a gigantic guillotine, the huge blade withdrawn again into the sky. Further along ferns and grassy clumps edge into the crevice, dirt and undergrowth narrowing the gap.

By the wet trunk of a fir tree we sit in our yellow raingear to decide how we want to proceed. After setting the flashlight upright in the mud and securing it with soil, Rummy produces the bottle of Belvedere and we drink – I take huge swallows. Brenna drinks after me, then wipes her mouth, but her face is wet anyway.

'I love vodka.' She tongues the lip of the bottle. 'No calories.'

'Let's get on with it,' Rummy says.

I reach into the bag, the plastic wet and cold, to find what it is we've come to bury. I already know that Trainer's Cleveland Indians hat is stained, the inside rim yellowed and shiny with forehead grease. I took it from the road where he'd fallen and, still holding it, answered all their questions. There is no blood on it, though I want there to be. Without the blood it's just his hat. Bryce tried it on a few times, but it's too big for him.

I couldn't keep it in the room with me, even hidden away in the closet – Trainer's bloody beard brushed against me as I slept and the sounds of his choking came at me from the walls. In one dream he was dressed like the Virgin Mary and waving to me frantically from a lifeboat, his hat missing from his head. I wondered about sending it back to his family with some kind of note, like everything else that's been shipped off in boxes. But what the fuck would I write?

Something seemed right about putting a piece of him underground, in a place where he wanted to be.

Trainer and I discovered the Crack in the Island on the Mackinac map hanging above the employee table. He laughed, while pointing out its location, marked just above the airport.

'Sounds ominous,' I agreed. 'Biblical, or something.'

'Sounds like a giant ass,' Trainer said giggling.

Rummy has been here before, and we agreed it was appropriate to give Trainer his send-off in the island's giant crack.

Brenna takes the hat from me, and smells it. In the narrow light of the flashlight, both she and Rummy appear as shadows, the beam floating upwards and disappearing above our heads.

'Smells like him,' she says.

She places the hat before us. From the pocket of her raincoat she pulls out a small wooden zebra and places it inside Trainer's upturned hat. The zebra's about three inches high, with a wiry mane and tail. The stripes look hand-painted.

'I'd bought it for him at the toy shop,' she explains.

Rummy takes a drink of Belvedere, and says nothing.

'Why?' I ask.

She draws her bright yellow legs up to her chest, leaning back against the pine tree.

'He was my friend too,' she says. 'He told me about the African resort.'

A burst of thunder interrupts her, then lightning, and the air feels full. Brenna looks at me. I look at Rummy, but he's staring down into the ground as he drinks.

'What resort?' I ask.

'Thanda Private Game Reserve,' she says. 'In South Africa. His aunt lives out there and said they were looking for experienced foreign waiters.'

She pauses, her hood covering her face.

'He was going there in October. So he didn't have to go home.'

The light of the flashlight dims suddenly, then returns to full strength.

'A *game* reserve?' I say, unbelieving. 'He didn't like being outside.'

'It's a five-star resort,' she says. 'The staff get free fucking body massages, rose petal baths, everything. He showed me the website.'

I look at Brenna, feeling as if I've underestimated something this summer.

'I didn't know that.'

'Neither did I,' Rummy says.

She motions to the tiny wooden animal upturned in his hat.

'He really wanted to see a zebra,' she says.

He never told me about South Africa. A whole other country, his plan for luxury and escape never mentioned. Sucking water from the end of my cold fingers, I try to remember if he knew about St. Kat's. If he knew how I craved the decadence of eating steak with expensive wine, to be the sort of woman at the table the waitress usually mocks in the kitchen, only she wouldn't – I wouldn't be pretentious. I would understand, because I had been there. I wouldn't demand that my mashed white truffle potatoes be substituted for green beans, or ask for an extra plate or more garlic sabayon when she was busy. I'd never even taste the wine, just motion for her to pour. I would have an understanding face. I would leave an extravagant tip. I've seen too much here to settle for anything less.

I pick up Brenna's offering and stroke its tiny wire mane with my finger.

'He's cute,' I say.

Brenna reaches for the bottle. 'I did my nails to match.'

She holds out a hand, each of her long fingernails striped with black, then white.

Rummy places his own contribution into the Indians hat. Trainer's Spice Girl playing cards. Covered in clear packing tape to protect them from rain, there are only a few cards left. Some were lost on the road as he slipped under the carriage that night. Some he lost earlier, or traded. On the back of each is a figure of a woman, leaning forward, posing and dressed in leopard print and leather.

'What ever happened to his bike?' I ask.

'They never shipped it,' Rummy says. 'Tom sold it to a guy over at the bike shop for ten bucks. He's gonna get a new wheel for it, straighten the fenders. I took the cards off before he sold it.'

'Did they have the Spice Girls up in Canada?' Brenna asks him. 'Their music I mean?'

Rummy glares at her. 'Do they not have an education system in Toledo?'

'I went to a Catholic school,' she says defensively.

'So did I,' I tell her.

The vodka makes everything seem important.

'You should know we've had running water *and* electricity in Canada for years now,' Rummy says to Brenna.

'So you *have* heard of the Spice Girls then. That's all I was asking, fuck.'

More rain falls, and Rummy wants to know if she's heard from Blue, and she tells him she hasn't. In a voice uncharacteristically kind, she asks him to forget Blue, and to move on.

There will later be some debate as to what exactly we were talking about when we first noticed. It's true that sometimes a presence is felt before it is seen.

We all look up together.

Holy shit.

Standing just yards from our gathering, through the rain and just across the narrow crevice in the ground, is the dark, real form of an animal, larger than anything I've ever seen. Its legs are long, three times taller than a horse, its body beginning somewhere up in the darkness. We stare – just four impossibly long and muscular legs, longer in the front than the back. Rummy shines the flashlight silently along its body. The sleek coat is perfect except for a bare patch of pale skin near its neck, as if the hair had been rubbed away or fallen out from disease. Its back rises up into a hump before descending again to meet its elongated head. His face is long, endless, and serene, undisturbed by our light and presence. Rising above him are antlers – huge, bone-colored protrusions like delicate driftwood stretching out and up towards the sky, and it doesn't seem they can be so big, that his head can hold them up. Enormous, silent, his one wet eye reflects the light, and blinks. The rain falls around us, the tops of the trees bend and there is thunder. He exists here in just one small beam of light. It is monumental, the moment so intense, so drawn out as the three of us sit with legs crossed in front of a hat, a zebra and some playing cards, but somehow something else has come, and I don't know if I'm breathing.

'It's a goddamn moose,' Rummy says, disbelieving.

A powerful rush of spirit enters into my stomach, and I am positive this feeling of something beginning must be the same perfect appreciation and awe that any one of us, anywhere, must feel when confronted with such an impossible vision. I think of all three of us and the entire world stranded together with a feeling of wanting more, and wanting meaning, and I think of the little boy in the lifeboat with three religions, but here, the island belongs to those who found it first, whose myths brought us here, to the place where the earth never ends.

He is slow, impossibly slow, as he bends quietly, bringing his elegant face to where the ground is split at his feet. His antlers bow before us, nodding at the ground, and he seems to smell the earth, or taste it, I cannot tell. He rises again. When he turns back into the darkness, I realize what I am about to lose. When the light can't find him anymore, we are alone again, and it is painful.

He is gone, and we cannot hear his footfall. We look at one another, then into the forest, waiting and listening for his return.

'That was a moose,' I say.

'How did the moose get here?' Brenna wants to know. 'I've never heard of moose on Mackinac.'

Rummy takes another drink of Belvedere. 'The ice,' he says. 'He came across the ice in the winter.'

'Don't they swim?' I ask.

'Maybe he swam,' Rummy says thoughtfully. 'We'll never know.'

It is almost one o'clock, and we fold the hat around the playing cards and the zebra. The rain is unrelenting, all three of us are wet through, our hands frigid, water dripping from our noses, drunk, elated. The three of us hold our offering together, fists touching, and Rummy yells, 'I'm fucking soaked, asshole. Don't say this Canuck never did anything for you,' but his voice breaks and he makes a choking sound.

Kneeling, our knees muddy, our brains suspended with vodka and the lingering presence of our visitor, we drop the hat into the crack in the island. Rummy pours some vodka in after it.

The offerings make no sound, they never reach the earth, they simply fall. We never hear them land. Bryce told me the Native Americans believe this a spiritual place, nothing dropped into the crevice ever reaches the bottom.

'I can't believe we saw a moose,' I say, as we begin the long ride back home.

His bike weaving dangerously back and forth across the path, Rummy agrees with me.

'But the moose was as real as I am,' he says.

St. Paul, 6:21 p.m.

Rummy stands on the doorstep. In the bright burning of the streetlight, his entire frame is lit up like an offering. He is wearing dark jeans and a brown leather belt, his gray hairline holding steady, his face with the same distinguished, wry expression I've become used to from studying his headshot on the university website. His hair and jacket are wet, though the weather around us is quiet, everything echoing like a too large church hall. I can feel the rain but cannot see it, yet. It is the eye of the storm – or perhaps it has passed altogether.

He is here just as I've imagined him these last three weeks – constructing this impossible meeting, considering the possibilities, what I will say and how he will respond.

'You're late,' I say, relieved.

'Drove through the storm,' he says apologetically. 'It's a big one.'

He holds up a bottle in a brown bag and waves it at me. 'You knew I'd make it.'

I hear in his voice that he is the same, that underneath the old skin I am not used to yet, he is there.

'Well, come *in*.'

As he passes through the doorway he is close enough to smell. The scent of somewhere I've never been. There is a brief moment, imperceptible as it passes, where our time is not all gone and the evening is still ahead.

In my relief at Rummy's arrival I feel dizzy, and look to my wooden crucifix above the light switch – but it's gone, and I don't remember what I've done with it. Aunt Lydia gave one to my mother as well, and I couldn't have thrown it away. Has Anna taken it? When did I last visit Resurrection Cemetery? As I age the graves accumulate along with the guilt at my inability to visit them all, but the drive is too far, the traffic so fast, and perhaps Anna will take me to my parents tomorrow.

Something has slipped, but I catch hold, and after a moment I am fine again.

Rummy. Saving me from time, delivering me from grief if only for an evening. Animated. Real. Covered in skin. He scratches his nose, briefly fingering a nostril, and we pause for a moment before he stretches out his arms – an angel, or something not so obvious – and says, 'Give us a hug then, Bell.'

We embrace and he is warm and solid, his body reliable and working properly, keeping his insides safe all these years. He feels now a better friend than ever before.

'When is Erik coming back?' I ask as we draw away, his watch clasp catching in my hair.

'At eight,' he says, disentangling himself from me. 'Nearly two hours.'

When his son returns they will continue on to Milwaukee. Down from Calgary through the Midwest and over to Wisconsin for the annual meeting of the Oral History Association. Rummy is the keynote speaker. I am part of his latest project, his bid to keep our small part in history alive. His wife Aileen is not strong enough to travel.

'Come and sit,' I tell him. 'I'll get the drinks.'

He follows me into the kitchen and sits obediently in my chair, making an *ahhhhhhh* noise as he leans back. His jacket is open, a navy-blue corduroy lined with fleece, and underneath his V-neck sweater is Hunter Green; I recall he had an almost identical sweater on the island. He puts both hands on his thighs as he takes in the kitchen.

'You've done well for yourself, Bell,' he says. 'Right part of town, right people. The house is white. Easier to sell if they're white, I hear.'

'It's true,' I say. 'That's true. And thank you.'

He raps the wall beside him with a knuckle while looking around.

'So are there different *shades* involved here?'

Pulling open the fridge door to retrieve my half of the promise, there is a single photograph held by a magnet in the shape of a sailboat – Russ meeting the President in Cheyenne, me in the background, plastic ID badge around my neck. I was close enough to sneeze on her.

With ice in each glass, I pour Rummy's liquor for us both, then add the ginger ale. The bottle slips, and when the floor dries it will be sticky. He takes the glass from me and holds it up.

'Rye and ginger, together at last.'

'Your favorite.'

'It's all I ever drink,' he says. 'Here's to old friends.'

We raise our glasses across the table from one another, our eyes full of the past. We sip carefully, and it seems unbearable to wait any longer. Rummy wipes the table with his sleeve, erasing the wet ring left by his glass. I had Anna's coasters out this morning, but they've disappeared.

'I'm glad to be here, Bell. I needed to come.'

'It's hard to believe you're really here.'

Something crashes against the window, but doesn't come in.

'Now,' he says.

From the inside of his jacket pocket he withdraws the tiny earpiece he'd described over email, and I fumble with its minute dimensions while he fits a similar piece over his own ear. A wireless, voice-activated recording device available in different colors, I've seen them only on television. Turning to Rummy with the device buried in my ear canal, he nods in approval.

'It won't record until I say *begin*,' he explains.

'You're the expert,' I tell him smiling.

He smiles back, shrugging his shoulders.

'We Canucks have always been better listeners than the rest of you.'

'What's it stand for?' Alan asked as I perused Rummy's latest title a few years ago: *The Demise of the Canadian Reservation: Personal Narratives by First Nations Peoples.*

'What does what stand for?'

'Rummy.'

'I don't know.'

It felt odd not knowing, and I refused to join him as he pondered the possibilities.

'Rumsfeld, Rump *Roast*, Romania . . .'

'Romania would be shortened to Rommy,' I pointed out.

'Rumpelstiltskin,' he continued, ignoring me.

'You should read it when I'm done,' I told him.

'Or I could stare at the author's photo and call it reading.'

Alan had fallen on an icy city sidewalk that morning, and I received blame by association; I worked at city hall, where the decisions were made about which neighborhoods to salt first after a storm. I put the book away.

Looking at Rummy, sitting across from me at my own kitchen table, I feel grateful; this figure sent to ensure my past remains real.

'What's your real name?' I ask him suddenly.

'My what?'

'Your real name. I never knew your real name.'

He shakes his head. 'You always knew my real name,' he says.

I lean back in my chair, Patty's red, faux-fur Tit-Bits in place. 'I guess I did,' I say, feeling oddly unsure.

'My mother's favorite card game,' he says. 'I thought I'd told you.'

Cupping his drink, relaxed and making no mention of our task ahead, his hands are just as I remember them, large with thick fingers – pouring coffee, wiping tables methodically as everyone else passes them over briefly with a damp cloth, holding the pages of the *Sunday Star*, gesturing as he comments on other people's lives with a kind of balance and tolerance that makes him seem older than he is. As he leaps onto Trainer's back I watch the two of them galloping down Main Street, both alive and vital as only the past lets us be.

I've drifted again, I can tell. Rummy is polite and says nothing, sitting exactly as I've left him.

'You remember Trainer's favorite joke?' I ask Rummy tentatively.

He doesn't hesitate. 'What's the difference between a Canadian and a canoe?'

'Canoes tip!' I say loudly.

He chuckles, and then looks thoughtful. 'It's not really fair though. It's the exchange rate you know.'

I refill his glass and mine, this time with no ginger ale. He doesn't complain, and the phone begins to ring – Anna, checking on me. Rummy waits, but I wave the noise away.

'My daughter,' I say explaining. 'I have a daughter. But I'll speak to her later.'

He nods, understanding. This evening is just for the two of us, as planned.

'I'm not sure exactly what you need from me,' I confess.

He leans forward. 'It doesn't matter what *I* need,' he explains. 'It's what you need to say. Oral history is a very organic process. It's about giving memory an audience,' he says.

This idea has been his life's work. This listening. His dedication to passively recording the truth with no interfering questions, no *tampering with the narrative* has brought him a Governor General's Award for Non-Fiction.

'Who else will you speak to?' I ask.

He coughs deeply from his chest, and for a moment I am worried he will die here, leaving me alone. He recovers.

'Everyone,' he says. 'Street sweepers, volunteer firefighters, the mayor, tourists, the governor, the governor's gardener, school kids, dock porters, carriage drivers, State Park tour guides, the police, hotel owners, ministers, chefs, the fake British soldiers, ferry captains.'

As Rummy speaks the island streets become busy again, peopled with figures I'd forgotten to record. I begin to sweat, the air hot from the island sun, uncomfortable; perhaps I've turned the furnace too high.

'Your chapter will be called *Restaurant Worker*,' he continues. 'I've already thought of an epigraph.'

'What is it?' I wonder.

'You'll have to wait and see,' he says. 'Velvet died,' he says as an afterthought. 'Dickweed too. She was over a hundred.'

'Guess all the flags were at half mast,' I offer.

We both take a sip of our drinks and I know what he will say next.

'I was sorry to hear about Alan.'

'Thank you,' I say. 'I guess you know what it's like.'

We both take another quick drink in silence.

'Do you ever wish you could go back?' he asks.

We have not begun recording, this is an answer for him

alone. I think of my journals. The envelope at the bottom of my closet, the way everything ended so horribly, and I realize what I have always wished.

'I want the possibilities back. The feeling that something better was ahead of me.'

Rummy leans forward, wise with whisky and says, 'Most people have never even had an island. We're the lucky ones, because if we didn't miss our past then we didn't live enough.'

The phone begins to ring again, and the house shudders from a change in atmospheric pressure. I am safe.

'It's just nice that someone wants to listen,' I confide.

'That's what everyone always says,' he tells me.

He hesitates.

'There is another reason I'm here, Bell. But that can come later.'

I'm curious as to what it could be. He sets his drink back softly on the table, the glass empty.

'Jesus, Rummy,' I say. 'Where did the time go?'

'Well,' he says. 'I'm here now. Let's begin.'

I start at the end.

'I still believe he was a good person,' I say. 'Even after everything that happened.'

Mackinac

Oct 12?
  Sunday
  He is gone
XXXXXXXXXXXX
Where?
*Everything before, everything has been drowned, suffocated and even here,
the island, even here nothing keeps the world from us and my mother is
dying and Trainer is gone his blood all wet in the street and Bryce . . .*

Is gone. And no one knows where. Six nights ago he was
not at the Cock, and he was not in bed, and the next morning Dickweed remembered seeing him on the two o'clock
ferry the day before. One oblong duffel bag. Everyone agreed
he must have missed the last returning ferry, and would arrive
from the mainland having slept in his car overnight. But he
never appeared. In the afternoon I made a list of places he
could have gone nearby – the pubs he'd told me about on the
mainland. After six phone calls there was no one left to call.

That first day I sat beneath the pay phone at the ferry docks
until it was dark – still hopeful and worried whether he had
enough money and if he'd remember to call. That evening,
when the last ferry docked, he was still gone. His BMX was
still in the bike rack near the docks. It was an expensive bike
and he never left it unlocked, but there it was. It was this
careless disregard that terrified me most, as if I'd found his car
abandoned and unlocked at an airport or train station.

My blood began to feel too full for my body, pulsing, frantic, and wanting to escape. A girl I didn't know stopped me on Main Street to ask where he was. Casually, I told her he'd gone to the mainland for a while, but she'd probably see him around soon. She looked at the ground, told me how Bryce came to her rescue one evening, punching a man who molested her.

'He was arrested that night for fighting,' I told her meanly.

She shrugged, turning awkwardly to leave. 'He was doing the right thing, you know?'

'He's a real saint,' I said flatly, and she left.

From Main Street I went straight to church so that I wouldn't have to sit at the Cock and listen to F 12 on the jukebox or have John give me free pity drinks while everyone discussed where he'd gone.

St. Mary's was open. It felt like the logical place to be.

I believe God pays careful attention to these island people. They are all happy and eating well. They can afford to be here, and not at a roadside diner eating waffles and having to piss without letting their ass touch a greasy unisex toilet seat. They are here and I serve them, work for Velvet, pay bank fees and taxes and still this island is only on loan and we can disappear from it because we are nothing. Actors. Even wearing our nametags we pretend we are more.

With *real* money comes the attention of waiters, dock porters, credit card companies, cameramen, travel agents, secretaries, photographers, politicians, accountants, models – so why *wouldn't* God pay attention to the well-maintained island steeples and women who worship in high-waisted designer dresses, the men with tans wearing khakis by Tommy Bahamas? Maybe I could borrow some of their good fortune. Their ability to arrive at different ports of call with highball glasses and fresh clothing and know that in each new port they are valued, their patronage is welcomed and no one would ever leave them behind.

Swimming is for the losers.

I asked reverently for a misunderstanding, a simple flat tire, a drunk-driving arrest even, anything to have made that day alone without him my last. On my knees I held onto his name, his prophet name, and wondered if thinking *Lehi* loudly enough would have any effect. If it would keep him afloat, wherever he was. If the existence of it would bring him back.

But all that kept surfacing was *he left me he left me he left me . . .*

St. Paul

'And what did I ask for?

'Oh, Rummy. There was only one thing. In retrospect it was too late – even as I knelt staring up at the Virgin arriving by boat onto Mackinac – it was too late, but then I didn't know what I should be asking for. I didn't know what he was about to do. All I asked – foolishly – was that he still loved me. That he would come back. Even then, with Trainer gone, if he'd just turned around and driven back for our last week together he would have been saved. But there was something wrong even then – that first day – and I couldn't quite figure out what I felt I should know. I never have. The reason why.'

Rummy listens and says nothing. The earpiece feels warm inside my ear, as if it lives.

He was a good person. You can't taste someone and not know what's inside them. So young. He did everything like he wouldn't ever get the chance to do it again. As if he knew.

He *was* a good person. And I couldn't have known what was about to happen. Supposing I had? Supposing I'd received a message of some kind before he'd done it? Or any indication I *meant* something. That I was not so easy to leave.

There must have been a reason for what he did. I don't blame him. I just wish I'd paid more attention. I wish there was some way to know for sure.

Are you recording all this?

Mackinac

For the first three days after his disappearance I drank only water, vomiting even the chocolate croissants Rummy brought me out of sympathy. There were no car accidents or bodies discovered anywhere in Michigan, Wisconsin or Canada. The Tippecanoe received no phone calls, and searching through Bryce's apartment there was no indication he planned on leaving – there was no letter addressed to me. I spent the evenings holding his pillow.

I became responsible by association for his disappearance, meeting with Velvet in her office about the disconnected phone line in Bryce's Grayling apartment, his parents' unlisted number. *Did he have money troubles?* she wanted to know.

But I don't know. I know nothing about him – our entire summer constructed around our own imagined wealth, our faith in the exact moment and nothing else. Everything was, and is, horrible. In his absence Bryce became dead, married, a narcotics agent, manic-depressive, kidnapped, on the run, and nothing made sense. It was none of these things, but it could also be all of them – what I knew for certain was the very real fact of the island, without him.

The island police told me there were almost 6,800 missing persons registered in Michigan, and that most of these people disappear of their own accord. A report was filed, but I didn't have a photograph. I couldn't be sure of his eye color.

I spent my mornings with Rummy drinking coffee and convincing myself that Bryce was unreliable, from a different faith, that our romance was seasonal, and that I believed what I was saying. Rummy listened, put his hand over mine, and said many nice things.

'You'll be okay, Bell,' he said. 'Forgetting will be easier than you think.'

– and when he said it his eyes were a nice shade of brown. For a moment I turned my palm upwards so we were holding hands across the Voodoo altar table. His was warm and dry, and he was right. For an instant, I was okay with his comfort and the possibility that some day Bryce could return and we could resume our summer together.

But it couldn't remain so. The problem with time is the way it has of ruling out certain possibilities as it passes.

My world folded in on itself, imploding, exploding, and everything else impossibly terrible as Brenna came running into the Tippecanoe holding the *Detroit Free Press* above her head.

'You won't *fucking believe* it,' she said slamming the paper down onto the table between Rummy and me. 'You won't fucking *believe* what the fuck he's done.'

She pointed triumphantly to the headline on the first page. Our table was surrounded quickly by Velvet, Chef Walter, and everyone else wanting to know the news – but there was no one else there as I read the one, black headline that told me where Bryce had gone.

It was worse because, suddenly, I knew.

With the first word followed by another and another and one short paragraph in black ink I read over and over and over again while everything turned inside out and I knew this summer had taken *two* people from me, and somehow this was much, much worse. Inside of me something clean was gone.

Rummy stood abruptly from his chair saying, 'Oh, God, oh,

no,' as the restaurant erupted into excited gossip, shock, and speculation, so many questions unanswered and the article maddeningly short. Someone put his hand on my shoulder which made it worse – everyone knew he had been mine, everyone suddenly sorry for me all over again, and wondering how I could have loved someone so awful.

Velvet gave me the day off and I ran to the beach, slipping on the uneven shore beneath me. Would I have rather not known? My body was empty, then full again with anger and hurt and disbelief as I battered a large gray rock over and over against my wrist bone to see if it would shatter under my skin, wanting the stone to leave a bruise. The lake was empty. In the mingled waters of Lake Huron and Michigan I careened out into the waves and waited until my bare feet turned cold and unfeeling, until my toes wouldn't move and I had to wait until I could walk again. The clouds hung gray overhead and for the first time, there was nothing else up there.

There were no bicycles and no tourists and I walked down Main Street wanting someone to ask what was wrong so I could tell them. So they could be horrified as well, and puzzled, asking, 'Did you ever suspect? Have you heard from him since?' So I could shake my head and begin to cry.

Past Marquette Park I hesitated outside St. Mary's, feeling the need to decide something quickly – feeling I was very close to needing saving. I compromised by doing five vodka shots before entering the church.

But on my knees all I could do was imagine him unclean, his face and clothing covered in hot blood.

Oct . . .
Bryce, I prayed for you at you with you today can you hear? You stupid fuck.

227

I'm left. There must be a reason why.
Was it really you?

The press arrived along with the police. Men with black recording devices atop shoulders and microphones covered in fur, wearing baseball caps and trailing wires behind them, went from bar to pub to restaurant, asking questions and drinking beer. Those who never knew Bryce were the most eager to talk.

From work I returned straight home each night, avoiding everyone until it was my turn to speak. My interview was scheduled after Rummy's, and he looked nervous as he left the station.

'They want to know if there's been any *contact*,' Rummy whispered.

But we both knew there had been none.

Sergeant Mann was wearing shorts even though it was cold, and the navy-blue canvas made him look more like a mailman than a cop. He offered me a shortbread cookie baked by one of the island women, and I told the Sergeant I couldn't see how the two events were connected – the island had nothing to do with what happened. Bryce never told me he was leaving. He hadn't tried to contact me. I'd never met his family. I couldn't give them a motive.

Sergeant Mann wrote everything down and I was free to leave.

Dickweed didn't tell them about the duffel bag, but they found out anyway from one of the dock porters.

From everything left behind, I've reclaimed my calendar of the Pope, and taken only his Mormonator T-shirt, the one he let me wear to bed. 'Won't answer my knock?' it reads over the image of a sunglass-clad missionary with arms crossed. 'I'll be back.' There is a watery brown beer stain near the collar, and it smells like the woods and alcohol and the sharp sweaty sting of deodorant.

Now standing on the dock at eight o'clock, I cannot believe that the island will end this way for me.

There is no color in the sky – the wind cold, the water black, a family of mallards bobbing brown near the shore. In the early morning light everything seems more important, and it's cold enough for mittens, but I haven't got any.

Last night a fly died on my windowsill. Moving slowly for hours it was too weak to climb the glass, and finally turned onto its back, legs waving, quietly buzzing before being still. This morning there was frost on the windows.

My suitcase stands beside a Mackinac Mart bag full of things I've accumulated over the last few months:

One Petoskey stone.

A Tippecanoe mug with the logo of a birch bark canoe.

Four stolen packages of souvenir walnuts from dry storage.

An unreturned library book that I'll probably throw away when I unpack.

Velvet's business card in case I want to return next summer.

Phone numbers on paper coasters and slips of paper: Rummy. Brenna.

A small brown scab from the floor of Bryce's bathroom.

Two journals.

The dock porters secure my luggage onto a large metal trolley and wheel it away onto the boat, leaving me without my possessions. The marina on my right is nearly empty and Marquette Park above it is green without the busyness of people. The Tippecanoe on my left is now closed for the winter, its two stories white and clean, its plate-glass windows obscured by massive sheets of plywood. The piece covering the third window from the left holds a fresh pair of initials carved in the bottom corner; I have a splinter, Rummy a cut from the kitchen knife we used. I stand facing Main Street, facing him.

Our breath is cold, white, and winter advances, though neither of us will be here to see it.

The lake will freeze.

The school will stay open.

The hotels will close except for one or two that stay open for cross-country skiers.

The pubs will close, but for one or two that do a brisk business helping everyone that's left forget about the snow.

In winter the island reverts to those who really belong, I suppose, and when the horses have gone back to green fields on farms and when bicycles become ridiculous, skidding and sliding, when the streets are covered in a foot or two of snow, the island isn't really timeless after all – there are snowmobiles.

Velvet has informed us she will be spending the winter in Lisbon.

'I've always wanted to go,' she said. 'And I've nothing else planned.'

She has rented a furnished villa in the countryside that is being let out by one of Lisbon's most renowned orchestra conductors who will be touring southeast Asia for the winter. She expects she will be able to cycle to and from the city quite easily.

I imagine there must be more like Velvet. People rich enough to escape, knowing how far luxury lies from the island in the months of February and March. Chapped lips and hands, air that hurts to breathe and ice forming on beards and scarves, the wet, cold ends of socks – these are not romantic things. St. Paul has taught me this much.

The ones left behind will check the temperature daily. After two weeks if the ice is white and hard the call goes out, and bare Christmas trees emerge to line a pathway in the ice to St. Ignace – these used-up symbols of faith will guide the islanders home again. For weeks the island is no longer that – there is land where once there was water. Caught and frozen in flux, the surface will be uneven and slushy with the afternoon sun. Snowmobiles will spray plumes of winter lake water behind them. This is just what I have heard.

Rummy and I hug for a long time. Pulling away slowly I feel a moment of forever; a lifetime caught suspended in our goodbye. Brenna arrives pulling a designer suitcase that must be fake, and wearing white furry mittens. The three of us stand for a moment. She gives me a kiss.

'I bet you a million dollars he writes you,' she says. 'From jail or whatever.'

Then, dismissively –

'What a weird fucking summer.'

With her suitcase she boards the ferry and is gone.

I ask Rummy what his plans are for the winter.

'I'm going to live in a Californian monastery in the mountains and drink only tea,' he says.

And it's okay to laugh.

I step onto the wet ramp of the ferry, then up the metal steps to the top deck. With an aisle down the middle, the plastic benches have been laminated to look like wood. I sit next to an orange life preserver hanging on the railing, a yellow coil of rope keeping it in place. It's too cold and my hair is black and fierce in the wind, sticking to my lip-gloss. Brenna is on the lower deck, inside.

The ferry backs away from the pier. Reversing slowly, it does a three-point turn before the engines begin, low and thick, the water beginning to churn behind us. The white spray rises from the back of the boat, but it's going too slow and too fast all at once. I wave and Rummy waves until our hands are too small to see.

Curving in a watery arc, we pass between the lighthouses, the white one on my right, Round Island on my left. A Star Line ferry approaches, passing us and heading towards the island, but there is no one on it, the top deck empty. Across the widening gap between myself and land, the huge white line of the world's longest front porch stands grand and expensive atop the west bluff, but soon that is gone as well. A dark-black break in the autumn-colored trees marks the hidden outcrop that is Sunset Rock. The stone balcony looks like nothing from down here, just space. Bryce's wine glass is still in the water somewhere below.

The wind increases, sharp and cold, turning my fingers red as the ferry emerges past the shelter of the island's north western end, the sky still thin and gauzy, empty. A seagull shits on the seat beside me.

In fifteen minutes I will be in St. Ignace again, the sharp smell of gasoline strange and immediate, forgotten. The cars will all look hard and too big. In the parking lot I will load my one blue suitcase and Mackinac Mart bag into my white Ford Focus and begin the twelve-hour drive through the Upper Peninsula of Michigan and towards St. Paul – towards United Hospital and my mother. 'Head 'em off at the pass,' she said.

In the distance the mainland is dark and thin, but slowly it gets bigger.

St. Paul, 8:05 p.m.

Arriving slowly back at the table, with a shudder I try to disembark, to gently let go – but I can't. I never could.

He could have done it differently. Run, maybe. So young. I would have gone with him. And where would I be now, what place and with who after all this time? But he didn't run. And so he could never have asked me to go with him. He didn't ask me anything at all.

These thin and yellowed newspaper articles aren't the most important part of the story, but they're the only part I don't understand. Folded neatly into the last pages of my red journal are clippings from the *Crawford County Avalanche*, the *Detroit Free Press* and the *Sunday Sun*. Rummy agrees as I offer to read them aloud, though he knows what they contain.

The headlines – still black though the paper has yellowed – are blunt. First, the small article from the *Crawford County Avalanche*:

Alcohol May be a Factor in Father/Son Hunting Accident
A hunting trip turned deadly for a local Grayling man and his son this weekend after a firearm accidentally discharged during their excursion. Brackley Russo, 47, was fatally injured by his son's high-powered shotgun around 3:30 p.m. in the afternoon on Sunday. Police are investigating to determine whether alcohol was a factor in the accident after finding several beer cans in the vicinity.

Then one day later, the headline Brenna brought to us so long ago – the revelation that made the major papers. The cause of his father's death: four rounds to the chest and groin area. From a Remington 7600 pump action rifle.

Son Remains Silent on Motive for Killing

AP – A Michigan man has been arrested for the murder of his father during what was supposed to have been a routine hunting expedition this weekend in Grayling. Initially reported by local police as an accident, Grayling Sheriff Al Codder is now charging Lehi Bryce Russo, 21, with homicide in the second degree.

The cause of death for Brackley Russo, 47, is listed as four gunshot wounds to the chest and groin area.

Lastly, the *Sunday Sun*:

Excommunicated Mormon Murderer Says Only God Can Judge Him for the Brutal Slaying of his Father

The sleepy town of Grayling, Michigan has been rocked this week by the murder of long-time resident and 'Mormon elder' Brackley Russo. Home of the world's longest canoe marathon, this small northern community has been coming to grips with what appears to be the calculated, cold-blooded murder of a well-respected father by his own son.

Sources say the son lured his father out into the bush under the pretext of a father/son hunting trip.

The charge against Lehi Russo has been upgraded to murder in the first degree after officers discovered the accused to have transported the suspected murder weapon to Grayling from a previous residence on Mackinac Island, just days before the killing.

Local hunters have expressed disgust the two family members were hunting illegally with deer season over a month away, but were appeased after discovering that no deer were shot before the murder.

Neighbors describe son Lehi Russo alternately as a well-groomed, intelligent, and socially adept young man, and a troubled, unemployed drifter who repeatedly failed his college electrician courses and had a poor relationship with his father. A neighbor of the Russos told the *Sun* the accused left the family home last summer: 'He tried to take his sister with him, but Brackley went and brought her back. Said his daughter was staying with him at home until she turned 18. She was a quiet one – went and killed herself last week before all this happened. The whole thing's a tragedy.'

Russo has refused to speak with the press, saying only through a statement released by his lawyer that 'he did the right thing, and only God can judge him.'

Lehi is an excommunicated member of the Mormon Church, the fast-expanding American religion that was founded in Salt Lake City. Many of its claimed twelve million members are said to still practice polygamy.

A church spokesperson declined to comment on the case, saying only that the biased media coverage of the murder reflected an extreme ignorance of the Mormon religion.

This was always the hardest to read, and it remains so. These were the reporters who discovered the island so long ago and wanted to know *exactly how many* women *Lehi* was seeing at the time of the murder, and did he believe God spoke to him, and whether or not he wore the sacred LDS undergarments under his clothes – only the *truly* faithful wore these full cotton jumpsuits, the press reported ecstatically. He became a caricature, and without him I became uncertain of what he really was. As I am still.

I put the yellowed pages back onto the table. Rummy shakes his head, but we've both lived too long to be angry about these sorts of things anymore. Rummy can only do his job to lend other voices to the story.

What we missed that summer was what came first. What caused him to leave so suddenly. The tiny clipping is an obituary, too small for me to read now:

Suddenly on October 13th . . . Odette Russo died alone in her apartment – her brother's empty apartment, with medication she'd taken from Mercy Hospital.

Bryce had left us to attend his sister's funeral. Three days later he had murdered his father with the contents of the oblong duffel bag he had taken with him from the island. Premeditated murder in the first degree, he received mandatory life with no parole. He never contacted me, and we never spoke again.

My hip bothers me suddenly, sharply. Shifting painfully in my seat there is more I need to say.

'That's only the end,' I tell Rummy. 'I can start at the beginning if you want. It's nicer.'

He says nothing for a long while, and I can't think of what to say to make him stay. Like a Buddhist chant I think *Rummy* over and over again, to keep him here with me.

'Bell,' he says.

We both wait.

'Bell. I'm an old man now. I need to make things right.'

He takes an envelope slowly from his corduroy jacket, handing it to me, and it is old. Old stamps and a very old postscript. I don't understand and feel panic – wondering if I've been left behind again.

'There were two good reasons I kept this, at the beginning,' he says. 'You were sad and I wanted to help. And I never heard from Blue again. You remember her? I thought if you and I were alone, we'd be alone together, it would be fair. And after that, it was too late.'

The envelope is addressed to me.

'It came early,' he says. 'To the restaurant. While I was reading the paper.'

There is no return address, but the handwriting is his.

A letter from Bryce.

Rummy's eyes look wet and suddenly I am not the only one who has been haunted by what happened that summer. Across borders and time, I have lived wondering why he left me with no goodbye, and Rummy has lived knowing he denied me an answer, or at least some kind of explanation.

'I'm sorry.'

Something heavy in me is cut from its moorings and I feel buoyant, light and light-headed all at once.

'I thought he never wrote,' I say.

'He wrote you,' Rummy says softly. 'How could he not?'

I am now holding an envelope containing a letter addressed to me written fifty years ago by a man who I knew for a few months and who has spent most of his life in prison. It is wonderful. Even now, after everything, there are still things that surprise me in this life.

'I thought it was best for you then,' Rummy tells me. 'To think he was gone. To have me instead. I kept it for your benefit, and mine.'

He pauses, embarrassed.

'But afterwards, it was too late. When I realized it wasn't a standard break-up letter.'

He bows his head – the top of his skull showing pale and

white underneath the hair. After a moment he looks up, wiping his cheek.

'What if it was a confession? What if he was asking you for help? What if keeping the letter had caused it all to happen? I'd lied to the police, I'd lied to you. I was terrified.

'I never opened it,' he adds.

It's true, the letter is sealed. It could be a grocery list or a request to forward his mail.

'Why didn't you?'

'It wasn't addressed to me,' he says sheepishly.

But it is here now. There is a brief moment where I wonder if there is a need to read it at all, if I could put it in the kitchen wastebasket under the sink and be content knowing of its existence. But of course I cannot do this – whether a confession or simply a hello, I must know. Will he mention the murder? The stamp has a Christmas theme, dark night with an angel and a halo and I remember all my island prayers which I believed to have been unanswered until this moment. The envelope is light and thin, and the letters are small, so small:

Bell (STAFF)

The Tippecanoe

Mackinac Island, MI

49757

The letter is dated 14th October, and the pen is black and permanent, each alphabet character in the address separate from the last. It has been printed with no clue as to whether it was written in haste.

I tear open my letter and begin to read. It is very short.

Dear Bell,

I spoke with my father on the phone yesterday and please understand I had to come to Grayling. I don't think I'll be back – would have left you a note but couldn't find a pen. Tell V. I quit. Odette took a bunch of

pills at my apartment – I guess she'd been sleeping there to get away, but
I'm going to put it right. I wish you could have met her, but it's all gone
to hell now, and I guess it doesn't matter. Most likely I won't be talking
to you for a while. Hopefully you'll be able to come and visit me though.
If you want. But I understand if you feel you can't. I'm all torn up over
this, the past and future, but I think I'm doing the right thing for my
family. I'm going to fix everything. I'll wait to hear back from you.

    Your angel (wearing tights)

    B

    Rev 19: 11–13 (if something happens, please tell them I had to)

The verses are from Revelations, and I wonder if he didn't
believe in salvation after all. The idea of *goodness* floating just
above our heads, waiting for us to ascend. Waiting for us to
sin in order to save others from something worse.

I saw heaven standing open and there before me was a white horse,
whose rider is called Faithful and True. With justice he judges and
makes war. His eyes are like blazing fire, and on his head are many
crowns. He has a name written on him that no one knows, but he
himself. He is dressed in a robe dipped in blood, and his name is the
Word of God.

Delivered after fifty years, the letter is not too late and I tell
Rummy so. Rummy looks at me, his entire life dedicated to
telling the real and true story – using everyone else's voice but
his own. I wonder if his calling became more urgent over the
years when my unopened letter was hidden away in his
conscience.

    The mail always finds a way, I guess.

    'Neither rain nor sleet nor snow,' I say quietly.

    Crying might be the thing to do, but it's too long ago, too
old now to mourn the decisions of others.

'Guess I can pass on now, knowing I did the right thing.'

He pauses for a moment, looking at the letter I am still holding tightly.

'I always wondered why he did it. I suppose that explains it, more or less.'

I imagine the headline in the *Sun*, the one which should have been printed all those years ago.

Vigilante Justice Stops Father's Reign of Terror.
Distraught Son Avenges Sister's Suicide

Bryce's last free decision in this world had been an honorable one it seems, though Trainer had been wrong about his craving for martyrdom – he never told anyone the reason why. Until now. Bryce chose to avenge his past, and in doing so forfeited his future. I believe I will see him again. He'll have to wait in line after Alan, of course.

'When did he get out?' Rummy asks.

'He's still in.'

I lay the letter on the table and remove my earpiece, leaning back in my chair exhausted.

'I'm done now,' I say. 'I guess we've both learned something.'

Taking out his own earpiece he puts them both in his pocket.

'Thank you,' I add.

He nods, relieved, and we are quiet for a moment.

'It's a crime to get this old.'

But I don't know which one of us it is that speaks.

Moving to the front door to wait for Erik, the air is colder now, but still there is no storm. Rummy does not shiver in his thin jacket, he looks comfortable, warm. Across the street the old-fashioned lamppost suddenly flickers, bright. Only the best

St. Paul neighborhoods are graced with these romantic relics from the past and I realize I've earned this neighborhood, this house, my expensive health-care policy, my good bottles of whisky and each scar on my body. But I know enough to value my sadness too – knowing I'd trade this future to have the possibilities of that summer back. Poverty, youth, water, blind faith, and the one man who lived it with me. It was the beginning of a new century then, before the weather had taken over, the skies yellowed, before New York and everything after. Before the clashes of fundamentalists within our own borders, before my sickness and Alan's death.

I think of the lighthouse suddenly, not Round Island, the other one. White and solid in the lake, its electric signal too far away to save the ship that broke in two, like a heart. I wonder about those twenty-nine men of the *Edmund Fitzgerald* and how long they stayed afloat, treading water, believing someone would come before they drowned. I wonder how long any man can stay afloat on his own, alone, before giving in.

Headlights advance towards us from the end of the street.

'How old is Erik?' I ask.

'Forty-nine this April. Why?'

I add the years slowly in my head, but I already knew. As old as Mackinac. We look at one another.

'Found me when he was eighteen,' Rummy says. 'Aileen and I never had kids.'

'Remember the moose?' I ask at last.

'As real as I am,' Rummy says.

He taps his jacket pocket containing the two earpieces with everything we've recorded.

'Some good stuff here, Bell.'

A huge Ford Chippewa with Alberta plates turns into my driveway, the stereo loud. The windows are rolled up, his son nothing but shadow beyond the tinted glass. I don't know what he looks like, I can't picture what's behind the glass.

With a smile that makes him look twenty again Rummy asks, 'So, Bell, where do you get virgin wool?'

'What?'

'It's a joke.'

'Fine. I have no idea. Where do you get virgin wool?'

Rummy turns and waves to his car, then gives me a hug. I breathe in the scent of him, his sweet and gentle odor. He walks to the passenger door and before he gets in the car he says, 'Ugly sheep.'

I am still laughing as they drive away.

At 10:05 the Virgin Mary is tired. Her right hand angled down, palm up, her left points towards the heavens. Two glasses stand empty on the table, both marked with lips, the glow from their contents long faded. Bell is cold, her knees and shoulders stiff, her stomach empty, she feels wonderful. Between the two of them, only Mary knows that he is horribly late.

10:07.

The Virgin's hand scoops time upwards, collecting.

From a cloudy orange container on the kitchen counter Bell takes three white pills, then one yellow from a dish on the counter, but she doesn't remember what they are for. She is sure she isn't supposed to have been drinking.

In the living room she sits slowly in her reclining chair, the bottom worn threadbare from the past year where she's slept every night, and she arranges the yellow blanket around her, tucking the edges underneath her body so she is wrapped like a cocoon. *Like a dead sailor before they throw them out to sea*, Bell imagines happily, *one stitch through their nose to make sure they are dead*. She goes to sleep. Her last thought before drifting off is that it was nice to see Rummy again, after all this time. She dreams contentedly of a masked avenger, a man on a horse who reveals his pink face only to her. Slowly then, for the first time in fifty years, she dreams of nothing at all.

In the open sky the black-yellow swirl of cloud is smaller now, the government employees at the digital radar information building on West Avenue recording its dissipation from their screens. The data is relayed to the environmental emergency response team in the basement of city hall, and a call is made. The siren gives five long blasts from its location in the low squat building next to United Hospital. The city has survived.

First reports indicate St. Paul received eight inches of precipitation over a six-hour period, initially rain, then hail, measuring five inches in diameter. An RWP enthusiast is reported to have drowned in the contaminated waters of the Mississippi while filming the storm. The year-old headstone of Althea Morris in St. Mary's cemetery was damaged by a falling tree. Traffic accidents were numerous, and fatal.

The weather helicopters film the remnants of a pile-up involving nineteen cars north of the city, and from the sky the metal shines dull under white spotlights. Three of the license plates are out of state, and one is from Canada. A brown loafer lies in the road, absent of a body. As the temperature warms the hailstones begin to melt, the lights from each ambulance burning red, white, and blue, reflecting on the wet interstate.

The interlodge lifted at the Sushi Palace, Anna is already on her way. The unanswered phone leading her to imagine her mother wandering the streets during the storm, looking for friendships and relatives that can no longer speak to her. Imagining her past is reality.

She never knew what her mother was preparing for this morning.

Bell's journals lie open on the kitchen table, her last correspondence from a long ago lover beside them. In the morning the envelope and letter will be misplaced, but it doesn't matter anymore.

These are her monuments to those many summer months. Built out of bicycle grease and pine gum and horseshit and the paper frail dreams of youth.

Your right hand, palm inward, thumb out, is the state of Michigan.

Mackinac Island is off the tip off your middle finger. You can imagine how small it is compared to the rest of your body, the rest of the world.

She makes the journey sometimes as she lies awake in her chair, more often these days than before. With a carton of icecream or a photograph album or a particular article in the newspaper or with the certain slant of the sun at midday, Bell will stop for an afternoon or an evening, take the ferry over and watch everything coming closer, the houses getting clearer, and see if she can spot the carriages before the ferry docks with the low sound of its horn.

If she stays until the evening, it is to watch the sun set in the west on the straits of Mackinac, on the lighthouse, on the rocks, on the wide white building called the Tippecanoe. Everything glows pink, gold.